THE DOME

A Thriller in the Age of Climate Change

W.F. VAN DER HART

First published in 2020

First edition, 2020

Cover and interior book design by W.F. van der Hart

ISBN 9789464007343 (paperback)
ISBN 9789464007350 (hardback)
ASIN: B08NFCFSQC (eBook)

To all the children of the world

THE DOME

1.

The rain had been pouring for days, but today was probably the heaviest rainstorm Dylan had ever seen in his life. The noise on the roof of the car was deafening, and he was frightened. Outside it was all dark, even though it was the middle of the day.

His mom had tried to persuade him not to go. She worried about the heavy rain and the rising water levels of the river downtown. She didn't feel comfortable. Dylan was only ten years old but did not hesitate for a second. He had no choice; he had to go. They were playing against the Wildcats, a basketball team from the northwestern part of town. A few weeks ago, they had lost against them and this time they had to beat them to still have a chance in this year's championship. His dad convinced his mom that everything would be fine and brought him to the sport complex in downtown Augusta.

After the game, Dylan felt triumphant, and the torrential downpour outside did not bother him initially. They had just beaten the Wildcats in an intense and exciting game. He ran to the car behind his dad and the strong wind slashed the raindrops against his face. With his hands, he protected his eyes from the streaming rain. Soaking wet, he climbed into the car. His father smiled at him and pushed the start button of their electrical car. With the pounding rain, Dylan heard nothing else than the rumbling noise on the roof. He just noticed the screens in the dashboard light up and they entered the main road.

The heavy rain blurred the windshield. They drove slowly. They could barely see anything in front of them. Luckily, there were few cars on the road. The rain showers had gotten heavier than earlier that morning, and they flooded the streets with water. Normally it was only a ten-minute drive home, but this time it took a lot longer to get home. His dad parked the car on the road in front of their house. Dylan saw his mom already waiting at the front door. She waved at them and looked worried. His father got out first. The look on his face changed the moment he stepped into the water next to the car. He looked stressed and gestured with his hand.

"Dylan, take my hand and step out of the car on my side! There's too much water flowing through the street."

Dylan moved over to the driver's seat and grabbed his dad's firm hand. He stepped outside. To his surprise, he was up to his knees in the water. The strong current pulled on his legs. The level seemed to rise fast and water was filling the car now. His dad pulled him away from the car.

They waded through the water toward the steps leading to the front door, but they could feel the current getting stronger and the murky water rising higher and higher. His father looked worried and lifted him up in his arms. He held him tight against his body, and Dylan felt his father's strong arms around him. For a moment, he felt safe as his dad slowly continued dragging his feet through the rising water.

The raindrops poured on his face, water streamed against his legs, and he had the impression the water level was rising quickly. He heard his mother screaming through the wind, but he could not see her as he was looking over his father's shoulder. The car started floating and moved, and then a few seconds later, his father tripped. The heavy stream of water swept him off his feet. They both fell down in the water and the murky water dragged them along.

Slowly, he slipped out of his father's arms. Suddenly, he heard his mother's voice through the rain and wind.

"Lawrence, please don't let Dylan go!"

Dylan felt his dad grab him with two arms, pulling him close to his body. They both drifted away with the water, and as they turned, Dylan saw his mother standing in the doorway with her hands on her face. He had never seen her so terrified. She disappeared out of sight as they floated through the street. Another car hovered just behind them, but their own car had vanished from sight. The murky water was full of debris, and his dad struggled to stay afloat. Dylan tried to swim with his legs to help his dad to stay above water. But then they got pulled down, and their heads sank underwater, just to surface a moment later.

As the water continued to drag them through the streets, suddenly his father screamed and seemed to have hit something under the water. While he squirmed in pain, his grip around Dylan loosened for a few seconds, but he quickly tightened his grip again. His dad was not letting go of him, although he noticed the agony on his dad's face. Slowly, the car behind them got closer and his dad pushed him toward the car.

"Climb on top of the roof, Dylan!" he shouted, sounding out of breath from the struggle to stay above the water.

Dylan reached with his arms to the car and grabbed the roof. As he tried to climb on top, he felt his dad push him up. Then his dad climbed onto the hood of the car and then onto the roof next to Dylan. They drifted like that on top of the car for a while through the streets, and the current seemed to slow down a bit. The car drifted toward a balcony. His father reached for it, still holding on to Dylan, but missed. It was too far. They slipped and slid off the back, back into the murky water. It took them a while to climb back on top of the car, but when they finally succeeded, they rested to catch their breath. The car continued floating along the street.

"We have to get off this car, otherwise we'll end up in the Savannah River. Do you see that balcony coming up over there? Let's try to get a hold of the railing."

"Okay, dad!"

They were lucky, since the car passed relatively close. A moment later, his dad told him to jump. They jumped together, grabbed the railing, bumped into the balcony, and slipped. Dylan fell back into the water, but could just grab his dad's trousers. His father was hanging on the edge of the railing with his body in the water. With one hand, he quickly reached for Dylan's arm and dragged him back up to the railing. Dylan quickly clung onto the railing and started climbing over it while his father gave him a push from behind. As soon as he stood on the balcony, he turned to help his father climb onto the balcony. While he was turning around, he noticed a big, white van coming toward the balcony.

"Watch out behind you!"

His dad turned his head while he tried to climb further, but then the van smacked into the balcony. He moaned in pain. His hands immediately let go of the balcony, and he sunk back into the water. Dylan could not see him anymore. Terrified, he looked around the balcony and at the white van drifting away along the street, but he did not see him. Then, out of the blue, he saw a dark shape surfacing, but he was not sure if it was some object or his father. Desperately, he screamed,

"DAD!? DAD!?"

The dark shape disappeared, and he felt fear rushing through his body. He stared at the murky water floating by in the street, and the white van drifted out of sight. This could not be true. A shock of fear hit him, leaving him stunned. Tears were pouring down his face and he desperately continued scanning the debris, but he did not see his father anymore.

2.

When the buzzing sound of the alarm clock woke him, he slapped the snooze button and turned to his other side. When it went off ten minutes later, Dylan knew it was really time to get up. He jumped out of bed. The lights in his bedroom turned on automatically and the screen on his wall lit up, showing the Swiss mountains covered with snow on a sunny day. Even though the picture was over thirty years old, he programmed the screen to show it, since it always put him in a good mood. Today was an important day, and he rushed to get ready in time.

He walked to the bathroom and took a shower. He tried to be as quick as possible not to waste too much water, since his mother always complained about it. He would have skipped the shower normally, but he wanted to look his best today. After drying off, he looked in the mirror and felt excited. He had been working hard for it the last years and today was the big day.

He shaved, dressed and took his new dark suit out of the plastic cover. It got delivered to their compound a few weeks ago. It was custom made for him based on the body scan he had sent to the shop. He tried it on and it fit like a glove. He looked one more time in the mirror and walked to the living room.

His mother was busy preparing breakfast in the kitchen. She had also dressed up in her best clothes and looked ready for the big event. He gave her a kiss on her cheek, and then they sat down for breakfast. His mother looked healthier than usual with all the make-up she had put on. Quite a difference from her typical pale and gray face. He asked if she had slept well and she pretended all was well, but he had heard her coughing horribly at night again. He worried about her, but she always tried to avoid talking about her health.

He checked the time on his wristwatch. It was fifteen to nine already and they would have to leave in five minutes. She looked at him and asked,

"What time will the taxi arrive?"

"At nine o'clock."

"Did you check the weather warnings?"

"Yes, same as yesterday. Not too good. We should try to stay inside as much as possible."

"Are the respos fully charged?"

He stood up and walked to the desk in the entrance hall. The respos were standing in their charging station. These air masks were indispensable to breathe the air outside comfortably. His eye fell on the picture in the silver frame standing next to the respos. He looked so happy in this picture. He was standing between his father and his mother, with his dark face with a big smile exposing his white teeth. The picture was taken fifteen years ago, one of the last ones with his dad on it. His mother noticed him staring at the frame.

"Your dad would have been so proud of you today."

"Yeah, I guess he would…"

He checked out the respos next to the frame and lifted them out of the charger.

"They're fully charged, so we should be fine for the day."

He gave one to his mother, who came walking with her cane to the entrance hall. They left the apartment and took the elevator downstairs. His mother strolled out of the elevator toward the main hall. There they both put their respos on their face. Their breathing sounded heavier through the mask. He smiled at his mother. When she was ready, he pushed the button to open the door to the airlock. The door behind them closed with a hiss and when it was completely sealed, the outside door opened. They both stepped into the underground hall, where a white taxi was waiting.

Dylan took his identity card and held it in front of the door of the taxi. The sliding doors opened with a buzz and a voice resonated from the speaker:

"Good morning, Dylan Myers."

They both took a seat inside the four-seat vehicle. The sliding doors closed automatically behind them and they heard the air-filtering system starting. A few minutes later, a green light went on in front of them. It was safe now to take off their respos. His mother coughed after she took it off. Then a voice asked,

"Where would you like to go to Dylan Myers?"

"To the Swiss Federal Institute of Technology in Lausanne, please!"

"All right, your expected arrival time is 9:15."

The vehicle started moving, and his mother looked a bit stressed.

"I never get used to these driverless vehicles."

He smiled at her as the vehicle drove out of the underground hall. He saw the large red doors opening in front of them and the vehicle drove into the exit tunnel. When the doors closed behind them, the gray doors ahead of them started opening and the light from outside blinded their eyes. The vehicle drove onto the main road, and he looked outside. The sky was gray. On the horizon, he vaguely made out the shape of the gray mountains through the brown and gray smog. The forest fires in southern France made the pollution worse the last few months and going outside without a respo was irresponsible and dangerous.

As they drove through several neighborhoods in Lausanne, he felt privileged to be living in their apartment's compound. It was located north of Lausanne and relatively high tech. Most of the other students lived in much less sophisticated houses or apartments. Most buildings were gray from the pollution and neglected. Most of the buildings in the richer neighborhoods added air cooling and filtering installations. Most of the poor ones had to do without the sophisticated air purifiers.

The streets were deserted and the only things moving were a few taxis and several delivery drones flying back and forth through the sky. A freight truck passed them over, startling his mother. The driverless truck looked unnatural to her, a large container on a platform without a cabin moving through the streets. Fifteen minutes later, they arrived at the campus of the most prestigious science and technology university in Switzerland.

Technology and science had fascinated him since he was young. He remembered how he used to design complicated electrical circuits with his dad. His father was an electrical engineer and had taught him many things. Dylan held on to the memories of his dad, although they could never fill the emptiness of growing up without him. Today especially, he could not help thinking of his father.

The taxi slowed down in front of the main entrance.

"We arrived at the Swiss Federal Institute of Technology. Air quality is insufficient. Respos are recommended. Push the green button when you are ready to leave the vehicle."

They both put on their respos and he made sure his mother was ready before pushing the green button. The doors opened with a buzz and he helped her out of the taxi. The air was warm already. It was going to be another hot day. He briefly stared at the horizon, and through the smog he saw the sun. The state of the climate often depressed him, but not today. Today was a big day. The end of one period and the beginning of another.

They strolled through the main doors and entered the airlock. It closed back behind them, and he heard the hissing sound of the polluted air clearing out. They waited until the green light appeared, after which the doors opened automatically. They entered the large entrance hall of the university campus and took off their respos. He put them in his locker and they walked to the auditorium.

Besides some staff members who were preparing the stage for the big event, it was still empty. He had promised to give his mother a tour of the campus. Now, at the end of his study, he had realized he had never shown it to his mother. She had reacted enthusiastically, as always, when he proposed to go earlier to show her around. He hoped the walk would not be too tiring for her though, since lately he worried a lot about her health. They had diagnosed her with chronic obstructive pulmonary disease several years ago. Since she had never smoked in her life, the doctors thought it was most likely caused by air pollution. The doctors had proposed to grow new lungs from her own stem cells to replace her current damaged lungs. To his surprise, she had refused the idea, claiming it was not up to humans to play God. He respected her decision, but never really understood it.

For the last few months, she felt constantly exhausted and often needed extra oxygen. Her condition suddenly improved last week. She said she wanted to be there for him on this big day. He showed her the entire campus, and when they arrived back at the auditorium, it was filling up with people. They walked up to the front of the stage and he greeted some of his professors and introduced his mother. While she talked to one of his professors, Dylan scanned the crowd.

But he did not spot her face anywhere and wondered where she might be.

3.

His mother had taken a seat in the front row and he was still standing to look for Elizabeth. The dean approached the lectern, and Dylan sat down next to his mother. He turned his head one more time in the entrance's direction. She had promised she would be there. It was not like her to be late; he wondered if something had happened to her.

The dean welcomed everybody in the auditorium, and while he continued with his introductory words, Dylan noticed his mother looked tired. As soon as she had noticed his concerned look, she grabbed his hands and gave him a look as if he was not to worry. They listened to the speech.

"… these last weeks we are celebrating several graduations. Today it is time for our students in Environmental Sciences and Engineering. This program prepares students for the multidisciplinary nature of environmental engineering problems on our planet. In the last decades, we have seen the climate change and the resulting destruction of our planet caused by humanity. Our program aims to educate students to address this issue. One of the biggest challenges is to buck the trend and to bring our climate back to normal. We hope that one day our engineers will restore the balance on our beautiful planet. Solutions like capturing carbon dioxide, methane and nitrous dioxide from our atmosphere are challenges that are being addressed by engineers educated in our Environmental Sciences and Engineering program. They are our hope and our future. Today we will add several new bright engineers to help in this daunting task…"

About an hour later, the dean finally started calling the graduation candidates forward. One by one, they came forward in alphabetical order. As they arrived at the letter M, he rearranged his clothes and was slightly nervous.

"Our next student has excelled in critical thinking and creativity, and it is my pleasure and honor to announce that Dylan Myers has graduated Summa Cum Lauda and earned his Master's degree in Environmental Sciences and Engineering!"

Dylan stepped onto the stage while the audience applauded louder than before. As he approached the dean, he glanced at his mother, who had never looked so proud. The dean handed him his diploma, and he continued to shake the hands of the rest of the faculty members. Just before leaving the stage, he peered into the crowd, looking for her face. Elizabeth had promised she would be there. To his relief, he saw her waving with a big smile at the back of the auditorium. She had made it. His mother got up to kiss him, and he took her in her arms for a moment.

"I am so proud of you. I am sure your dad is enjoying this moment from up there. Our boy… Summa Cum Lauda!"

He noticed the tears in her eyes and he kissed her on her cheek.

After the applause for the last graduate faded out, the dean completed the ceremony with some final words and, for the last time, the crowd applauded. It felt to him like the closure of an important period in his life and as if someone had fired the starting pistol for a new phase. He got shaken out of his thoughts when Elizabeth jumped in front of him out of the crowd. She swung her arms around him and kissed him on the mouth to congratulate him.

"My Summa Cum Lauda hero," she said with a smile on her pretty face.

He noticed his mother's smile, satisfied, as she observed them. After letting go of him, Elizabeth hugged his mother and congratulated her on her son's graduation. They got along very well, and his mother always spoke highly of Elizabeth. She grabbed his mother by the arm and walked toward the large hall in front of the auditorium where the celebration drinks were taking place.

"Let's get our glass of champagne!" she said enthusiastically while she moved her chin up and swung her long brown hair backwards.

He followed them toward the hall, but got slowed down as several of his professors and fellow students came to congratulate him. In the hall, he noticed Elizabeth entertaining his mother and one of his professors, so he felt comfortable to talk to his friends for a while. Peter, one of his best friends, and a Scottish student who graduated a week earlier with a Master's degree in Energy Science and Technology, handed him a glass of champagne.

"Cheers, my friend! To our future!"

Dylan smiled back and their glasses touched briefly in the air before they took a sip of the champagne.

"So, what are your plans now?" Peter asked him.

"Well, I'm thinking of applying for a job at the largest conglomerates focused on Environmental Sciences. Ideally, I would like to work for Enviro Technologies A/S, the market leader. I understood they've developed the most advanced carbon dioxide capture technologies in the world and plan to roll out a network of factories globally. The rumor goes they've also developed a highly efficient technology to capture methane gas on a large scale. If this is true, it would be a breakthrough because removing methane from the atmosphere is a trickier task than capturing carbon dioxide, mainly because it's far more diluted in the atmosphere. But I'm also going to apply with the numbers two and three in the market, since I don't want to put all my eggs in one basket."

"Enviro!? Wow! That's one of the most prestigious and most mysterious companies on the planet. I understood it's one of those companies wielding the geopolitical power once relegated to states and nations. It's probably the most successful company on the planet and one of the best employers to work for at the moment. Also, one of the most difficult ones to get in, but hey, a Summa Cum Lauda from one of the world's top universities should help."

"Yes, let's hope so. And you? What are your plans?"

"Well, I'm first going to take a long summer break and then I'll join my father's company to work in the nuclear fusion field."

"Wow, sounds interesting, Peter. So, I guess you will move back to Scotland?"

"Yes, after the summer."

"We should plan another mountain climbing trip before you leave."

"Yeah, definitely. Let's hope the air quality improves soon so we can be more comfortable on the outside."

The conversation got interrupted as several people came over to congratulate Dylan on his graduation. While talking to different people, he kept an eye on his mother and was happy to see that Elizabeth kept her company and introducing her to different people. She seemed to enjoy the entire event, which pleased him.

They took a taxi back to the compound after the event. He felt excited about this new period in his life. His mother looked exhausted, but happy, and she kept repeating she had really enjoyed it. During the trip, he could not keep his eyes off Elizabeth. She must have noticed since she smiled with a loving look at him and she put her hand on his hand. Her hands were fresh, and he loved her soft skin. They had been dating for several years, but they knew each other much longer.

The streets were empty besides a few taxis, which was common during those days when it was hot and the air quality was poor. Most people avoided going outside. After driving for a while, he spotted the gray, bunkerlike shape of his compound at the end of the road. There were no windows in the structure, which ensured it could sustain the storms and other extreme weather events. The taxi continued toward the gray doors under the structure. While they entered, he wondered about his future career.

His dream had always been to find a way to repair the damage caused by climate change in the world, restore nature's balance and make the planet a more livable place again. At the same time, his mind remained restless, and he kept wondering about himself and his roots. He always sensed there was this big unanswered question in his life. He had to find the answer, and it would probably be best to do that before starting to work.

Upon arrival he woke up his mother, who had dozed off. He helped her put on her mask and they went back inside. After the hissing sound of the airlock stopped, the doors opened, and they walked into the entrance hall. Elizabeth assisted his mother as she looked exhausted. She was always kind and helping his mother, probably because her parents also suffered from respiratory illness and she knew what it was like. They entered the elevator and went to their floor. Elizabeth lived on the same floor with her parents. In front of the door to his apartment, they said goodbye. She kissed him on the cheek.

"See you after dinner!" she said with a sweet smile on her face, while she entered the apartment next door.

4.

After dinner, Dylan cleaned up the kitchen and told his mother to lie down so she could rest before the guests arrived. He prepared the drinks and placed the snacks on the bar. When he passed through the entrance hall, his eyes fell on the frame again. On a day like this, he missed his father the most. The nice memories of his father made the loss bearable. Still, he sensed the emptiness. He always felt a bit out of place in Switzerland, like it was not his country and he would never really fit in.

It was his mother's country. She was born at the beginning of the twenty-first century in Boudry, a town north of where their compound was located. Her family name was Schneider, and she still had some family in the region. She had met his father, Lawrence, in Lausanne. He was an American working as an electrical engineer on an international project for a multinational company. The moment he laid his eyes on her; he felt attracted to her. Eva, his mother, had been distant and reserved. She was studying at the university in Lausanne and they first met at a bar where she was with her friends. She had explained that Lawrence was quite a charmer. He was very kind to her, and she liked him from the beginning, but she had been the type of woman who did not easily give in to the advances of men.

After asking her several times, she finally agreed to go out with him. They dated for quite a while, and when he returned to Florida for his work, she missed him tremendously. They would see each other a few times a year. On one of her trips to Florida, he proposed to her during a short trip to Key West. Dylan remembered the story very well, since his mother had repeated it often. Her romantic trip to Key West was one of her best memories. Because of this, the destruction of the Keys several years later by a hurricane devastated her. The rising sea levels made living there impossible, and they never rebuilt the destroyed buildings in the Keys. The population was evacuated and the Keys slowly vanished in the ocean. It was only the beginning of a much larger catastrophe.

After their marriage, she moved in with him in his house in Boca Raton, Florida. She found a job in Fort Lauderdale, and Lawrence created his own electrical engineering company. Eva did her best to fit in, but she missed the mountains and her own country a lot. She tried several jobs, but none of them gave her much satisfaction. His company grew fast, and they were making quite a bit of money. She assisted him in doing administrative work for his company. Soon, they moved to a larger house in Boca Raton. The evacuations for the hurricanes became more frequent and a few years later, they bought a large second house in Augusta, Atlanta. Every time they had to evacuate; they would move temporarily to Augusta.

They had tried to have children, but after several years of trying desperately, they registered for adoption. Friends recommended In Vitro fertilization, but they thought it would be better to create a new home for one of the many orphans in the world. Normally, it would have taken years of waiting before one could adopt a child, but a disaster on the other side of the world created a multitude of orphans.

A heat wave in India, combined with a large power failure in and around New Delhi, created what was then the deadliest heat wave ever. Almost half a million people died in just three months. The high humidity and heat killed many, especially the poor. Air conditioners did not work because of the power failure, and it took weeks before they had restored power. The government had tried to move people to underground basements, but they lacked space. The press all over the world had presented this disaster as a record catastrophe and an exceptional once-in-a-lifetime event. Unfortunately, they proved wrong not too long after. It was only the beginning.

Several months later, the adoption agency contacted them. Eva and Lawrence were besotted with their new son. A beautiful Indian boy with a smile that melted even the coldest of hearts. In his mother's bedroom, Dylan often looked at one of the frames on her desk with a picture which was taken at that time. His father was holding this tiny, dark-skinned baby in his strong arms. The look in his father's eyes always touched him deeply. He had wept with happiness when he took Dylan in his arms for the first time. His mother had often told him it was the only time she ever saw his father cry. They showered the boy with love and did everything to raise him well. They made it possible for him to have the best education in the world.

Dylan realized his luck and grabbed every opportunity he could get to learn. The result was there, and his father would be proud of his accomplishment. The ring of the doorbell took him out of his thoughts.

5.

Elliot said goodbye to his colleagues as they entered the elevator. He took the staircase up. It was quite a climb, but he felt like moving after his hard day of work. He had been working for more than a year in the nuclear fusion development center. Before this job, he had followed the Master of Science program in Nuclear Fusion and Engineering Physics program at the Clara Futura University. The Council founded the university twenty-four years ago, and it claimed to be the best university in the world. It worked together with the most prestigious universities around the globe, but developed the best research by itself, which remained exclusive to the Clara Futura University. Students could follow online courses at other universities around the world, in addition to the courses available at Clara Futura.

His father, Amos, had been a proud man when Elliot graduated with honors last year. On the day of his graduation, he had wished his mother could have been there. She would have been so proud. His girlfriend, Elsa, was at his graduation and he had celebrated together with her and his fellow students afterwards. Elsa was still a student at the Clara Futura University, and she studied Medical Engineering and Science and hoped to graduate next year. After his graduation, the Council gave him a job as a trainee in the nuclear fusion development center. He would rotate for several years between different departments in the center and build experience. After the trainee program, the Council would decide on a permanent job for him.

As he climbed the stairs, he thought about his passion. Nuclear fusion fascinated him, and he believed it was the solution to the global energy challenges. With nuclear fusion two lighter atoms merge into a larger one, as opposed to traditional nuclear reactors which are based on nuclear fission, or the splitting of an atom into two separate ones.

About twenty years ago, the Council ordered the construction of the world's first large-scale hydrogen-boron reactor. Several years later, they finished construction. The reactor was a great success. The energy it supplied was more than enough for their community. They even stopped the traditional nuclear reactor they had used before for their energy supply. They stored all overproduction as hydrogen, and the stock had been growing over the years. This technology fascinated him. With the use of special lasers using so called Chirped Pulse Amplification technology, they sent hydrogen at high speed through boron. When it hit the boron, it set off a fusion reaction and the cascading avalanche of reactions that followed created a tremendous amount of energy.

These reactors were a huge leap forward from the traditional fusion reactors, as they did not produce the extremely high temperatures and unstable and difficult to control reactions created by traditional nuclear fusion reactors, like the Tokamak. With the hydrogen-boron reactors there was no risk of a meltdown, no super-heated steam and no nuclear waste. They were working on up-scaling and optimizing the technology further, and about ten years ago they built a second, much larger reactor about thirty kilometers away from the community. This technology was going to solve the world's energy problems. He was sure of it. He had heard that the Council, through one of its companies, had already built several reactors in different countries.

He arrived at the top floor and opened the door to the entrance hall. The bright sun shone through the hall. He passed through the airlock in the door and stepped outside. It was another beautiful day, and he walked through the lush green gardens before going back to the apartment. His father usually arrived home later than him, so he had enough time. The breath of fresh air always did him good, and he strolled amongst the green plants and brightly colored flowers. Above him, the sky was blue and there were no clouds at all.

The long walk did him good. After sitting inside the entire day in his office downstairs, it was great to be out here. It always fascinated him, the beauty of nature, and to observe the fruits hanging on the trees. He stared at the green pears on a tree next to him and continued to the herb section in the extensive garden. Some more people were strolling through the gardens, enjoying the evening sun.

Around this time of the year there were no dark nights, only a few hours of twilight, and Elliot preferred the summer over the winter. The daylight and the sun made him feel good. In the winter months, there were only four hours of daylight, and he would often go for a walk during his lunch break to enjoy the few hours of light. But now it was great to go after his work and enjoy the sun. During the winter the only place where they could get a bit of the feeling of daylight in the evening was in the large greenhouse further down in the gardens, as they illuminated brightly to stimulate plant growth.

He was in the mood for strawberries tonight, so he walked toward the greenhouse. As he got closer, he looked up at the enormous glass construction in front of him. The structure towered above him, and he always felt small next to it. He went inside and the smell of herbs came to him. The smell was strong. He climbed the staircases to the fourth floor. He smelled the strawberries before arriving upstairs. All the way in the back, he spotted a familiar figure. A tall, slender woman with long blond curly hair was picking strawberries. It was Elsa. He waved at her when she looked up. She had just filled a basket with strawberries, and he walked up to her. He smiled at her and gave her a kiss. She looked pretty under the mixture of sunlight and artificial light from the lamps above the strawberries.

They met at the Clara Futura University about four years ago. Medical science fascinated her, and during her study she specialized in Tissue Engineering. Last year Elliot's father had gotten a heart transplant, and he had talked about it at length with Elsa. She explained everything about it to him. He learned that his father's heart had grown out of his own stem cells in a laboratory downstairs. The fact that it comprised his own cells minimized the risk of rejection by the body after the transplant. He had been fascinated with everything Elsa had explained to him.

Amazing that science had evolved so much. Elsa believed that the people in the community would break all longevity records of the world. She believed life could be extended indefinitely with the current medical science. Time would tell, but so far, the oldest person inside was a hundred and eighteen years old. He was one of the Council members and founders of their community. She had explained to him that everybody took special medical injections starting at the age of thirty, which rejuvenated all their cells and body functions. That's why most people in the community, despite their age, looked much younger. His father was a good example. Despite his seventy-four years, he had no wrinkles, no hanging skin, and still had his original hair color.

Elsa hoped to get a job at the hospital laboratory to continue in her specialization in Tissue Engineering. Elliot filled a basket with strawberries while they talked. At some point, Elsa asked,

"So, any news about your visit to the outside reactor?"

"No, not yet. The head of my department said he is still waiting for the green light from the Council."

They continued talking and when they had enough strawberries; they sauntered back. Downstairs, he kissed her goodbye and returned to his apartment. When he opened the door, he was curious to see if his father had arrived home already.

6.

Dylan rushed to the door. After hearing the doorbell ring for the first time, he had continued adding the glasses on the bar until the doorbell rang a second time. His mother had even gotten up and entered the living room. She looked more rested, but still quite pale, and she was coughing again.

It was the Muller family, Elizabeth with her parents and her older brother, Matteo. They all congratulated him on his successful graduation. Elizabeth's parents sat on the couch to talk to Eva, while Dylan offered Elizabeth and Matteo a drink at the bar. Matteo had always been very fond of Dylan. They had been neighbors for more than ten years and when they were younger, they had spent so much time together. Often, they could not go outside because the weather was too extreme or the pollution too high, and they would play in the compound building. They knew every corner of the place.

During the periods when they had to stay inside, they would attend online classes and they would help each other with their homework. After secondary school, Matteo was the first one to attend Military Service and, two years later, Elizabeth and Dylan followed the same program. Dylan had found its military training useful, especially with all the survival techniques he had learned, but he had a different ambition in life. The firm belief drove him that humanity still had a chance to turn around the dire state of the planet and that technology was the tool to make it happen. After their military service, Elizabeth and Dylan both joined the Swiss Federal

Institute of Technology, while Matteo stayed in the Swiss Army and joined the elite Special Forces Command.

Elizabeth had chosen a different field than Dylan and had studied Energy Science and Technology. They started dating during their time at university. To Dylan's surprise, Matteo, who always had been overly protective of his little sister, reacted positively. They saw Matteo less often, since most of the time the army stationed him in Isone in the south of Switzerland, but when they met, they always had a good time. Matteo had always been physically stronger than Dylan, and the army training had made him even stronger and he had a square, muscular body. Matteo and Elizabeth handed their gift to Dylan. It was the newest type of Swiss Army survival knife, fitted with the latest gadgets. Dylan loved it, but barely had the time to thank them when the doorbell rang again.

Slowly more of his friends started arriving and eventually, both the living room and the kitchen were filled with people. He had a great time and at some point Harry, one of Dylan's university friends, challenged Matteo to an arm-wrestling contest. Dylan could barely hold his laughter as Matteo, with his macho manners, could not resist the challenge. Elizabeth knew and stumped Dylan lightly in his stomach.

"Tell him, Dylan!"

He gestured her to lower her voice.

"No, it is okay, he can take a joke."

It was too late to stop him anyway, as he was already getting ready to arm-wrestle with Harry. He let Matteo try a few times to move his arm until Matteo's face had turned red from pushing. It took Harry only a few seconds to push Matteo's muscular arm on the table. Matteo looked flabbergasted. With a big grin on his face, Harry rolled up his sleeve completely to show the point where his bionic arm connected to his upper arm. They all laughed and even Matteo got a smile on his surprised face, realizing they had tricked him.

"You bastard, that's one realistic bionic arm you have there."

Harry had lost his arm in an accident during a storm last year, and his father was the president of one of the largest companies in the world, specializing in medical science and robotics. They had fitted him with one of the most advanced bionic arms out there, and except for the connection point, it was a perfect copy of his lost arm. Most people could not afford this expensive technology and had to settle for cheaper variants.

Later in the evening, Elizabeth put her arm around Dylan, who was talking with his friends in the kitchen. Her parents had gone home already, and he looked at her while his friends continued talking. In a low voice, she said,

"I helped your mother get to her bedroom. She looked exhausted, and she coughed a lot."

"Thanks for helping her. Yeah, I'm worried about her."

Harry suddenly interrupted the two of them.

"Matteo tells me you're both going to apply to the same companies?"

"That's right. Elizabeth has already started applying to Enviro Technologies in Denmark and to three of its competitors, one in Norway, one in Canada and one in China. I'll do the same in the coming week. We're hoping to get hired at the same company, so we can move together to Denmark or one of the other countries."

"Enviro, huh? That's the market leader, no? They make our respos. Impressive company, but I heard it's one of the hardest to get into."

"Yep, that's what I understood as well. Elizabeth is going to have her first video interview next week with them."

Suddenly, the power cut and all the lights went out. It happened regularly during the hotter periods as the heavy usage of air-conditioning and air-filtering units drained energy and the hot weather made the power grid more sensitive.

"Power outage. Don't worry! It shouldn't be too long before our back-up system will start."

Just at that moment, the lights came back on and everybody in the room cheered. They had equipped their building with hydrogen fuel cells, which were the perfect back-up during outages. Dylan could not help thinking of the poorer people who did not have back-up systems for their power. Their houses would slowly get warmer and the polluted air would enter their homes. Even in Switzerland, the life expectancy continued to drop, although not as dramatically as in other countries.

The rest of the evening, he had a blast with his friends, and by the time the last one went home, Dylan felt tired. He had enjoyed the evening and while he cleaned up the apartment; he again had that strong feeling that a new phase was starting in his life. Still, something was troubling him and he had so many questions running around in his head. His mother's coughing took him out of his thoughts, and he went to check on her.

7.

Two weeks later, Dylan was sitting next to her hospital bed with tears in his eyes. His mother looked exhausted and breathed through an oxygen mask.

Several days earlier he had called the emergency services, after his mother had fainted and dropped onto the floor in the living room. He tried to wake her up again, but she did not respond. The paramedics arrived ten minutes later and luckily could reanimate her.

She had been in the hospital since that day, but she remained weak and had to stay for observation. He stayed with her most of the time and would talk with her when she was awake, especially about the past. He asked her many questions, as he knew deep down that her end was near. They would talk often, as long as she could, but she slept mostly.

One day he asked her about his birth parents and she tried to respond, but had difficulty breathing.

"We've talked about that in the past. I…I'm really sorry, but I've little information about your biological parents. They didn't tell us at the time. I know they're from New Delhi, but that's all I know."

"I know I keep bringing it up, but I've this feeling deep down that something is missing from my life. I mean, you've been the best parents a child could wish for, but I've to find out more about them. Do you understand?"

She smiled faintly at him and then muttered,

"I understand. All the information I have is in a file…a folder…in the vault."

"A vault?"

He had never noticed a vault in the apartment. His mother looked exhausted, and she closed her eyes for a moment. A moment later, she opened them and continued explaining.

"The vault is in my bedroom… in… the… the… wall, be… behind my clothes… haaaahh," she sighed, and her head dropped to the side as she fell back asleep.

She slept for a long time, and he stayed with her in the hospital. Later that day, he came back from a walk through the building. He looked at her, and she was still asleep. He took a seat and read a book.

At some point, she opened her eyes and looked at him. Dylan noticed and moved closer to her and gently put his hand on top of hers. She looked exhausted, but she tried to speak. With her other hand, she moved the oxygen mask to the side and, in a trembling voice, she spoke.

"You're a sweet boy… and I'm so proud of you. I feel my time has come… just promise me one thing."

Visibly moved, he looked at her. She put the mask back on her face for a moment to catch her breath before continuing.

"Follow your heart in life and pursue your dreams! You ne… never know how much time you'll get on this planet, so make the best out of it and li… live your life."

She put back the mask and he gave her a kiss on the cheek.

"I will. I will. I love you."

His mother smiled at him, but looked so fragile. He held her hand while she fell back asleep. That was the last time he spoke with his mother.

8.

After the funeral, Dylan returned home with Elizabeth and her family. They all had been a wholehearted support to him, but now he wanted to be alone. As he entered his apartment, the sadness came back to him. His mother had always been there for him, so the emptiness and lack of life in the apartment weighed heavily on him. He felt his mother had died too young at fifty-two, and he had hoped she would have been much longer in his life.

The last years his mother had suffered from chronic obstructive pulmonary disease and gotten weaker every year. Her death was not a surprise, but still saddened him. It also triggered thoughts of his father. The memories of that horrible day he had tried to push away, but they were part of him and now they came back to him. He was alone now, with both his father and mother no longer there.

All alone in this harsh and savage world, scarred and angered by the climate change caused by humanity. His parents no longer needed to struggle for survival. They had found their peace now. The thought that his parents were finally together soothed his grief. Deep down, he knew his love for both of them would keep them alive in his memory. He thought of one of the ancient poets, Khalil Gibran, who said, "For life and death are one, even as the river and the sea are one." His mother used to read his poetry to him when he was young, and some of his poems had touched him deeply.

In the living room, he sat for several hours staring at the picture of him standing between his parents. They were the best parents he could have wished for, and he thought back to her last words. They had marked him and he planned to live by them. His dream was to construct efficient factories that would capture carbon dioxide from the atmosphere. He would like to construct as many factories as possible all over the world so they could bring the concentration of carbon dioxide in the air back down to healthy levels and nature could restore itself on the planet. And he would like to do the same for the other greenhouse gases like methane and nitrous dioxide. This had driven him to study Environmental Sciences and Engineering and to excel in this field. Now his ambition was to go work for the best company in this field and to realize his dream.

Still, there was something else tormenting his thoughts regularly. Now, with his mother gone, the urge had grown even stronger. He knew this would keep haunting him and would distract him from pursuing his dream. This could not continue like that. He had to do something.

9.

As Elliot entered the hallway of their apartment, he heard noises further away. A strong smell coming from the kitchen filled the room, and he recognized it immediately. He stuck his head round the corner of the kitchen and his father looked at him with his dark brown eyes. He smiled at him, which did not happen so often. His father was making his favorite Indian dish, Chana masala, a tangy chickpea curry.

"Chana masala, nice! That has been a while," Elliot said as he tore a small piece from the freshly baked naan bread on the table.

"Yeah, I finished early today, so I thought to surprise you with your favorite dish."

His father was in a good mood, apparently. He wondered what the reason was, while he was swallowing the naan. Over the last few years, his father had become grumpier and less cheerful. Often, he would not say much and stare at the television for hours. Elliot asked him why he was in such a good mood, and his father explained he had a good day at work.

His father was in charge of the defense department of the community, and he reported directly to the Council. In the past few years, Elliot had asked his father questions about his work regularly, and as he grew older, he understood things better. His father was responsible for protecting the community, and amongst others, he advised the Council on which defense systems to buy. In addition, he advised them which military or defense companies in the outside world to invest in. The Council decided which investments or divestments the community would make. They invested in equipment or machinery for direct use, but they also invested in or bought companies which they believed would generate a nice return or which could help extend the power of the community.

When Elliot was younger, his father had taught him the concept of money, which was new to him since inside the community there was no money. Nobody had money. He found it weird that people needed it. Inside the community, everything he needed was freely available. His father had explained that outside, the world worked differently. If you wanted to have something on the outside, you would need to pay money for it. His father had also explained that even though nobody in the community had money, the community as a whole had money and the Council decided what to do with it.

Today, apparently, his father had presented a new investment proposal to the Council, and they had given him quite some praise for his work. They had approved his father's proposal and now they were going to buy a company that developed a new military drone technology. This technology could enhance the existing security system to protect the community. Elliot understood the good mood of his father now, as it was a great honor to get praise from the Council.

His father always spoke highly of the Council, which comprised the wisest men and women in the community. He explained to Elliot that they had done extremely well with their investments in the outside world and that it was one of the reasons the community life was so comfortable. At school, Elliot had learned that life outside was completely different and difficult. People were struggling to survive in the harsh and inhospitable world outside.

Despite all the videos he had seen about the world, he still had difficulty imagining the reality of life outside. It fascinated him, and often he thought about how it would be to live outside. They allowed almost no one in the community to go outside. Only a few persons went occasionally as part of their work and only after explicit approval by the Council. Elliot often asked his father about it. His father was one of the few people who would regularly go outside since he was in charge of defense. Although most of his visits were within the vicinity of the community, where the defensive security system was located. He rarely went beyond the vicinity since he settled here twenty-four years ago.

Still, he taught his son a lot about the world. Although his father always presented things with more drama and horror than his mother had done. She died when he was ten years old. She used to tell him about the beauty of the world in the past and how she hoped that one day they would restore the climate to how it was before. About how they traveled around the world and visited the beautiful places it offered. He missed her a lot.

His father told him about the harsh outside world where life was a tough struggle for survival, especially for the poor. He loved to talk about the big disasters: the deadly heat waves, the hurricanes, tropical storms, tornados and typhoons, the enormous wildfires, the flooding of cities and countries, thunderstorms, extreme rainfall, gigantic hailstorms, landslides, the outbreak of deadly diseases, global pandemics, the droughts, food and drinking water shortages, deadly toxic clouds, acid rain and constant air pollution, wars and conflicts. All had resulted in many, many refugees. Climate change seemed to have angered the planet and changed the world into an inhospitable place. Elliot watched the news on the television. And every day there were disasters happening somewhere on the planet. It had become part of normal life, and the dreadful events all over the world numbed him.

His father did not hesitate to emphasize that they were part of the lucky ones. The ones who had planned ahead and realized in time what all the warning signals had meant. Each catastrophe in the past sparked a brief and justifiable alarm, followed by a collective shrug of the shoulders. Most people had not grasped the scale of the threat. His father always compared humanity with the famous experiment of frogs in a pot of boiling water. In this experiment, they put a frog in a pot with tepid water. The water temperature would gradually increase and begin to boil slowly. The complacent frog did not perceive the danger until it was too late. It did not jump out and eventually boiled to death.

People had failed to act decisively despite being aware of the threat, like the frog in the boiling water. He had explained to Elliot how the founders of the community had had a clear vision over thirty years ago and had acted swiftly. Their plans had convinced his father and mother to join them. The same year Elliot was born, they had moved in and had become part of the community. Although he was born outside, he had no memories of it and had learned everything about the world afterwards through school, television and the stories of his parents.

Elliot had always been curious and enthusiastic about the world outside. His father kept telling him he should lower his expectations and just count his blessings to be part of the community.

"Outside is an uncertain place full of misery and struggle for survival," his father had told him.

His father was always negative about it, and this fed his curiosity even more. He cherished the memories of the bedtime stories his mother had told him about the outside world when he was young.

He was thrilled when Elias, his boss in the nuclear fusion development center, suggested that he might join on a research trip to the external reactor. The external hydrogen-boron reactor was about five times larger than the one supplying the community with power and was a scientific masterpiece. It powered the villages around them and two of what they called climate plants, one capturing carbon dioxide and another one capturing methane.

The carbon dioxide plant had been built about ten years ago, together with the external reactor. About five years ago, they had constructed another plant to take methane out of the atmosphere. The nuclear fusion development center was working hard on improving and up-scaling the technology of the reactor, while the environmental science center was doing the same for the climate plants. Other research focused on the creation of other large-scale plants to deal with the excess of other greenhouse gases in the atmosphere, like nitrous oxide and fluorinated gases.

Elliot dreamed that one day they would roll out this technology all over the world and restore the Earth's climate back to a healthy level. A daunting task and his father had called him a dreamer, but his mother had always told him that the future belongs to those who believe in the beauty of their dreams. He held on to that thought, and it gave him the courage to pursue his dream.

His father told him not to get his hopes up too much, since the Council barely approved trips to the outside. He annoyed Elliot when his father added that he was only a trainee who had just started and was not the most likely person to go on a research expedition. Was that how his father thought of him? His boss Elias had given him lots of praise since he worked at the nuclear fusion development center. Few people graduated with honors in the Master of Science in Nuclear Fusion and Engineering Physics program. No, his father was underestimating him. Still, for now he could do nothing else than be patient and wait for news from the Council.

10.

It was quiet in the apartment. Dylan could only hear the low humming noise of the climate control system in the room. After getting dressed, he stepped into the living room and the place had never felt so empty. He looked at the picture on the table and he thought of his mother. All those years she had always been there for him. The sadness slowly transformed into sweet sorrow. Life continued, and he felt he owed it to his mother to make the best out of his life.

The days after the funeral, he had slowly started arranging his mother's belongings. Elizabeth had helped him by sorting and packing her clothes in boxes to give them away. Tonight, the Mullers invited him again for dinner. He had eaten there a few times since his mother's death, and they had been supportive and kind to him.

Elizabeth had advanced in her job application and they had invited her for a last round of interviews next week at Enviro Technologies in Denmark. She was excited about the prospect of working there, and it spurred Dylan to apply. He had just had a first video interview, which went very well, and next week they had planned a second round of video interviews with him. Ideally, they would both find a job at Enviro and move together to Denmark.

Today he had other plans, though. Yesterday, when they emptied the wardrobe in his mother's bedroom, he had found the hidden vault in the back of one of the cupboards. Just like she had told him in the hospital. Unfortunately, it was locked and his mother had not told him how to find the key.

Yesterday evening, he had searched for the key in vain until late in the evening. Now he was fresh and full of energy again, and in good spirits, he restarted his search for the key. He had convinced himself that the contents of this vault might answer the questions about his past that troubled him all his life. No cupboard was spared as he searched everywhere. He worked meticulously and searched through the apartment in a logical way. He did not just search for a key, but also took the time to sort out all her belongings and decide what to keep, what to throw, or what to give away. Time passed quickly and at the end of the morning he had still not found the key, but he had found a box with old pictures, some documents and several memory sticks. He looked at them in the kitchen while having some lunch.

Most of the old pictures he had seen before, like the wedding pictures of his parents. The pictures of the ceremony at the Château de Cormondrèche were lovely. His parents looked beautiful in their wedding attire. His mother had insisted that the wedding would be close to Boudry, where she had grown up. The view from the castle over the Lac de Neuchâtel was magnificent. The reflection of the blue sky with a few white clouds on the lake's surface was like a perfect mirror. Dylan looked even more astounded at the blooming and green nature around the lake.

The wedding had been in the year 2025, and things had changed tremendously since then. The memories of his visit to the castle about ten years ago were still clear. It was about a week after a heavy storm had passed over the region. The air pollution was relatively low after the storm, and his mother wanted to visit her sister in Boudry. Dylan and Elizabeth, who were already close friends at the time, had come along for the day. The storm had left a trail of destruction, with many houses having their roofs ripped off. Many trees had fallen and the heavy rain had caused several mudslides, leaving many parts of the landscape dark and gray. The castle had been heavily damaged. These violent storms became so common that the building sector adapted, and the more recently constructed houses resembled bunkers with concrete roofs. The visit had left a deep impression on him.

At the bottom of the pile, he found some childhood pictures of his mother. It marked him that most of the pictures were taken outside and how beautiful the weather and nature were. If only we could go back to that time, he thought to himself. He found some pictures of his parents' honeymoon to the Keys and a picture of his father holding him as a little baby in his arms. He looked so happy, with his light skin face next to this dark-skinned baby in a white jumpsuit.

After going through the piles of photos, he checked out the memory sticks. One of them had short movies on them. The first one he played was of their honeymoon in the Keys. His parents swimming in the clear waters of the Gulf of Mexico next to some dolphins. A scene you would not see today anymore. The oceans were too polluted, full of plastics, and many of the marine life had disappeared. Vast areas of the oceans had been transformed into dead zones. In other areas algae bloomed and dominated the seas. Jellyfish also proliferated in some regions and were so abundant in the oceans that in some places the waters were infested with these stinging creatures. A fall in those waters full of jellyfish could end your life instantly.

Subsequently, he watched a movie of his parents picking him up at the adoption center. It touched him to see the tears of happiness on his father's face when he held him in his arms. Another movie showed his father carrying him on his shoulders and playing with him in the garden of their house in Boca Raton. After this the movies were no longer in Boca Raton but in their house in Augusta. He must have been five or six years old when they moved permanently to Augusta and he started attending school there.

In between the happy family movies, there was one different movie which shocked him. It showed the house in Boca Raton, or at least what was left of it. The house had been completely destroyed and flattened, with only one wall still standing. Debris was everywhere and the lower parts were all underwater. In the past, his mother had talked several times about this disaster. An enormous hurricane had created a storm never seen before in the region. The sea level had been slowly rising over the years, but with the construction of sea walls, Miami had kept the water out for years. This storm combined with a springtide was too much though and had ravaged Florida. Most of Miami and the cities and towns around, like Fort Lauderdale and Boca Raton, had been flooded and destroyed. The storm had relatively minor casualties since the government had evacuated the region. Consequently, the American government had made an extraordinary decision and did not allow people to return to rebuild their homes. The rising sea levels were becoming too big a threat, and the whole South and all the coastal regions in Florida became an uninhabited zone. They created many more of these zones thereafter.

Later movies showed his cheerful youth, and watching the movies made him realize what a lovely couple his parents had been. During their time in Augusta, they looked happy as a family. He checked another movie and noticed it was the first movie in Switzerland. He must have been twelve years old, and he was playing with Elizabeth and Mateo on the lake shore of Lac Léman near Lausanne. While checking the memory stick, he noticed that after a period of frequent movies there had been no movies for several years after that horrible day in the year 2039 in Augusta when he had seen his father for the last time. He had been ten years old at the time, and it had left a deep mark in his life.

His wristwatch vibrated and shook him out of his thoughts. It was time for dinner at his neighbors. He couldn't believe how fast the time had passed. He freshened up in the bathroom, put on a clean shirt and went next door. The Mullers were very warm and understanding with him, and their company distracted him from the sadness he had felt before.

During the dinner they discussed all kinds of topics. At some point Matteo started talking about some of his colleagues who had been drafted for a mission with a European joint army task force to reinforce the security at several large food storage warehouses. With this year's drought all over Europe, food production had been much lower and food prices had gone up. Several warehouses had been plundered, and they called upon the military to protect food transports and storage places. They were also upgrading the security making future ransacking more difficult.

The last few years the food supply was disrupted regularly after a drought or another disaster and this had resulted in many people starving all over Europe. Even rich people like Dylan and the Mullers, who were living in protected compounds, had been affected. They had stored large quantities of food in the compound, but for months they had eaten only a limited choice of starchy foods or canned food. They had reduced the portions to make the stock last longer.

After dinner, they continued their lively discussion in the living room. Matteo disagreed with his parents about the severity of the security measures that should be taken.

"The current system is too soft. People still dare to pillage warehouses. Look at countries, like China or the U.S., that have implemented stricter security measures like police drones and robots in the streets and have increased the punishments. They don't have riots or plundering."

"Please, I hope they will never implement those systems in our country. Those police drones and robots are horrible. They execute looters on the spot. Monstrous! Those poor people have little choice. Starvation causes desperation and turns people into cornered animals," Matteo's mother said.

She wheezed, a sure sign that the conversation had deeply affected her. She had the same lung disease as his mother, although less advanced. Many older people suffered from some kind of respiratory illness. The number of cases had been rising tremendously in the last decades because of the increased global warming and related air pollution.

"Thanks to their technology, we have solved the refugee problem in Europe, though."

"Please don't talk about this horrible border. I am going to bed," and she left the room.

She always had difficulty discussing the harsh measures that had been taken in Europe. It had taken years of discussion, but eventually the European countries had no choice anymore. The food shortages, poverty, wars and armed conflicts, natural disasters, harsh living conditions and misery all over the world had caused huge streams of refugees.

On the east side of Europe, they had built electronic fences, with cameras and drones flying around to control the borders. Any trespasser would get one warning, after which any refusal to return would lead to one of these drones firing their high-tech guns. In a second, the drone would obliterate the trespasser, barely leaving a trace. On the south side, a long string of floating border buoys, which detected any trespasser, guarded the Mediterranean Sea, and within ten minutes, a drone would show up and convince the trespasser to return immediately or obliteration would follow.

Elizabeth, also displeased with the topic, intervened at some point and abruptly changed the subject.

"How is it going with your mom's things? Are you making any progress?" she asked Dylan.

"I packed all her clothes and started sorting through her other documents and stuff, but I got distracted when I ran into these old photos and movies. I spent the entire afternoon looking at them."

"Ah, but that's nice. After someone passes away, memories become the treasures in which that person lives on."

"Yeah, I ran into this picture of us when we went altogether on this mountain hiking trip from Grindelwald to Faulhorn."

"That was an amazing trip!" Matteo said. "I remember it was one of those rare months that the air was relatively clean. That view over the Brienzersee was spectacular."

They continued talking about their hiking trips until late in the evening. After kissing Elizabeth goodbye, he returned to his apartment. The documents and boxes still lay scattered throughout the apartment the way he had left them. Still, he had not found the key to the vault in his mother's bedroom, but it would have to wait till the next day. He felt exhausted and went directly to bed.

11.

His frustration had grown to immense proportions, as Dylan had been looking for the key for almost a week now. After combing through all her belongings, he had searched in her computer files. The search for a clue about those documents became almost like an obsession for him. The last few days, he had been busy also with several other matters.

A few days ago, Elizabeth had gone to Denmark, taking the hyper-loop connection between Bern and Copenhagen. A day later, she had called him. The last round of interviews at Enviro Technologies had gone well, and they had indicated they were going to make her an offer to come work for them. Meanwhile, they had shown her around the compound where all the employees lived. She had been ecstatic over the phone.

"It's an amazing place, much more luxurious than ours. They have a large swimming pool, great sport facilities and a leisure center with games, bars and clubs. They even have these human looking robots that assist you if you need anything. Did you know they have about a hundred and twenty different nationalities working for them?"

"Wow! That's truly international, and those robots sound fancy. Any idea what they're going to offer you?"

"Not yet, but they want me to come work at their Energy Development department and I understood that they require all employees to live in the compound. It looks like a safe place to live, probably safer than where we are now."

She was really excited about the prospect of working and living there. So much that he worried about his own job application now. What if he would not get a job offer at Enviro Technologies? The other companies where he had applied for a job were in other countries. Would she still move to Denmark without him? They had not really discussed all this, but now it came so close. He did not really believe in a relationship at a distance. They were both also applying at other companies, but Enviro was by far the most prestigious firm to work for.

The day after, he had his second round of video interviews and he was nervous. The whole morning, he had prepared himself by going through research about the company and the department he would like to work for. The fact that Elizabeth was going to get a job offer increased his nervousness. He realized he really needed to get hired, otherwise they might get into an awkward situation.

In the afternoon, he sat prepared and well-dressed behind the video camera. The interview was with three people from Enviro Technologies and lasted more than three hours. The interviewers were razor sharp, and he felt exhausted afterwards, but he thought he did not do too bad. They gave no feedback afterwards, just that they would get back to him the day after. This left him feeling unsettled for the rest of that day, and in the evening, he had no news to tell to Elizabeth when she called from Denmark.

After a restless night, he took his time to have breakfast, after which he continued going through the files on his mother's computer. Early in the afternoon he was going to have an appointment with the notary in Lausanne, about his mother's will, and this also kept him from sleeping well.

While searching for the missing documents and the key, he had found several bank statements. His mother seemed to have some funds available on these accounts, but nothing spectacular. If this would be the total size of his inheritance, he could probably manage for a year without income, but then he would really need a job. Even so, he was not sure if he had a complete insight into the financial position of his late parents.

He had been only ten years old when they moved from America to Switzerland. He remembered they moved into the compound quickly after emigrating and only later, when he was an adult, he realized how expensive their apartment in the compound was. Consequently, he always assumed they were richer than most people, but this did not match the total balance of all his mother's funds on the bank statements he found.

After twenty minutes in the taxi, he arrived at the Avenue Général-Guisan where the notary had his office amongst the many office buildings. He put his respo back on his face and pushed the green button to open the taxi's door. The doors opened with a buzz and the hot air fell on him like an uncomfortable, warm blanket.

Summers had become so uncomfortable that he limited the time spent outside to an absolute minimum. Only on the fresher days he would go for a walk or some other outdoor activity. Unfortunately, each summer there were less of those days. After passing through the airlock, he walked to the reception in the building while he took off his respo.

A moment later he entered the office of notary Laurent Meister. He shook the hand of this gray and meager man who welcomed him in his office and invited him to take a seat.

"Mister Myers, first of all my condolences for the loss of your mother."

"Thank you."

"They've appointed me as the executor of the estate of late Eva Myers-Schneider and I prepared you a copy of her will. Let me walk you through it."

The notary handed him a document and started reciting the will to him. He listened attentively while staring at the document.

Later, in the taxi on his way back to the compound, he still could not believe it. His mother had left him a sizable inheritance, enough for him to live a comfortable life without working. He could retire now before ever having worked in his life. It felt surreal to him. His modest mother never had mentioned anything to him.

Apparently, after his father had passed away, she had inherited his wealth and had invested most of the amount in a fund focused on so called 'green' investments, companies focused on activities beneficial to the environment. These investments had flourished, and his mother had accumulated a sizeable amount of money all those years.

In the evening, Elizabeth came over to his apartment. She just returned from Denmark and was so excited about her trip and the prospect of living in the Enviro compound. It took a while before she finished talking about it and asked Dylan about his day. He explained about his meeting with the notary. It baffled her when she heard the amount of the inheritance.

"Wow, with an amount like that you can retire immediately!"

"Yeah, I still have difficulty believing it. My mother, such a prudent investor."

"So are you still going to continue to apply for a job then?"

"Funny that you ask, since I thought about that today, but I guess deep down I realize all this money does not change much. My dream is to help speed up the capturing of carbon dioxide and other greenhouse gases to make this world a livable planet again. What good is money if our life expectancy keeps plummeting the way it does?"

"True!"

"Anyhow, time for something else…" he said, and he started kissing her, "… I missed you last week!"

"Yeah, me too!"

They hugged on the couch, and her touch and smell absorbed him. He kissed her and stroked her long, brown hair. He started undressing her slowly while he caressed her all over and slowly the passion took over.

Later that evening, she gathered her clothes from the floor as she came out of his bedroom. While she dressed, she peered into his mother's bedroom and noticed the piles of paper and the emptied drawers in the bedroom.

"Did you have any luck finding that key?"

Dylan came walking to her in his bathrobe and gently kissed her on her lips.

"No, it's a mystery and a damn frustrating one."

"Well, I'm sure it will show up eventually. Are you joining me tomorrow for a swim in the Olympic pool in the Lausanne Sports Club?"

"Ah, nice! Absolutely! What time?"

"I will pick you up around two in the afternoon."

They kissed one more time, and she left the apartment. He watched some news, after which he walked back to his bedroom. While he passed his mother's bedroom, he glanced at the cardboard boxes and piles of documents. One more time, he tried to imagine where his mother could have hidden the key. His eye fell on the paintings and frames with photos on the wall. He rushed into her room.

Frantically, he started taking everything off the wall, checking if she had hidden anything behind. Nothing behind the paintings. Nothing behind the frames, except for one. Behind the wedding photo of his parents, there was an envelope taped to it. He opened it and there was a letter inside. It was from his father to his mother when he was back in Florida, while she was in Switzerland. A beautiful love letter and he got tears in his eyes reading it. He sensed the profound love his father had felt for his mother.

After reading it, he continued looking in the room for spaces he might have missed in his search. In a wave of desperation, he moved the furniture away from the walls to look behind it. After looking behind the last piece, his mother's desk, he had found nothing again. He felt so frustrated and enraged that he pushed the desk away from him with so much strength that the drawers fell out on the other side, onto the floor. Rubbing his hand through his dark-brown hair, he calmed down and started picking up the drawers one by one to put them back inside, until suddenly he froze up. There it was. A silver-colored key taped under a drawer. That must be the one.

12.

Jubilant is the only word to describe how Elliot felt the moment his boss told him that the Council had approved his participation in the research trip to the external reactor. On the day of the good news, he rushed home after work. He knew his father would still be at work, so he rushed to Elsa's apartment. When she opened the door, he said ecstatically,

"The Council has approved the research trip! My first time outside!"

What he said was technically incorrect, since he was born outside and had entered the community a few weeks after. Since his birth, he had never been outside and his excitement was understandable, since they allowed only a few people to go.

"Wow, congratulations!" Elsa said with a smile on her face.

"Congratulations Elliot. Although you'd better be careful! Outside can be quite a dangerous place," Elsa's mother said.

"I will, ma'am! They're going to prepare the entire visit in the next few weeks, and we're going to get some training before."

"Yes, I can't image the Council would leave anything to chance there," she responded and walked to the kitchen.

"So, when is this research trip going to take place and is it for the day or longer?" Elsa asked.

"Two weeks from now, and I believe it's just for the day. But a long day since we will leave early in the morning and come back in the evening."

"Exciting! I've never been outside and I'm not sure if I would dare to go."

Elsa had been born inside about a year after her parents had entered. Her entire life had always been inside this confined space. Their world was a small one, and they knew the place like the back of their hands.

They went for a walk together and climbed up to the higher parts of the greenhouse, where the views could be breathtaking. They looked at the horizon. On one side there was a high, gray mountain range, while on the other side the mountains were lower and more green-grayish. His father had explained that when they had just moved in here, the mountains were still covered with snow in summer, but that was a long time ago.

He returned home after a while, but to his disappointment, his father had not yet returned from work. He prepared some tea and watched the news program until he heard the electronic lock on the door. He got up and rushed to the entrance hall.

"Hi dad! Guess what?!"

His father looked tired and puzzled at him, and Elliot did not wait for him to guess.

"I'm going to the outside! They approved the research trip!"

"Congratulations, son. I'm happy for you," he said with a faint smile on his face and added, looking slightly worried.

"I hope it will be safe though. The outside can be a harsh place."

"Yes, don't worry, dad. They're going to prepare for the trip for weeks and we'll get a lot of training. Also, Elias told me they'll only go if all the conditions were perfect. They're not taking any risks."

"Okay, I guess they know what they're doing. Well, I better prepare you a perfect meal than to celebrate."

They both walked to the kitchen, and he helped his father prepare dinner. After dinner, Elliot told his father he was going to meet up with Elsa. As he opened the front door, he overheard his father making a call, and he waited at the door to listen in.

"Hi Elias, it's Amos here. Sorry to disturb you so late. Elliot told me they allow him to go outside with you on a research trip. I'm worried about my son. Are you sure it is safe?"

Elliot could not hear what Elias answered and did not want to eavesdrop any longer. He closed the door and rushed to Elsa, but he thought his father worried too much. What could possibly go wrong?

13.

He rushed in his bathrobe to the vault in the back-wall of the cupboard. It was after midnight already, but Dylan could not wait another second anymore now he finally had found the key. Excited, he tried the key. Thank God. It fit. He turned the key, and the lock made a sliding noise, after which the heavy door opened. He opened it completely. Inside, he found a pile of documents with two dark boxes on top. He took everything out of the vault, and to his surprise one of the two boxes was very heavy, as if they had filled it with lead or something. He put everything on the desk.

Even though the information he was looking for was most likely somewhere in the pile of documents, he could not resist opening the dark boxes first. They looked magical. The first box contained his mother's jewelry, and he recognized her diamond necklace immediately, a gift from his father on their wedding anniversary. He briefly scanned through the jewelry before opening the second box, which was much heavier. As soon as he took the lid off, he understood why it was so heavy. Many one-ounce gold bars lay neatly arranged in rows inside the box. He counted sixty of them in the box, almost four pounds of gold. His mother had been a wise investor.

With the economy in a continuous recession for the previous two decades and many countries collapsing in financial distress, investing in gold was basic financial prudence and his mother had always been very conservative with money. They wasted no money on unnecessary luxury, but she spent on the things that mattered in life, like the university education of Dylan or the apartment in the compound.

After putting the gold bars back in the box, his eyes focused on the pile of documents. One by one, he started going through them, scanning them carefully to check if it was the document he had been searching for. He felt tired but still could not resist, and he continued going through the pile. The financial accounts, which the notary had told him about, were all there. They went almost thirty years back, and it reminded him of a famous quote from Albert Einstein, "Compound interest is the eighth wonder of the world. He who understands it, earns it; he who doesn't, pays it."

About an hour later, he got to a folder with some documents written in English and some papers with some weird letters on it. He recognized the letters. It was Hindi in the Devanagari script. His heart started beating faster as he realized he might have found what he was looking for.

First, he read the English documents, which were his adoption papers certified by the District Court of Palm Beach County in Florida. Then he found a form on which they had marked "Child's name after adoption: Dylan Myers". He read the document carefully and noticed that the section with information from the original birth certificate was incomplete. The child's name at birth was filled in with only Yagnesh, with no last name. It marked his birthdate seven of April in the year 2029 and the birth certificate number. At the box "Child's Birth Place" it stated New Delhi, Republic of India. Below this, they had left the box with the biological mother's and father's name blank. Disappointed, he continued reading the other papers.

Another English document titled "Amended Birth Certificate" stated his name and his late adoptive parents. The number on the certificate did not match the number that was marked on the adoption papers. Then he found two return plane tickets to New Delhi in his parent's name and one ticket to Miami from New Delhi in his name. He never realized before that his parents actually had traveled to New Delhi to pick him up.

He scanned through the other documents and started now on the ones written in Hindi. Unfortunately, he did not know how to read Hindi and, to his relief, there was an English translation on the backside of the papers. One document was from the court in New Delhi approving his adoption. It had the same birth certificate number on it as the one on the English adoption papers. So, he figured this must be the number from the original birth certificate. On another document, it stated the name of the orphanage where he was registered before his adoption. Nowhere he could find the names of his birth parents.

At three o'clock in the morning, he felt exhausted and disappointed at not finding anything about his biological parents. The only useful leads he found were the original birth certificate number and the name and address of the orphanage where they adopted him from. This search could get more complicated than he had figured. Tired, he put everything back in the vault and crawled into bed.

14.

Full of hope and anxiety, Dylan opened the e-mail from Enviro Technologies in his inbox. It was already late in the morning. He had slept long and deeply last night and felt rested now. He felt a wave of relief when he read that he had passed to the final round of interviews. They invited him to come to their head office in Denmark next week. They would make all the reservations for the transportation and he would sleep there for two nights, just like Elizabeth had done. He was excited and confirmed the invitation.

With fresh energy he continued the search for his birth parents, although his chances to find anything looked slim. The only useful leads he had found in the documents were his name, a birth certificate number and the name of the orphanage. First, he reexamined all the documents from the vault to make sure he had missed nothing. This did not give him any extra information, so he continued his search online and focused on the orphanage. To his relief, the Udayan Ghar orphanage still existed, which was quite a wonder given how many disasters had struck the city of New Delhi. It had made the headlines in the news so often in the past few years, that people had nicknamed it "The city of death". He found a phone number of the orphanage.

It was twelve o'clock and Lausanne was three and a half hours behind New Delhi, where it was three thirty in the afternoon now. He called immediately. The phone rang a few times before a woman answered the line. He explained to the woman that he wanted some information about an adoption and she passed him on to the manager of the orphanage.

"Garima Patel speaking," a woman with a strong Indian accent answered.

"Good afternoon, Miss Patel. My name is Dylan Myers, and I was adopted twenty-four years ago by Lawrence and Eva Myers, who lived at the time in Florida in the United States of America. I'm calling to get some more information about my adoption…"

He continued explaining his entire case to the woman, and she listened patiently, after which she replied.

"I understand your request, Mister Myers, and I'm really sorry, sir, but we never give out any information about birth parents. The law doesn't allow us to do so."

"There must be a way to get this information. What do other people do in such a case?"

"I'm sorry, but there's no way. The law forbids it."

"Would it make a difference if I come over there? Could I maybe look into the files?"

"No sir, you can't. I'm sorry, but I've got to go now. Have a nice day, sir!"

She hung up the phone before he could even say goodbye. That did not go so well, he thought. It sounded logical, what Garima Patel had said. If it was the law that forbade to give out names of birth parents to adopted children, then over the phone she could only state these rules. Still, he would not give up so easily. He looked for a solicitor specializing in adoption laws in New Delhi and emailed him, explaining his case. Tomorrow he would call to follow up.

Quickly he prepared his bag and checked if his respo was fully charged. A few minutes later, the doorbell rang. It was Elizabeth. She stood with a big smile in front of his door.

"Guess what?"

"Uhm!?"

"I just received the offer from Enviro! They offered me a job as a trainee in their Energy division. The package looks great: well-paid, and an apartment in their company compound is included. I can start two weeks from now."

"Wow! Congratulations! You must be thrilled," he said as they both walked toward the elevator.

"Yes, I am. And you? Any news?"

"Well, I got invited to the next round. I'll have a last round of interviews in Denmark next Monday."

"Great! I'm sure you'll do fine."

"I hope so," he said while he put on his respo just before going through the airlock. He smiled at her and spoke with a louder voice through his mask, "Ah, I didn't tell you the good news yet."

She looked a bit puzzled at him while they both got in the taxi and Dylan commanded.

"To the Lausanne Sports Club, please!"

"All right, your expected arrival time is fifteen minutes past two."

Suddenly, Elizabeth smiled, and while she took off her mask she said,

"You found the key!?"

"Yes, I did! Last night. I found it hidden under a drawer in the desk."

"And? Did you find the documents?"

"Yes! I stayed up late last night to examine all the documents I found in the vault. Apparently, the name given to me at birth is Yagnesh."

"Yagnesh!?" she repeated while she stared outside and then she said, smiling, "Well, I prefer Dylan."

"Don't worry, I'm not planning to change my name, but it's nice to learn more about my roots. Apparently, Yagnesh means sacrifice. Can you imagine they named me like that and gave me up for adoption?"

"I'm sure they must have had no other choice when they gave you up for adoption. Anything about your biological parents in those documents?"

"That's the peculiar thing about it. They left the birth parents blank on all the documents. It looks like this search is going to be more difficult than expected," he said with a sigh, after which he continued explaining to Elizabeth all the things he had found and about his call to the orphanage.

The whole search had frustrated him so far, but he knew he would have to be patient. He wanted to try everything he could to find his birth parents. For all those years, he had wondered about his roots. He knew it would not be easy. Maybe they were dead already. Although deep down, he knew speculation was useless and he should focus on getting the facts; whether they would be pleasant did not matter. As soon as he dove into the fresh water and started swimming, he felt the weight and stress wash away. He pushed himself and swam for about an hour. The physical activity emptied his mind, and he felt recharged after.

As they arrived back at the compound, Elizabeth invited him for dinner with her family that evening. He felt like company and accepted, then he continued to his apartment. He freshened up and put some clean clothes on. He made some tea and sat down at the table behind his computer. His eye fell on a new email in his mailbox. It was an answer from the solicitor he had contacted. He read it and then he looked at the clock. It was late already in India, but he thought he should try it and he called the solicitor's number. To his surprise, he answered the phone.

"Sorry to disturb you so late, Mr. Bakshi. I just read your email and I wanted to check my options with you."

"No problem, Mr. Myers. As I explained in my email, in cases like yours with a so-called closed adoption, the law forbids the revelation of birth parents to adoptees. That's also why you found nothing in your adoption papers. They don't allow the orphanage to give out that information."

"I'm sure there must be some kind of legal procedure I can start to get access to the names?"

"No, I'm sorry, Mr. Myers. I can imagine this must disappoint, but there's no such procedure."

"You mean there's really nothing I can do?"

It was quiet on the other side for a moment, and Mr. Bakshi hesitated before he answered.

"Well Mr. Myers, this is India and there might be another possibility for you…"

15.

Today was the big day, and at the sound of his alarm clock, Elliot woke up with mixed feelings of excitement and anxiety. Except for being born outside, he had never gone outside and that made this day so special. Only a few people in the community were allowed to go, and the news about his trip had spread like a wildfire. Elsa was so proud of him and she had told it to all her friends. He had even overheard his father, who never showed much emotion or excitement, talking to the neighbors about his trip.

After taking his shower, he looked at the clock. It was ten minutes past four in the morning. It was going to be a long day, and his boss Elias had told him they would come back late in the evening.

He dressed and took some yoghurt from the fridge. He added some fresh strawberries and blueberries. While eating, he prepared himself an espresso. The caffeine would do him good, he figured. He quickly finished his breakfast and moved toward the door when he heard his dad's voice.

"Elliot?"

His dad stood in the door opening of his bedroom in his bathrobe and looked sleepy.

"Morning dad."

"Just wanted to wish you a marvelous trip. Enjoy it and I'll see you tonight."

"Thanks, dad. I will. Although I might be back quite late. You don't have to wait up for me."

His dad smiled at him, and Elliot rushed out of the door. On his way out, he passed Elsa's apartment and he couldn't help thinking of her. She must be deep asleep now. What if something would go wrong and he would not see her anymore? He pushed the thought away. Elias had told him the trip would be perfectly safe. They had chosen today for the trip, as the weather forecast was ideal. He left the underground apartment area and took the stairs up.

After passing through the airlock, he looked up at the sky. It was still civil twilight, and above the towering greenhouses he saw the clear sky in twilight, as if the sun was about to rise. Around this time of the year, this was about as dark as it would get.

It was a walk of less than a kilometer to the entrance of the office, which was all the way on the edge of the community. He enjoyed his walk to and from his work, since it passed through all the plants, flowers and trees next to the greenhouses. It smelled nice and intense out there, and it reminded him of the many walks he had made there with his mother during his childhood. About ten minutes later, he entered the airlock to the entrance hall to the nuclear fusion development center.

Downstairs, he stepped out of the elevator and rushed to Elias's office. Most people were already inside and were chatting together. He noticed there were quite a few people he had never seen before, and it looked like he was the youngest in the group. Elias spotted him immediately and greeted him. He took a coffee from the table and spoke briefly with some of his colleagues while more people arrived. He noticed Elias talking to a woman with a determined look on her face. She looked the same age as Elias, although it was difficult to tell. Elias was born in the same year as his father in 1979 and was seventy-four years old. Although Elias looked fitter and more energetic than his father. The woman started addressing the group.

"Welcome everybody! For the people who haven't met me before, I'm Aurora, and I'm in charge of the environmental science center. Together with Elias, the head of the nuclear fusion development center, we'll lead the trip today. The past two weeks we all have worked hard preparing and training, and now the moment has come to go outside and visit our reactor and climate plants. The weather conditions are excellent. So, I propose we all walk toward the departure hall now."

They all followed Aurora and Elias through the open office space and the double doors leading to the underground tunnels, which connected the entire community in a mazelike structure. Although Elliot always preferred to walk upstairs through the gardens to his apartment, he could also use the tunnel network to get home. Today they walked in the opposite direction, though.

A few minutes later they arrived at the large graphene security doors. The armed guards waiting in front of them greeted Aurora and Elias and opened the doors. They all walked into the gray tunnel and inside there were more guards. Aurora guided them into a large room on the left. He noticed the white transporter vehicle in the large tunnel.

Inside the large room, one of the guards opened a door to another room. Inside there were large rows of plastic looking dark-gray suits. Every suit had a name tag on it, and he looked for the one with his name on it. Elias found it before him and handed it to him.

"Excited to go outside?"

"Yes, my first time… I mean, the first time I'm going outside that I'll remember."

"I still recall the day when your father and mother arrived here in the community. I believe you were only a few months old and a beautiful baby. Your father had looked so proud."

"And my mother?"

"Your mother was proud as well, but she was more stressed about…" Elias got interrupted by Aurora's announcement.

"Everybody got his suit on? Okay? Take a mask from the rack over there and make sure it's fully charged and then please take a seat in the white transporter outside!"

Elliot walked over to the rack and took one of the masks and checked it, then he walked through the airlock outside toward the white vehicle and took a seat next to someone else.

"Please wear your masks and buckle up your belt! We will leave in thirty seconds," Elias announced before taking the seat next to Elliot.

Everybody buckled up their multi-point harness and put on their masks. He breathed through the mask and tried to relax. The large doors closed and the driverless transporter moved through the tunnel. It quickly sped up, and Elliot got pushed back in his seat. At the end of the tunnel, he saw two doors opening and a bright light appeared in the middle. A moment later, they passed through and the road moved up now as the transporter drove out of the tunnel. The light blinded him and it took him a while to get used to the light outside.

After driving up, the transporter passed a security post, and another gate opened. They had arrived back on the surface, and Elliot felt overwhelmed with what he saw. First, he noticed the mountains behind this massive wall in the back of the flat concrete terrain in front of him. All around there were many large halls and buildings, and in the middle, there was an enormous platform with several electrical Vertical Take Off and Landing vehicles, the so-called eVTOL air taxis, on it. Inside some large halls, there were what looked like military vehicles and, on the surrounding terrain, there were several more parked. The wall in the back stretched to his left and to his right as far as he could see, and above, he noticed small dots moving through the sky. The way they moved around, he figured they were probably drones flying around.

His first time on the outside and all the buildings, vehicles and the wall in front of him made quite an impression, but nothing compared to what was about to come. At some point, he turned his head to look behind him, and what he saw overwhelmed him at first sight. Amazed, he stared backwards with his mouth agape. He had never realized the size of it before, but it looked enormous from here.

16.

Everybody around the table looked baffled at him after his announcement. Elizabeth's father was the first to break the silence.

"New Delhi!? The city of death? Dylan, nobody wants to go there. That's a very dangerous city."

"Well, I believe it's the only way for me to get more details about my birth parents. They'll never give out that information over the phone or by mail. Probably they live in New Delhi, so I might find out some more on the ground."

"Sorry to say it, Dylan, but I hope you realize that if they lived in New Delhi, they might very well be dead. Many lethal heat waves hit the city in the last fifteen years, and every year they've gotten worse. Last year about half a million people died because of heat waves. Although the deadliest heat wave was in the year 2039, with more than two million casualties in the city. From a documentary I saw during my military education, I still remember the enormous mass graves they dug outside the city. It was absolutely shocking. I believe that in the past twenty years, the population of New Delhi has decreased from thirty-five million to ten million people. Mostly the poor people died and the life expectancy has dropped tremendously," Matteo said.

"I know, but for me, it's important to know who my birth parents are or were. If they're dead, I prefer to know it, although I hope they're still alive."

"Jesus, I didn't realize so many people had died over there," Elizabeth's mother said with an astonished look on her face.

"Yeah, apparently the reason there're so many deadly heat waves in India has to do something with this wet-bulb temperature or whatever they call it," Matteo answered.

"Wet-bulb temperature?" Elizabeth's mother asked, puzzled, while her breathing whistled.

"Ah, that's something Dylan knows all about," Elizabeth said enthusiastically.

Everybody looked at him now.

"Well, let's see how to explain that simply. Normally, we measure the temperature with a normal thermometer. This is what they call the dry-bulb temperature.

"However, humidity is also important. When it's more humid, the same dry-bulb temperature feels hotter than when humidity is low. This is where the wet-bulb temperature comes in.

"If we put a wet cloth around the bulb of a thermometer, then the air will blow past the cloth and water will evaporate. This evaporation cools off the bulb.

"Wet-bulb temperature is the temperature you measure when you put a wet cloth around the thermometer. Typically, the wet-bulb temperature is lower than the dry-bulb temperature, since the thermometer cools off because of the evaporation of the water. However, the difference between the dry- and the wet-bulb temperature depends on the relative humidity.

"In the driest air, the difference between the two will be biggest and with a relative humidity of a hundred percent, the two will be equal."

"Okay, that I understand, but what does this wet-bulb temperature have to do with how deadly a heat wave is?" asked Matteo.

"Well, you know that the human body cools itself by evaporative cooling or simply said by sweating. A sustained wet-bulb temperature exceeding thirty-five degrees Celsius is likely to be fatal even to fit and healthy people. Even unclothed in the shade next to a fan.

"At a wet-bulb temperature of thirty-five degrees Celsius, the body can no longer adequately cool itself and our bodies switch from shedding heat to the environment to gaining from it and start overheating, which results in death. So humidity is key in determining how dangerous a heat wave will be.

"At fifty percent humidity and a temperature of forty-two degrees Celsius, we already reach the wet-bulb temperature limit of thirty-five degrees Celsius. In India we reach this limit regularly now, and the people who die first are the poor who do not have proper air-conditioning.

"The air pollution makes this even worse and causes people to die even with wet-bulb temperatures below this limit. This is one of the principal reasons India has become one of the most uninhabitable countries in the world, weirdly enough worse than the Middle East, where temperatures are higher but humidity is lower."

"All those poor people! Although the heat waves are a problem in most countries now. Here in Switzerland, we've regular heat waves during which people can't work outside or only for a brief period or they'll suffer heatstroke. I can imagine that must be much worse in India. No wonder those people are desperately trying to migrate to other countries," Elizabeth's mother said.

"That's exactly why we had our electronic border control installed in Europe. Without it, we would be constantly flooded with refugees and our societies would have collapsed even more than they already did," Matteo told his mother.

"Oh, no! Don't talk about this horrible border again. Just the thought of all those people who die every year trying to come to Europe," Elizabeth's mother said and she immediately left the table and walked to the kitchen.

"Stop it, Matteo! You always switch the discussion to this electronic border. You know Mom doesn't want to talk about that," Elizabeth told her brother agitated and Matteo looked like a punished boy now. Elizabeth continued,

"Anyway, Dylan, I don't think it's a good plan to go to New Delhi in summer, since there's a horrible heat wave over there at the moment."

"That wasn't what I was saying. Of course, I'm not going now, but maybe in a month or so when it's less hot. My first priority is this last round of interviews at Enviro in Denmark coming Monday."

"We really hope you pass this last round and get a job offer as well. It would be so nice if you could move to Denmark together," Elizabeth's mother added as she came back from the kitchen.

He wondered if this comment meant that Elizabeth would move to Denmark anyway, regardless if he would get a job at Enviro. They had not talked about it, but he had the impression she had not continued with her job application at other firms, which he could also understand since he would probably do the same if he got an offer from Enviro, the most desirable employer in the world. He really needed to pass this last round, otherwise it would mean they would get into a very awkward situation in which they would have to make some painful tradeoffs. He just hoped they would avoid that situation, since he had no clue if Elizabeth would choose the preferred job or choose to be with him. As if she could read his mind, she looked at him now.

"I'm sure you will do great in the last round. They gave me some cases and problems to solve; we could discuss them together if you like. It might help with the preparation for your interviews. We also had to do some role playing, and I had to give a brief presentation, but I had the impression the case studies were the most important part. On the second day, I even had a meeting with Amy Patterson, the head of the Energy division, a very impressive and smart woman. Did they send you the schedule already?"

"No, not yet. But it would be good to go over those cases together."

After dinner, Dylan and Elizabeth went to her room to discuss the interviews. Later in the evening, when he was back in his bed in the apartment, he could not help to think back of his conversation with the solicitor from India. This trip was going to be full of risks, and it was unlikely that he would get access to his birth certificate. Still, he felt he had to try everything he could, otherwise this would haunt him for the rest of his life and what the solicitor had suggested made sense to him.

17.

Monday afternoon Dylan rushed out of the taxi with his suitcase in his hand and his respo on his face. His taxi had taken longer than expected to get to Bern, and now he had to hurry. Otherwise, he might miss the hyper-loop to Copenhagen. Fortunately, Enviro had booked the ticket for him. All he had to do was present his passport at the entrance of the station. The system recognized his reservation, and he continued to platform two through the departure hall. It was only the second time in his life that he was taking the hyper-loop. During his university time, they once had made a trip with it to Berlin. Overall, he had liked it, although he found the acceleration and deceleration phase uncomfortable.

After taking his seat inside the hyper-loop cabin, which looked like a large cylinder, he buckled up. He heard the doors close behind him and he waited for departure while he listened to the safety instructions. He noticed an older lady next to him, who looked nervous. It comforted him to realize he was not the only one who was anxious. A hissing sound indicated the pod was about to leave, and on the screen in front of him, he followed the countdown to departure.

"… three, two, one, ignition… pfffoom!"

Dylan got pushed backwards in his soft chair for several minutes, after which the pressure slowly decreased. He tried to relax and selected a program to watch on the screen. With the low whooshing sound in the background from the hyper-loop moving at more than one thousand kilometers an hour through the pipe, he watched the documentary he had selected. It was about the growth of the cellular seafood industry. Lab-grown food had always fascinated him. Lab-grown meat had been around the longest, with the first hamburger eaten in 2013. Lab-grown fish quickly followed through with the first fish, a yellowtail amberjack, created in 2019.

About twenty years ago, most countries in the world abolished the traditional meat industry, and they forbid the use of livestock for meat production, as it was one of the largest polluters in the world, emitting methane gas in large quantities.

Governments had ignored methane gas for a long time, but the escalation of problems in the world caused by global warming had finally pushed them to make this step. Methane gas emissions were much lower than carbon dioxide emissions and the estimated lifetime in the atmosphere was only nine years approximately compared to an estimated lifetime for carbon dioxide of over a hundred years.

The problem was that methane gas was much more destructive. It was more than eighty times more potent than carbon dioxide at warming the Earth in the first twenty years after its release, and twenty-eight times more powerful over a hundred-year period. Together with the enormous amount of methane gas escaping from the thawing permafrost, methane had become one of the key factors that accelerated global warming to scenarios worse than ever predicted. Governments had finally acted, although hopelessly late.

The abolishment of using traditional livestock for meat production gave the lab-grown meat industry a tremendous boost, and prices for the meat finally came down. The development of lab-grown fish took off for different reasons and happened later than with lab-grown meat. The main trigger was the increase of micro-plastics and toxins in wild-caught fish, like mercury, poly chlorinated biphenyls (or PCBs), dioxins and pesticides. As the pollution increased globally, it became unhealthier to eat fish. More and more people ended up in the hospital after eating wild-caught fish. On top of this, overfishing and global warming had decreased fish populations tremendously, and wild-caught fish fell out of grace gradually.

Initially, fish farming or pisciculture filled the void, but open ocean farming suffered from the same problems as with wild-caught fish. Indoor fish farming compensated partially, but suffered from many problems like diseases, parasites and clean water shortages and the fish became very expensive. This development triggered the growth of lab-grown fish, fish grown from pre-muscle tissue cells in bioreactor tanks. As demand increased, production of lab-grown fish scaled up and this brought the price down to a more competitive level.

The documentary had not finished yet, but the announcement of their imminent arrival interrupted the screen. Dylan checked the time. It had taken him about an hour to get to Copenhagen. He braced himself for the arrival, which he liked least. The screen announced they were going to decelerate now. Soon after, he got pushed forward. Luckily, the five-point harness he was wearing kept him in his chair, while his head felt heavy. After several minutes, the pressure got less, and he slowly fell back in his chair.

Relieved, he stepped outside and into the hyper-loop arrival hall. It was not his preferred means of transportation, but it was efficient and the harsh climate and weather conditions had relatively little impact on it. With the many storms and increased turbulences in the air, flying had become much less comfortable and more dangerous every year. The hyper-loop had pushed flying out of the market on trajectories like this one from Bern to Copenhagen.

He left the hyper-loop station with his respo back on his face. It was hot and sunny outside. He scanned his passport at the taxi departure area, following the instructions he had received from Enviro. A white driverless taxi in front of the row of taxis opened its doors.

"Welcome, Mr. Myers. Your destination is the sky port. Your estimated arrival time is eight minutes from now."

After the hissing sound had stopped and the green light had switched on inside the taxi, he took off his respo. He had never been in Copenhagen and he looked around at the mixture of old and modern buildings. It was less hot here than in Lausanne. He noticed people walking in the streets with respos on.

A few minutes later he noticed the air taxi sky port in front of him. It was a rectangular building with circular platforms on the side of it sticking out at different levels, gradually going higher on the long side of the building. It looked like some gigantic staircase attached to the building. Just at that moment, he noticed an air taxi taking off from one of the platforms. It always impressed him to see those drone-looking vehicles hover through the sky.

As soon as he arrived, he put his respo back on his face and walked outside toward the sky port entrance. After passing through the airlock, he took off his respo and checked in with his passport at the self-service check-in. He had to go to platform three on the fourth floor. The air taxi was already waiting and he could board immediately. He rushed inside. There was space for ten passengers only. Five people were seated already. Looking at their neat clothes and young age, he figured they must all be there for the interviews at Enviro. He greeted them, took his seat, and buckled up immediately. The door closed right after him and from the speakers inside the air taxi an announcement followed.

"We'll take-off in five minutes. Please fasten your seat belt. Expected time until arrival at the Enviro headquarters in Ikast will be sixty-five minutes."

Several minutes later, the buzzing sound of the propellers above the cabin increased, and then he felt the taxi lifting off. It moved upwards and sideways, away from the platform. Then it accelerated fast. With the windows all around the cabin, he had a magnificent view of Copenhagen. He immediately noticed the sea, but his attention was drawn by what looked like a large wall or embankment between the sea and the edge of Copenhagen. From the sky, he noticed how a large part of the city was below sea level and protected only by this embankment. The taxi sped up further and Copenhagen disappeared out of sight. He looked at the young woman in front of him, who looked anxious.

"So, are you also interviewing at Enviro today?"

"Yes, I am. Which division are you applying for?"

"At Environmental Technology and you?"

"At the Medical division."

"Ah, they make the respos."

The air taxi changed direction, and the young woman looked startled.

"Nervous? These air taxis are quite safe, you know," Dylan tried to put her at ease.

"Yeah, I know, but I don't like it that there's no pilot. I read that last month in Great Brittan, an air taxi got hacked and crashed into a building."

"Well, don't worry, they would only hack into this air taxi if there would be some politician or CEO inside, not when it's full of job applicants," he said with a smile, and she laughed.

They chatted for a while until suddenly she got distracted and stared outside. She pointed her finger at something behind him.

"Look, I think we almost arrived."

He turned his head, and he noticed a town, but the air taxi was flying toward a massive black star-shaped building. It was on an immense terrain in the middle of a forest. There was an enormous wall all around and several platforms were visible, some with air taxis on them. About ten minutes later, they landed on one of the platforms. A white vehicle parked in front of the air taxi. They stepped outside, and they drove toward the tall black building in the white vehicle. Above the entrance, there was a big sign: Enviro Technologies.

Inside the building, six humanoid robots that looked almost human greeted them. Each robot addressed a different person. One of them stopped in front of Dylan.

"Welcome to Enviro Technologies! I hope you had a pleasant trip, Mr. Myers. Please follow me, then I'll first show you the room where you'll stay for the coming two nights."

He followed the robot through a door on the right of the entrance. In the corridor behind it, there were several doors and the other applicants were all escorted to their rooms.

"Here's your room, Mr. Myers. If you hold a finger here on the screen next to the door, the room will memorize your fingerprint. Next time you want to enter, you just press with the same finger on the screen to open the door. You can put your luggage inside and freshen up. I'll wait outside for you to bring you to your meeting with Miss Roland from HR in exactly fifteen minutes from now."

"Okay, thank you."

He put his finger on the screen, and the door slid open with a hiss. The room had a king-size bed and a bathroom. He quickly freshened up in the bathroom and unpacked his suitcase. The entire room looked modern and luxurious. There was no window but a large screen instead that showed a magnificent forest. He combed his hair in the mirror and rearranged his shirt.

A few minutes later, he stepped outside and followed the humanoid robot to his first meeting. He thought of Elizabeth. She had accepted the offer from Enviro last week and was going to start working next week already. She had started packing to prepare for her move to Denmark. He really needed to get an offer as well. He felt nervous.

Five minutes later, they arrived at a meeting room, which opened with a hiss in front of him. The hall and the meeting room were air-conditioned, but he felt hot and his hands were sweaty. Oh no, please, no sweaty hands now, not just before shaking hands, he thought. He entered the room and quickly wiped his hand on the side of his trousers. An older lady dressed in a black suit got up from her chair behind the large table and shook his hand.

"Welcome to Enviro Technologies, Mr. Myers."

18.

Elliot turned his head and looked straight toward the gigantic glass dome he had just left. To look at the top of it, he had to tilt his head as far as he could. There it was: the place where he lived since his birth. This was the first time he saw it from the outside. What an enormous dome. At this angle, the reflection of the light obscured any sight of what was inside, which was probably the reason he had never noticed the large military base in front of the dome.

Suddenly, the transporter braked, and he turned back to look in front of him. A huge drone flew in their direction, but contrary to the eVTOL air taxis, it did not have a cabin for people. It just had four large hooks under it in a rectangular position. It approached them until it was flying exactly above them. There was the buzzing noise of the rotors, followed by a large clunking noise, when the four hooks grabbed the vehicle in each corner. The drone attached itself to the transporter. He looked anxiously at Elias, who smiled at him.

"Don't worry, it's safe. Just hold on as we're about to lift off from the ground."

With a sudden shock, the transporter lifted off and moved up at high speed. He felt his stomach twitch as they moved upwards. The military vehicles and base quickly became smaller in front of him. He turned his head to look back at the dome. They soared above it, but even from up here, it looked gigantic. It stretched as far as he could see. With the changed angle now, he vaguely distinguished the shape of the high greenhouse structure inside, where he often went with

Elsa to admire the amazing views. As they flew away from it, while rising higher in the sky, he noticed the high mountain range behind the dome far away on the horizon.

They flew over the first wall and then he noticed there was a second wall on the horizon, separated by a vast terrain in between. They had done everything to keep the outer world away from the dome. Several minutes later, they flew over the second wall. When Elliot turned his head to look back at the dome, it had gotten smaller on the horizon and looked like some gigantic water bubble placed in the middle of the mountains encircling it. With the rising sun behind, it looked even more mystical.

"Impressive huh?" Elias said.

"Yeah, you can say that. So strange to be outside."

"I still remember your parents' face when they first looked at the dome in real life. They were with the last group of people to enter, before it closed to the outside world."

"Must have been weird to go inside this dome knowing you'll not go outside anymore after?"

"Yeah, it was, but everyone had already been confronted with the destructive effects of climate change and the deteriorating world outside. Going inside was a deliberate choice for long-term survival. We felt we were the privileged ones at the time, and I still believe we are."

"Don't get me wrong, I feel privileged as well, but you also lost the freedom to travel around the world freely. Don't you miss that?" Elliot asked while he continued to look around as they flew over the mountains and lakes further and further away from the dome.

"Well, I guess I miss the way we used to travel when I was young, but I also remember the years before I entered the dome. Traveling had become risky. The number of natural disasters had increased tremendously, and so did the amount of plane crashes. Traveling caused diseases to spread globally and several pandemics killed many people. The vast majority of the world became uncomfortable and too polluted to live in. Most of the year, it's too hot to go outside during the day. The people on the outside have actually the same limitations as us and have to stay inside most of the time. Only richer people can afford to travel now, and the way we used to travel around the world when I was young does not exist anymore."

Elliot looked at Elias while he was talking. He wondered why he was so much more comfortable talking to him than to his own father. Elias continued.

"When I entered the dome, the world population was almost eight billion people. They predicted it would reach about ten billion people in 2050. People underestimated the impact of climate change.

"Last year, in 2052, the estimated population of our planet was over five billion people. So many people have died because of the consequences of climate change.

"The life expectancy in the outside world has dropped dramatically over the last decades. In many countries it has even dropped below thirty years, while in our community it has gone up rapidly. Our medical scientists even believe our people could reach ages well above a hundred and fifty years. Some even say we might live up to two to three hundred years. The few dead we had in our community were all unnatural deaths. No, I don't really miss the outside world. All I miss are distant memories from a bygone era."

Elliot had to let his words sink in a bit, and while he looked at the horizon, he noticed a gray-blueish stripe.

"What's that?" he asked Elias, while pointing with his finger.

"That's the ocean. It seems we've almost arrived. Look!" Elias pointed at a gigantic dark-gray building with a dark gray tube-like extension stretching as far as he could see over the tops of the hills. Like an enormous snake slithering through the landscape.

"What's that long dark structure stretching over the hilltops? It looks endless."

"Well, that's the climate plant that captures carbon dioxide and methane. This one is about ten kilometers long, but we're designing an even larger…"

His words were interrupted by the voice of Aurora, who had just switched her microphone to the general speaker and started to explain about the structure in the distance.

"As most of you've noticed, we're approaching the hydrogen-boron reactor, which is the first building you see in front of us. For the people among us who've not visited before, I'll briefly explain what the structure. The two enormous connected buildings next to it are the climate plants, which capture carbon dioxide and methane from the air through the swirling structure attached to it. It sucks the air into the system where they capture the carbon dioxide and methane. To increase the capacity of this plant, we've expanded the swirling structure over the years and currently it's eleven kilometers long."

They approached the buildings, and the transporter slowed down but continued to fly over part of the swirling structure. It looked like a staircase of layered fans, which were all connected to the tubes coming out of the climate plant.

"The large fans on this side of the hill are sucking the air into the plant and on the other side of the hill they blow the cleaned air out of the plant and release it back into the environment."

The transporter hovered slowly over one side of the structure, giving the passengers a closer look at the large fans. A few minutes later it hovered to the other side, showing the exhaust.

"Inside the climate plants, we've several processes running that capture the carbon dioxide and methane out of the air. The carbon dioxide is separated from the rest of the air, and in this plant we run two key processes. In one process we sequester carbon dioxide by storing it in minerals. Under high temperature and pressure, the carbon dioxide reacts with widely available minerals like olivine to produce stable carbonates, which store it forever. This is very energy consuming, and that's where our large hydrogen-boron reactor plays its role. In another process, we heat the carbon dioxide to extremely high temperatures, so it splits into carbon monoxide and oxygen. The carbon monoxide is converted into hydrocarbons, from which we make plastics and synthetic fabrics."

The transporter had flown for a while over the large swirling structure, but had turned and was flying back to the buildings in the beginning while descending slowly.

"The methane goes through a similar process as the second carbon dioxide capturing process. We heat the methane at high temperatures and let it react with steam, which then yields carbon monoxide and hydrogen. The hydrogen is stored in fuel cells for later use, while the carbon monoxide is converted into hydrocarbons again. That is the whole climate plant in a nutshell.

"As you know we're working hard to expand the climate plant in the near future and also capture the other greenhouse gases in the atmosphere like nitrous oxide and fluorinated gases, but more on that later. We'll first visit the reactor, after which we'll go to the climate plant. Later today we'll split into groups and work with the people in the reactor and climate plants on the current projects. As you've noticed, we've started our descent and will land soon. After that, Elias will explain more about the hydrogen-boron reactor."

Elliot felt his stomach turn again as the transporter quickly descended and then slowed down just before the ground. They landed, and the doors opened. Everybody got out, and they walked toward the first building. There were several armed men in black clothes guiding them toward the building's entrance. He noticed they were all wearing masks, although they did not wear any special protective suits.

From the ground, the buildings that they had seen from the sky looked immense. He felt privileged to be amongst the few people allowed to visit. He was sure that his father was proud of him, and then he thought of his mother. She would also have been proud. She had always hoped they would find a solution to the climate problems. It had driven Elliot to pursue a career in this field.

As he walked toward the main entrance with the group and Elias talked about the hydrogen-boron reactor, he thought about something he had said. It had triggered his curiosity, and he should find some moment during this day to ask Elias. He might know more about that thing that had puzzled him for so long. He really wanted to find out more about it.

19.

On the last day, Dylan felt relieved when the head of the Environmental Technology division announced the good news. The day before had been intense, full of interviews, and in the afternoon, they did some role playing and he had to give a presentation. He was exhausted in the evening. After dinner, he had some drinks with the other applicants and several employees of Enviro. He soon returned to his room and slept quickly after.

Now he just finished his last interview with Olav Sorensen, the head of the Environmental Technology division.

"Dylan, I really liked your ideas about how to capture nitrous oxide on a large scale. We're currently developing a climate plant to capture it from the air. Nitrous oxide is a serious problem and has been neglected for too long. It remains in the atmosphere for about a hundred and twenty years; longer than carbon dioxide. Its global warming potential is almost three hundred times greater than carbon dioxide over a hundred-year period. With great pleasure I can inform you we would like to make you an offer to come and work at the Environmental Technology division and join the team working on our newest project, developing a climate plant to capture nitrous oxide from the atmosphere."

"Wow! Thanks! I feel honored, and that sounds like a dream job to me."

During this last interview early in the morning, Olav Sorenson had asked him several challenging questions, but Dylan answered them with ease. He was like a fish in water and had answered thoroughly and passionately. He had explained how they could break down nitrous oxide into nitrogen and oxygen by letting the polluted air flow over a catalyst, like titanium dioxide, while projecting sunlight onto the air, a so-called photocatalytic breakdown.

He suggested using a solar chimney power plant for this process. A large chimney with a turbine in the base and surrounded by a large greenhouse open to the air on the sides. The sun heats the air inside. The hot air rises through the chimney, turning the blades of the turbine. The turbine generates electricity while the air from the atmosphere passes over the surface of the greenhouse, coated with this catalyst breaking down the nitrous oxide. He had brilliantly explained how to use this technique on a large scale in a climate plant, generating electricity at the same time. He had left a deep impression on Sorenson, who grinned as he listened attentively to Dylan.

This job offer was exactly what he had hoped for, and the stress from the last few weeks finally fell off his shoulders. The rest of the morning, they got a tour of the modern compound, which housed the employees. Elizabeth was right about the compound being impressive. So many facilities were available and luxurious apartments to live in. There was a large choice in restaurants and shops. Almost no need to go outside anymore. The compound offered single apartments, but also apartments for couples or entire families. He thought it was time to live together in the same apartment. Although he was not sure if she would like that.

Later on, when he arrived in the hyper-loop station to return to Switzerland, he called Elizabeth and told her about the job offer.

"Congratulations! Although I'm really not surprised. I told you they would love to hire someone with your background."

"Thanks! Well now at least we can move together to the same country."

"I was already counting on that. I guess now is also the time to discuss what we're going to do?"

"What do you mean?"

"Well, if we each take our own apartment in the compound or if we take a two-bedroom one together? I checked with Enviro and they are fine with both options."

"You had already checked with them?"

"Of course! I mean, I had asked in general. Even if you wouldn't have gotten a job offer, we could have moved in together."

"Ah, okay."

"So, what do you prefer?"

"Well, I'd love to live together with you, that is, if you feel the same way about it."

"Of course, you dummy! It's about time! What time will you arrive back home?"

"In about two hours, I believe. If I don't miss the hyper-loop now."

"Okay, hurry then! I'll see you back home then. Have a good trip back."

"Thanks."

He rushed to the hyper-loop cabin and took his seat. As the doors closed and they departed, he thought about the new phase about to start in his life. His mother would have been so proud of him. The other thing he thought about was how he still had to negotiate some time off with Enviro to go to India in October when the heat waves would be over. They might not be so happy with it, since he would only have been working for about a month. In addition, he hesitated to go alone, since the trip was not without danger. Elizabeth already made it clear she would not come along with him. She preferred he would not go, either. He dozed off during the hyper-loop ride, but then a moment later he woke up with a great idea.

20.

A few months later, Dylan put his arm next to the scanner at the door. Almost instantly, the door to their apartment in Ikast opened. Lately he was so absorbed with the project he was working on that he arrived home late several evenings in the week. In the beginning they ate together after work, but often Elizabeth waited in vain for him when he had forgotten to warn her. After an initial fight, he adapted and made an effort to inform her well in advance when he would run late.

Tonight, he arrived in the apartment at eight o'clock in the evening and Elizabeth was still at the swimming pool. He had promised her to cook tonight, so he started preparing dinner. First, he zapped along the different channels on the large television screen in the kitchen, until he found some news program. While he cooked, he followed the news. The screen showed images of a violent hurricane hitting land in the abandoned Miami, which looked surreal. Almost two decades ago, the whole coastal region, including Miami, had been abandoned and declared a national park. Since then, sea levels had continued to rise steadily and Miami had become a permanently inundated city.

This hurricane was now threatening Orlando. They had evacuated the city before the storm, like the rest of Florida. About ten years ago, they had expanded the national park zone north, and cities like Jacksonville, Charleston and further up north Atlantic City had all been abandoned and declared uninhabited zones. For years they tried to protect cities like New York and Philadelphia and large parts of

New Jersey by constructing large seawalls and surge barriers, but they had all flooded in the end and were added to the large list of uninhabited and abandoned cities that had received national park status in the United States. Similar zones were declared in the Gulf of Mexico, where cities like New Orleans had suffered the same fate as Miami. The whole coastal line was declared a national park, and they allowed people to visit when conditions were good, but no one was allowed to live there.

Despite the interdiction, several homeless people had taken refuge in the abandoned cities. Every so often, the government tried to move them out of the national park zone, but it was a hopeless battle as they knew how to hide well in the abandoned buildings. The living conditions were so poor that the government figured most would die soon anyway, and they reduced their attempts to move people out. They were too busy fighting the many militant groups in the country that had taken power in several regions in the U.S. Anarchy ruled in those regions, and the government forces were constantly trying to reestablish the rule of law over there.

The electronic lock on the front door clicked as Elizabeth entered the apartment. They kissed and she checked out the food in the kitchen.

"Mmm, smells good. How was work today?"

"Good, we're making quite some progress. Today Mr. Sorensen approved the construction of the first large solar chimney power plant. They'll construct it on the Enviro terrain on the side away from Ikast."

"Nice! He doesn't waste much time huh, your boss!?"

"Yeah, that's what I like about this company. They can make decisions quickly and implement them immediately. Despite the size of the company, they still act like entrepreneurs. And you? How was your day?"

"Enlightening, actually. I finally got my head around the business model of the nuclear fusion business of Enviro. To my surprise, I learned today that we do not actually sell the nuclear fusion reactors."

"Ah, no? So how do we earn all that money then, since I understood that the Energy division is one of the most profitable of all divisions?"

"Apparently we construct them and exploit them ourselves, while the reactors remain our property."

"Interesting business model. It would explain though why most energy prices worldwide haven't gone down much, even though the operating costs of these reactors are so low."

"Exactly, I suspect Enviro charges market conform prices for their energy even though they could sell their electricity and hydrogen much cheaper if they wanted to. Combine this with the fact that Enviro is the world's market leader in hydrogen fuel cells and you understand how much power they have globally."

"Now I get why they are so extremely protective of all company information and intellectual property. As long as the competition stays far behind, Enviro remains the world's largest cash machine. It explains the thick pile of confidentiality and non-disclosure agreements we had to sign when we joined."

"Exactly, and that also scares me a bit, you know. It's remarkable that they've kept this nuclear fusion technology a secret for more than ten years already."

"Well, I heard they got the intellectual property well protected by patents."

"Still, the competition could hire some spies to work at Enviro and pass the information to them. Apparently, that hasn't happened yet."

"I guess their protective policies must work. I understood only a limited amount of people have access to the most competitive information."

"True, but I'm sure someone could infiltrate even this group of people. No, I'm more wondering if they don't have some kind of intelligent system to monitor all employees."

"Well, there're cameras everywhere in the building, so it's possible they monitor everyone."

"Yeah, but I'm suspecting they might have something more sophisticated than that. Remember, we had to implant this chip in our arm when we joined?"

"That chip to open the door and to pay automatically in the restaurants and shops?" he asked while he looked puzzled at her.

"Yep, I hesitated to accept when we joined, since I found it quite invasive. They had made it clear though that you couldn't join the company without the implant, since it was part of their company's rules. This chip could also be an excellent way to check on your employees the whole time."

"That's true, but I believe you're a bit too paranoid here. Don't worry so much. I'm happy to be part of this company. They're paying us well with excellent benefits, like living in this luxurious compound. I'm not so worried about them spying on us. It's not like we would do something wrong, anyway. I consider it more like an easy replacement of a key card, since it gives easy access to our work space and our apartment."

"It's more I overheard someone saying he believes they trace us with this chip everywhere we go."

"Even if that would be true, would that be such a problem? They trace us the whole time through our phones as well, and you don't seem to have any problem with that."

"I guess you're right. By the way, any news from Matteo?"

Dylan had asked Matteo about a month ago to come along on his trip to New Delhi to help him find out more about his birth parents. He had offered to pay for all travel expenses, and Matteo was thrilled to come along.

"Yes, he called me this morning. Apparently, he has sent some of his gear ahead already to New Delhi by freight plane, since he's bringing some army gear which isn't allowed on the passenger flight we booked for next week. Some colleague of his has helped him get the customs papers for all of it. He's quite excited about the trip."

"Yeah, since you asked him to come with you to New Delhi, he doesn't talk about anything else anymore. My parents are even getting tired of it."

"I know! He treats it as some kind of military mission. I learned so much from him these last few weeks about crime, diseases and all kinds of stuff relevant to our trip. He even got an entire weather and air analysis report. Next week the weather predictions are good. The worst part of the heat wave is over and if we don't stay outside for too long, we should be fine. Air pollution levels are still quite high though, so we are taking an extra set of respos and plenty of spare filters and extra battery packs. He talked to some people in the Indian army, and they gave him some travel tips. He even got all our routes in New Delhi mapped out to avoid all dangerous areas."

"Initially, I was quite worried when you insisted on going to New Delhi, but now, with Matteo coming along, I feel a lot better. At least you can help each other if something happens."

Dylan also felt better this way, especially after Sorenson had warned him about New Delhi. He had not told this to Elizabeth, since he did not want her to worry too much. His boss explained to him that although the Indian government claims to be in control of the entire country, parts of India are in total anarchy and gangs rule the streets there. Matteo had heard similar things from his military friends, but neither mentioned it to Elizabeth nor his parents. His boss had agreed to no more than one week of unpaid leave, which he thought should be more than enough.

The days passed so fast since he decided to go to New Delhi. He even was hoping deep down to get lucky and be able to meet his birth parents in New Delhi. He knew well that this was pure hope, as his chances of finding them looked slim. Given the history of the city, there was a large chance they died in one of the previous heat waves that struck New Delhi or they could have moved away to some other place. Still, he was determined to find out. He felt it was a quest he had to pursue. Nobody was going to stop him. Although at this point, he could not have known what trouble was waiting for him.

21.

At Frankfurt airport, Dylan scanned the crowd looking for Matteo and he continued to do so for about fifteen minutes until suddenly he spotted his dark short hair above his broad-shouldered, muscular body. With his short buzz cut, he looked like a soldier and his heavy build made it clear he was not a person to mess around with. Then Matteo noticed him, and his face showed a friendly smile as he waved at Dylan.

That morning, he had woken up at four thirty in the morning. He kissed Elizabeth goodbye, and she repeated that he should be careful. He missed her already. He had taken the hyper-loop in Copenhagen to Frankfurt from where their plane would leave for New Delhi. They booked a ticket with the relatively new hydrogen-powered supersonic stratosphere plane. He had never flown on it before and even Matteo had not done so before, even though he had flown in many military aircraft that reached similar heights up to eighty thousand feet.

Matteo hugged him and slapped his powerful hand on his back. Dylan was happy to see his good friend, with whom he had experienced many adventures during their childhood. It felt funny to go on another adventure with him after all these years.

"Hey buddy, are we all set?"

"Yep, our flight appears to be on time and the weather conditions are good."

"Well, the luggage I had sent ahead with the freight plane has arrived, and we just have to pick it up at the airport in New Delhi."

"Great, let's go then!"

They checked in at the automated check-in desk and continued to the security check. After that, they continued toward the gate. The thin stratosphere plane was already waiting outside. It fitted a maximum of a hundred passengers, but looking at the few people waiting at the gate, it would not be full. The ticket prices for this flight were high. The average person could not afford to fly, and Matteo had thanked him several times. For Dylan, the hefty ticket price was no problem since had received his inheritance. He considered it money well spent, especially if it would allow him to find out more about his origins. Excitement filled him while he waited at the gate with Matteo. About fifteen minutes later, they boarded the modern plane.

Later, on the runway, the plane accelerated with a tremendous force. For about fifteen minutes, the thrust of the plane pushed him backwards in his seat while they lifted off and climbed sharply into the sky. Outside, he watched the city of Frankfurt getting smaller fast. The plane climbed higher and higher. Dylan had never gone so high into the stratosphere. His nerves were tormenting him since he hated flying. The fear of something happening to the plane while being locked up inside like a sardine with nowhere to go always frightened him. He tried to relax by meditating and focusing on his breathing.

Matteo was sitting next to him, completely relaxed. Initially, he showed Dylan some photos and maps of New Delhi to explain which areas they would have to avoid. Eventually he realized that Dylan was too stressed to focus, and he read a book on the e-reader he had brought with him.

Two hours later, they landed in New Delhi on the Asian continent. Dylan felt relieved when he stepped out of the plane and touched solid ground. They picked up their luggage and exited the customs area. When they entered the main terminal, the dark crowd of people was overwhelming. Dylan blended in easily, but Mateo, with his Caucasian face, looked clearly foreign in between all the Indian people. They left the terminal through the airlock. With the respos on their face, they walked toward the taxi stand. The heat felt heavy on them.

There were two lines, one for chauffeur-driven taxis and one for driverless taxis. Matteo looked at him.

"With driver or without?"

"Maybe without, at least we can take off our respos in the driverless taxis."

They entered a white driverless taxi and put the luggage inside. An electronic voice asked.

"Good afternoon. Welcome to New Delhi. What's your destination?"

"To the Palace Hotel, please."

They took their seats, and the doors closed. There was no familiar hissing sound of the air filter doing its work, nor was there any green light in front, as usual. Dylan took off his mask, but the hot, dirty air immediately irritated his lungs. He had difficulty breathing and started coughing. Matteo grinned at him.

"Welcome to New Delhi, the city of death!"

Dylan put his respo back on his face and took a deep breath to recover a bit.

"The air is horrible, nothing compared to the air at home."

"Yeah, I guess we're going to be in for more surprises like this."

Suddenly, Matteo seemed to remember something.

"Please take the elevated expressway to the hotel!"

"Yes, sir. Destination Palace Hotel through the expressway. Your estimated time to destination is fifty minutes."

"That should be a safer route," Matteo explained.

On the elevated expressway, Dylan looked down toward the endless slums stretching to the horizon. Thousands of small roofs were glued together as far as he could see, most made from wood or corrugated plastic sheets. In the streets, the people were walking without wearing respos. Most wore mouth masks. They looked young and had dirty clothes. He wondered how people could live in this hot, polluted air.

Poverty was all over New Delhi. People in these slums die young. He had read somewhere that the life expectancy in India had dropped dramatically over the last thirty years, mostly as a result of the polluted air and the deadly heat waves. The government had constructed more and more air-conditioned communal basements, but the capacity was so low they could only fit a fraction of the population.

A moment later, Dylan peered at the horizon, and what he saw shocked him deeply. Behind the slums, there was a large thermal plant, and he recognized it immediately.

"Amazing, they still generate their power here with coal. Even now, after all those decades of climate warming disasters on our planet, they just continue burning coal to generate energy. Pumping more carbon dioxide in the already heavily polluted atmosphere."

"People will never learn," Matteo said as he looked at the coal plant.

So here he was in India, his country of birth. His roots were here. This was his motherland. On the one hand, he was happy to be here, and he hoped to find his birth parents. On the other hand, he realized how dangerous it was. Most of his colleagues at Enviro thought he was nuts, that he wanted to travel to such a poor and devastated country.

India lacked the means to adapt decisively to the ruthless climate change, and it was probably one of the hardest hit victims of it. Many islands in the Pacific and others like the Maldives had lost their territory completely because of the rising sea levels. They had simply vanished, but India held the questionable honor of the most climate change related deaths on Earth.

Here he was in search of his birth parents in the most populated country and one of the most dangerous countries in the world. Thank God he was there with his best friend and member of the Swiss elite Special Forces Command. Observing all these slums and poor people, he wondered if his plan would work. It was a big gamble, after all.

22.

After walking through the airlock, the local management team welcomed them into the large hall of the reactor. They greeted them, which felt awkward since they were all twenty dressed in dark-gray plastic suits wearing masks, while the management team members were all wearing normal clothes without masks.

During the preparatory training program, Elliot had learned that the special suits and masks prevented any contamination. They did this to keep the community free from diseases and infections. Without the suits, they would have to stay in quarantine for at least three weeks in the decontamination zone just before the entrance of the dome, while now they could return home the same day.

Elias had explained in the past that they had recruited all the employees working in this outside reactor and the climate plants from outside the community, through one of the many companies they owned in the outside world.

The first hour they got a tour with the entire group through the immense hydrogen-boron reactor. The reactor was impressive, but to Elliot, it was just a larger version of the reactor inside the dome. After the tour, they continued to the climate plants next to the reactor. They did not have to go outside anymore as the reactor and the climate plants were connected to each other. The climate plants fascinated him much more.

Aurora explained passionately as they walked through the climate plants about how hard they were working to optimize them further. She explained they would need thousands of these plants all over the world. If they all would run continuously, then it should be possible to reduce the carbon dioxide and methane in the atmosphere gradually back to the levels of the beginning of the twenty-first century. They were planning the construction of another climate plant to capture nitrous oxide from the atmosphere. They were still completing the design and development of this plant, but they were hoping to start the construction next year. The climate plants consumed quite some energy, and therefore the fusion reactors were crucial.

In the afternoon, they split up in groups. Elliot's group worked the entire afternoon together with a group of employees from the reactor. Before the trip, they had selected several issues to work on. The whole day he looked for the right moment to talk to Elias, but the program was quite full and either he was too busy or Elias was in meetings with the management team.

He talked to several employees of the reactor during the day and he learned they all lived in a large compound a few kilometers further away. They asked him about life in the dome and he explained how it was inside. That the dome was all green inside with plants and trees and that you could walk there without wearing a respo impressed the employees the most. Elliot was amazed with their reactions, since he always had taken the walk in the park and the greenhouse for granted.

Late in the evening they finished, and it was time to go back to the dome. They said goodbye to the employees and walked back to the transporter. Outside, the sky looked beautiful and mysterious. It was what they called civil twilight. Tonight it would only get slightly darker for about three hours in what they called nautical twilight, but during this time of the year there was no proper night without light. After entering the transporter, he took a seat next to Elias. Now was the moment to ask him.

Elias turned his head to him while they were taking off. The reactor and climate plants looked smaller and smaller.

"And did your first visit on the outside meet your expectations?"

"Yes, it was impressive, especially these gigantic climate plants…"

He stared at the horizon, at the mysteriously lit sky before he continued.

"…although the stories of all those employees left a deep impression on me as well. It made me realize that what they miss most is actually to walk outside and breath in the fresh air without the need for a respiratory mask filtering the pollution out. Something I always took for granted inside the dome."

"Funny you mention that. Since that is exactly what got humanity in trouble in the first place."

"What do you mean?"

"Well, about thirty years ago, before the construction of the dome, people were well aware of the fact that we were polluting the environment. Still, since the air we breathed in was free, everybody took it for granted and we continued polluting and adding greenhouse gasses to the atmosphere. Everybody thought things would not deteriorate that fast, and we would have plenty of time to reduce our emissions of carbon dioxide and other greenhouse gases."

"Didn't they to stop the pollution?"

"They tried, but they excelled in procrastinating the important measures that had to be taken to avoid a catastrophe. Life was good, so why worry about the future. I remember the endless discussions about carbon emission targets and measures, like putting a price on carbon dioxide emission, but the follow up and implementation progressed too slowly. People were busy with their own lives and believed a few degrees warmer would not harm that much.

"They also underestimated the many feedback loops, exacerbating the global warming. Like the thawing of the permafrost, which led to extra emission of greenhouse gases. Especially methane, which is over eighty times more potent than carbon dioxide at warming the Earth in the first twenty years after its release.

"Another feedback loop was the albedo effect. The melting of the polar ice and glaciers all over the world resulted in less sunlight reflected back into space, heating the planet even more. This resulted in ice-free summers in the Arctic with no ocean ice, reflecting less sunlight and deteriorating the situation further.

"The hotter temperatures created perfect conditions for wildfires, releasing more greenhouse gases and shrinking the forests. The extra carbon dioxide in the atmosphere made the trees grow faster, however not enough to recover, and subsequent droughts and wildfires destroyed them, resulting in younger forests with lower trees and more carbon dioxide in the atmosphere.

"Another problem was the hotter air, especially above cities. The heat created a stagnant layer of air above ground level, capturing pollutants and increasing their density in the air. Because of the heat, the usage of air-conditioners increased tremendously, resulting in a much higher power consumption, emitting more pollutants in the air. The sun and heat transformed pollutants into even more toxic ones, like ozone and ultrafine particles.

"All these feedback loops started strengthening each other, and the temperatures increased much faster than anyone could have imagined. The air became so unhealthy and hot that life expectancy around the globe dropped fast. On the worst days, staying outside without a respo could kill you, and on the best days it still shortens your life expectancy. The clean air we all used to take for granted is a thing of the past now, sadly enough. Luckily, your parents understood in time where the world was heading and they acted determined by joining our community."

"Yes, thank god they did. I wouldn't like to live outside of the dome. Speaking of my parents, there's something else I'd like to ask you."

"Tell me, Elliot. What is it you want to ask?"

"This morning you mentioned the few unnatural dead in our community, and since you've known my parents for a long time, there's something that has been puzzling me. It's about the death of my mother."

Elias looked puzzled at him.

"What do you mean?"

"Uh… well, I never really understood how she died?"

"Didn't your father explain what happened?"

"Not in so many details, just that she died in an unfortunate accident."

Elias stared at him in silence, agape, until he said,

"Accident? Oh, my god… he didn't tell you!?"

23.

The Palace Hotel was a modern hotel close to the Yamuna river. They equipped it with one of the best air-filtration and air-conditioning systems in New Delhi. This was one of the reasons Dylan had chosen this hotel to stay in. Matteo was delighted with the stylish, spacious room fitted with a king-size bed and a warm teak floor. Their rooms were next to one another and on one of the higher floors of the hotel.

Early in the morning, Dylan woke up after he had slept like a baby. He opened the curtain and looked at the horizon. This was it: the country where he was born. It was his first time in India and he was thrilled to be there. The sky was gray and yellowish from the smog hanging over the city. He could barely distinguish the roof of Humayun's Tomb through the hazy sky. Yesterday, the man at the reception had proudly explained about the famous view. Unfortunately, the smog spoiled it today.

At breakfast, he discussed the plans for that day with Matteo. Yesterday after arriving in the hotel, they had talked mostly about their youth and the pleasant holidays they had spent together when they were young. They laughed a lot and had a great time. Today, Matteo focused on the tablet he had brought with him and he showed him a map of New Delhi. Dylan looked at Matteo while he explained about the dangers of the neighborhood they were planning to go to. He was happy he had invited him to come along. Somehow, he felt a lot safer, and it was nice to share this experience with his good friend.

They planned to visit the orphanage, like the solicitor had suggested. While they drank some tea, a waiter approached them.

"Gentlemen, your taxi is waiting in front of the hotel."

"Thank you, sir. All right, Matteo, it's time to go."

Matteo put on his sunglasses and his baseball cap, which matched the khaki army vest he was wearing. They took their backpacks and walked toward the entrance. While they put on their respos, Matteo looked seriously at him.

"Did you take a spare battery for your respo?"

"Yep! All set!"

They walked through the airlock and stepped outside. The heat dropped on them like a heavy bag. A few meters away, a yellow taxi was waiting for them, this time a taxi with a driver.

"Good morning! Where to misters?" the shabby-looking driver asked them when they entered the taxi.

"To the Udayan Ghar orphanage in Janakpuri West, please!"

"All right sir."

The taxi left the secluded hotel terrain and passed the security post at the hotel. A few minutes later, they entered the flyover, called Baba Banda Singh Bahadur Setu, named after a legendary Sikh warrior. India was a country with such a rich history, and he felt proud to be of Indian descent. While they were driving, he noticed the driver coughed a lot and his breathing made a wheezing noise through the black cloth mask he was wearing. Matteo noticed it as well and asked bluntly,

"Sir, don't you need to wear a respo?"

"A respo? I wish I owned one, but they cost a fortune. The mask I have helps to keep most dirty particles out."

Matteo looked astounded at Dylan. One of the most polluted countries in the world and people do not have the money to buy proper protection. About thirty minutes later, they left the main road and the streets were smaller and buzzing with activity. Most of the people looked poor and malnourished. Almost everybody was wearing mouth masks, but none were wearing respos. He knew India was a poor country, nevertheless the poverty struck him. They all looked so young. It made him realize even more that where you were born determined your fate. The world was an unfair place.

The taxi was cruising at a walking pace now through the crowded streets. The people slowly cleared the way for the taxi. Staring at all those poor souls, he thought for a moment that he could have been one of them had he not been that fortunate to be adopted. As they continued, the street became a little less crowded. Five minutes later, the taxi stopped in front of a large gray building.

"Udayan Ghar orphanage, sir!"

Dylan paid and asked,

"Could you please wait here for us? You can start the meter already. We'll pay for the waiting."

"Of course sir."

He felt sorry for the taxi driver with his wheezing lungs. He thought the least he could do was to ensure that the man made some extra money today. They stepped out and walked to the front door of the orphanage. Dylan rang the doorbell, and a few seconds later, they heard a voice through the intercom.

"Hello?"

"Hello, we're here for Miss Garima Patel."

"And what's your name?"

"My name is Dylan Myers. I spoke to her a few months ago."

It was silent for a few seconds, after which there was a buzzing sound, and the door opened. They entered, and it closed behind them. Inside it was a lot cooler, and they heard a low buzz coming from the air-conditioning vent in the ceiling. In the reception hall, a young man of about their age came toward them. He did not wear a respiratory mask.

"Mr. Myers? Welcome to the Udayan Ghar orphanage!"

He looked at Matteo now.

"Who can I announce to Miss Patel?"

"Hello, oh, I'm sorry. My friend here is Matteo Muller."

"Okay, just a moment, gentlemen. Please take a seat. I'll be back soon."

The hall was artistically decorated with wooden ornaments in a clear Indian Mughal style. The sound of children playing and talking was vaguely audible in the background. They waited for almost thirty minutes, and Matteo was getting impatient. Then suddenly the young man returned.

"Gentlemen, Miss Patel can see you now. Please follow me."

They followed the man through what looked like a maze of hallways. There were no windows, but from time to time they passed some open rooms full of children, until the man stopped in front of an open wooden door. He gestured with his arm that they should enter. The room was large and filled with several smaller desks. In the back, there was an older Indian woman sitting behind a large wooden desk. She looked up at them.

"Mr. Myers and Mr. Muller, welcome to the Udayan Ghar orphanage. Please take a seat. Would you like something to drink?"

"Hello, Miss Patel. Some tea, please."

"For me as well, please," Matteo said while taking a seat.

Miss Patel gestured at the young man and he left. Now she peered at them over her glasses, like a strict schoolteacher.

"You can take off your respos if you like. We're blessed with a good air-filtering and air-conditioning system. A gift from our government after the death of all the orphans in the horrible heat wave in 2039. Anyway, that was before I worked here. What can I do for you, gentleman?"

Slightly hesitating, they both took off their respos. The air was better than what they had experienced the day before in the driverless taxi. Still, it was not as good as in the compound at home. The young man came back with the tea and put the cups in front of them, while Dylan explained what they came for. The young man stared at him and took a seat behind a desk, closer to the door. Garima listened, but her face turned grim, and slowly she started shaking her head.

"Mr. Myers, I thought I'd been clear over the phone. You could have spared yourself the long trip. We never give out the names of birth parents in adoption cases. The law forbids it."

"Yes, you've made that clear, Miss Patel, but I thought maybe we can work something out," Dylan said as he took a small, dark velvet bag out of his backpack. He took one of the one-ounce gold bars out of the bag and put it discretely on the table. She stared at the shiny gold bar, but she did not seem impressed.

"I see where you're coming from, Mr. Myers, and I know it often works like this in India, but I'm not like that."

"Would you accept a donation to the orphanage?"

She smiled awkwardly and replied,

"We welcome donations to our orphanage, but it changes nothing to my position. We never give out names of birth parents."

"No problem, I'd still like to make a donation."

Dylan moved the gold bar toward the woman, who looked perplexed.

"We do not accept donations in cash or in kind. Only electronic donations are allowed. This is also the law."

"Okay, could you give me the bank details?"

The woman looked in a drawer and gave Dylan a form. He took his smartphone and made a donation on the spot through his banking app. He showed the woman and her eyes almost seemed to fall out.

"That's very generous, Mr. Myers! Thank you in the name of all the orphans. I'm sorry I couldn't help you any further with your birth parents."

"No problem, Miss Patel. I understand. Please, if you change your mind, I'm staying in the Palace Hotel."

He handed her a card with the phone number and address of the hotel.

"Maybe you'd like to visit the orphanage before you go?"

"Yes, that would be nice, since I stayed here as well."

"Okay, Pradnesh will show you around. Thanks again for your donation and I wish you a pleasant trip back home."

They got up and said goodbye. The young man gestured them to follow him and he gave them a tour of the orphanage. He took his time and showed them the whole place. Looking at the young children, Dylan grasped how lucky he was to have been adopted. He thought back to what Garima had said, and he realized very well that without his adoption, he would probably have died in this deadly heat wave. After the tour, the young man accompanied them to the door. When they arrived at the entrance hall, the man said,

"Gentlemen, thank you again for your donation. This means a lot to us. I'm sorry that Miss Patel couldn't help you any further. You're good people."

They thanked him, put on their respos and left the building. The heat hit them in the face, and the noise from the busy street overwhelmed them. They looked around in the street for the taxi, but they did not see it anywhere. Suddenly, they heard a car honking and their taxi arrived from one of the side streets.

"I'm sorry, sir. The police sent me away, since there's no parking allowed here. I had to circle around," the driver explained.

"No problem. Return to the Palace Hotel, please!" Dylan said and felt sorry for the poor man.

"That visit was not what we had hoped for," Matteo said, as he felt bad about the whole situation.

"Yeah, I guess it was a wild, foolish attempt, anyway. At least I visited the place I lived in before my adoption."

"What do you want to do now?"

"I don't know."

A silence fell in the car and they both looked outside while the taxi brought them to the hotel.

24.

In the morning, the sky was hazy and still gray-yellowish from the smog. The sun glimmered through the smog as if someone had put a screen in front of it to dampen its force. Dylan sat there in front of his window in his hotel room. Yesterday was one big anticlimax for him and he lost faith. The night before, he had spoken to Elizabeth on the phone and she had tried to cheer him up. It had worked for the evening, and at least he had fallen asleep quickly that night.

That morning the disappointment came back to him, though. He had no clue what to do next. Matteo had suggested they hire someone to break into the orphanage and try to steal the birth certificate. But it didn't feel right to him, and he thought it only had a slight chance to succeed, anyway. How was a burglar going to find those documents since they had no clue where to look for them?

Yesterday he called the solicitor, but unfortunately the man did not have any other ideas either. Deep down, Dylan realized that his search ended here. They should probably take an earlier flight back home. But first, he wanted to check what Matteo wanted to do. His friend had come along with him, and they should at least try to make something nice out of this trip. Maybe some sightseeing or visiting some museum.

A moment later, Matteo knocked on his door to have breakfast together. They walked downstairs and sat at a table in the large restaurant. Matteo had made a list of top things to visit in New Delhi, and it cheered him up. His list was quite long; ample choice for several touristic tours. They wanted to start with Humayun's tomb, since it was next door to the hotel. Matteo really insisted on visiting the Red Fort. The Mughal Emperor Shah Jahan built this seventeenth century fort, and it served as the capital of the Mughals until the year 1857. India truly had a rich history. Dylan even suggested visiting the Taj Mahal, which was about two hundred kilometers south of New Delhi. Matteo like the idea, but he wanted to check first if it was safe to go there.

While they were discussing the day over a cup of tea, suddenly the concierge interrupted their conversation.

"Mr. Myers? Sorry to disturb, but there's a young man at the door asking for you."

"A young man? Did he say what he wanted?"

"No, but he insisted on seeing you."

They both got up and walked with the concierge to the front door. They stepped into the airlock to have a look at the man in front of the door. Outside, they noticed two security guards and behind them there was a nervous young man with a reddish mouth mask waving at them. Matteo looked at Dylan.

"That looks like the young man who was sitting in Miss Patel's office. The man who showed us around the orphanage. What was his name again?"

"Pradnesh!" Dylan replied and to the concierge he said, "please let him in, we know him."

"All right sir!"

The concierge gestured at the security officers and they let the young man enter the airlock. The door opened with a hiss, and Pradnesh stepped out. He took off his mouth mask and humbly bent his head down.

"Good morning, Mr. Myers and Mr. Muller. I think I might be able to help you out."

The three of them sat down at one of the tables at the window in the restaurant. Dylan looked curiously at the young man.

"So, how can you help us?"

"Well, I might be able to get you the information you're looking for."

"How are you going to do that?"

"My father used to be the director of the orphanage before Miss Patel became the director. What year were you adopted?"

"I'm born in the year 2029 and I was adopted that same year. Was your dad already a director at the time?"

"Yes, he had been a director since 2024."

"Do you think your father could tell me who my birth parents are?"

"I think he's your best chance."

"All right, could you bring us to your father today?"

"That depends…"

"Depends on what?"

Matteo and Dylan looked puzzled at Pradnesh.

"You know, mister? I'm a poor man."

Matteo showed a grin on his face and whispered in Dylan's ear.

"Obviously, he wants to be paid first."

Dylan took some money out of his pocket and put it discretely on the table.

"Here, this you can have now, and I'll pay you more when your father gives me the information about my birth parents."

"No, sir."

"What do you mean, no?"

The young man hesitated for a moment.

"I want the thing you showed Miss Patel."

"You want the gold bar?"

"Yes, sir."

Dylan contemplated for a moment before answering.

"All right. I'll give you one now and I'll give you another one when I receive the information about my parents."

"Thank you, sir! We can visit my father right away."

Then Pradnesh took the one-ounce gold bar that Dylan had put on the table.

Matteo looked warily at Pradnesh.

"Dylan, maybe you can get my backpack from my room and your own stuff while I wait here with Pradnesh?"

He got the message and went upstairs to get his backpack.

Half an hour later, they were in a taxi on the way to the house of the father of Pradnesh. Dylan couldn't believe his luck and felt hopeful again. Although he also thought it was too good to be true. Maybe the young man just wanted to rob them and lured them to some deserted place. He was glad that he was with Matteo. Alone, this would have been way too risky.

25.

He was full of anger after Elias explained everything to him. Why had his father not told him the truth? Elliot just didn't understand. It was his mother, and he didn't have the right to do that. Often, he had wondered about the way she had died. His father had explained it was an accident, but never had given many details. At the time, he was only ten, and he just remembered everybody being so concerned about him. Now he knew his father had lied to him.

After landing, the transporter drove toward the tunnel under the dome. The sky looked mystical, and he watched the stars until they entered. Inside, they sped up, and he stared at the light at the end of the tunnel. It looked like finally the truth about his mother was coming out. All those years he had believed it had been some unfortunate accident. But because his father had never wanted to talk about it nor had given him much details, he always had thought there was more to it than met the eye.

As they slowed down, he saw the large door and the hall where his journey to the outside had started this morning. They all stepped out of the transporter and walked toward the decontamination room. They stayed inside for nearly fifteen minutes while the disinfectants sprayed their suits. Then a green light went on and they could leave the room. Everybody took off their suit, and it felt good to be without it. The whole day he had felt like some kind of astronaut breathing through a mask. They opened the large security doors to the dome, and they walked back through the tunnels to the nuclear fusion development center.

At the center, he said goodbye to everybody and rushed upstairs to the exit. As he came through the airlock and stepped outside, he smelled the trees and the plants around him and it calmed him down a bit. Would he still be awake? He rushed home. Still catching his breath from running, he entered the apartment. To his relief, his father was sitting in the living room and seemed to have been waiting for him to come home.

"Hello. I was so curious to hear about your trip that I stayed up waiting for you. How was it?"

Elliot tried to control his anger and respond normally. Still, his voice was quivering.

"Amazing and a unique experience to be outside. Just at the end of the trip, there was an unpleasant surprise."

"Oh? What happened?"

"I found out you've lied to me all these years!" he said while his voice trembled and his father noticed the anger on his face.

"What do you mean?" he answered, astounded.

"Mother didn't have an accident! She committed suicide!"

"How…how do you know that?"

"That's not relevant… what I would like to know is why you lied to me!?" he yelled, with tears in his eyes.

Amos got up and tried to hold Elliot in his arms, but he pushed him away and shouted.

"Don't touch me! How could you lie to me all these years!?"

His father looked devastated now, and he noticed a tear in the corner of his eye.

"I'm sorry. I just couldn't tell you."

"Why not!?" Elliot yelled, crying.

His father sat down with his head in his lap and his hands on his head while he replied.

"I couldn't! I just couldn't! You were only ten years old! It broke my heart already to tell you that your mother had died."

His father was crying now, and for a moment there was a silence. Elliot still had too many questions running through his head and continued.

"You should have told me the truth instead of lying to me! How can I trust you!?"

"Somehow, I thought it would be easier for you to believe that it was an accident. I just couldn't tell you she had killed herself. I was devastated."

Elliot looked at his father and suddenly he felt sorry for him and realized the discussion caused him pain as well. He approached him and put his hand on his shoulder. His father touched his hand and wiped the tears off his face. A moment later, he stood up and looked at Elliot.

"I'm sorry for not telling you the truth, but you have to understand I couldn't tell you it was suicide. I knew your mother meant everything to you and when I told you she had died; I saw this deep pain and sorrow in your eyes. I just thought it would all be too much for you."

Elliot calmed down and said,

"I guess I understand, although I don't understand why you did not tell me later when I was older. Did you really think it wouldn't come out at some point?"

"You're right and I regret it."

"Do you know why she killed herself?"

His father looked at him, and his face looked frightened and distressed. He shook his head left and right and looked tired.

"She just killed herself. I'm sorry, I feel exhausted. Can we talk about this some other time?"

On the one hand, he felt sorry for his father, who looked exhausted by the whole fight. On the other hand, he still had the impression he was not telling him everything.

"Okay. I'm tired as well, but I would like you to tell me everything at some point."

"Good night."

26.

The taxi drove through the narrow streets in the south of New Delhi. Dylan looked outside at the poor people, and the amount of rubbish on the streets disturbed him. How could people live like that? He noticed black long plastic bags on the corners of several streets. At some point, the taxi braked for a red light next to one of the black bags and a horrendous smell entered the taxi.

"What the hell is that? What a horrible smell?"

Pradnesh looked outside and answered in a dull voice.

"Those are bodies from people who died during the last heat wave. There were so many of them that the city is still collecting them in certain parts of the city."

Dylan looked appalled at Matteo. The taxi continued and after a while stopped in front of a house painted in light green. Pradnesh stepped out of the taxi first, while Dylan paid the taxi driver and asked him to wait for them in front of the house. In the taxi, they learned Pradnesh was only one year younger than Dylan, but with his skinny body, he looked much younger. The heat outside was heavy and was humid. Some men in the street stared at them, possibly because Matteo was the only white man in the street or because they were the only ones wearing respos. Pradnesh opened the front door of the light-green house and they went inside.

It was dark in the hallway, and Pradnesh led the way inside. It was cool inside the old house. They passed a room with a woman inside who appeared to be reading to her four children. Dylan felt more at ease seeing the children, and his fear of getting robbed seemed ridiculous now.

"Follow me, please. My father is in the back. He's severely ill."

All the way in the back, they entered a room and there was a large bed in the middle of the room with an old man in it. The man was breathing through a mask and had a large bottle of oxygen next to his bed. They heard a wheezing and whistling sound while he was breathing. The man looked very weak, and he was just skin and bones.

"Dad, these are the men I talked to you about."

The man looked at them and gestured with his hand they should sit on the chairs next to him. His son helped him to sit, and he mumbled something to Pradnesh in Hindi. Pradnesh left the room for a moment. When he returned with some tea for everybody, he looked at them and at his father.

"Could you explain to my father about your adoption case and what you're looking for? He's suffering from lung cancer, but his memory is still excellent."

Dylan explained all the details about his adoption, including the dates and names of his adoptive parents. He also showed the adoption document, and the man looked at the number on it. He took off his oxygen mask for a moment and muttered something to Pradnesh in Hindi, who left the room thereafter. The man glanced at them for a few minutes before he spoke with a wheezing voice.

"I was the director of the orphanage from 2024 to 2039, then I lost my job after the great heat wave. So many people had died. It was horrible. Bodies laid scattered all over the streets, and they found many more inside the houses all over the city..."

The man paused for a moment to breathe through the oxygen mask and to catch his breath. He continued talking about the dreadful heat wave that had struck the country and had killed more than four million people in just New Delhi alone. Apparently, it had been deadlier than ever before, because it had coincided with multiple power failures in the city.

The power failures were caused by the combination of a peak load, because of the massive energy demand from air conditioning, and efficiency loss in the power plants because of the heat. It took the army months to take all the dead bodies out of the city and bury them in enormous mass graves. Many bodies laid rotting in the streets and diseases proliferated, killing more people. With tears in his eyes, the old man explained how all the children in the orphanage had died. The story deeply moved them and they listened attentively until about thirty minutes later Pradnesh returned to the room.

In his hand he was carrying some documents and Dylan's heart skipped a beat. Would he finally get to know the name of his birth parents? He gave the documents to his father, who took them in his shaky hands and looked at them for a moment before he said,

"I believe these are the documents you are looking for. You are lucky. I kept a copy of the whole archive in my home, since I understood the new director is applying the law mercilessly..." he read one of the documents and continued, "...Yagnesh wasn't it?"

Dylan nodded and had difficulty believing he might get the information about his birth parents. Suddenly, the man looked flabbergasted at the documents and murmured,

"No!? No!? What a coincidence! Everything truly happens for a reason. God moves mysteriously."

They looked puzzled at the old man and Dylan asked,

"What do you mean?"

"Mister, I remember your parents very well. They are the reason I'm still alive now."

The old man held the documents in his shaky hand, while he continued, "I still remember them standing in my office at the orphanage. They wanted me to take care of their son. Your mother cried the whole time and after signing the papers to trust their son in the orphanage's care, she left the room sobbing and crying. Your father stayed a moment longer and asked me to take special care of you. He wanted to ensure you would get priority in any adoption requests coming from rich countries. He donated generously to the orphanage and insisted on giving me personally a large sum of money. The money given to the orphanage ended up in the city orphanage fund, but the money he gave me I used to install an air-conditioning system backed up with an emergency generator."

He looked at his son and seemed to address him now.

"That system saved our lives during that dreadful heat wave and is the reason we're still alive. What a twist of fate to meet you here almost twenty-five years later."

The old man handed the documents to Dylan, who inspected them thoroughly. He noticed the names of the birth parents, but he wanted to be sure these were the correct papers. He took the document he had found in his mother's vault and compared the numbers. The number of the birth certificate and the number on the adoption papers matched. He read out loud the names of his birth parents.

"Vikram Singh and Tanvi Singh, father and mother of Yagnesh."

"I remember your father very well. He was a wealthy man in New Delhi and I had never understood why he gave you up for adoption. Your mother seemed to have agreed to it, although she seemed also deeply perturbed and saddened by it. I remember asking them if they were sure, and they claimed they had no choice. Your father really insisted that I should take special care of you and make sure you would get the best adoptive parents possible."

The old man seemed exhausted and his speech was trembling more than in the beginning. He put back the oxygen mask to recover. The young man turned his head to them after looking concerned at his father.

"I think my father needs to rest now. You can keep the documents."

"Just one last question. Do you have the address of my parents somewhere?" Dylan asked the old man, who was lying flat on his bed now.

The man murmured something in Hindi to Pradnesh, who then said,

"He says that if there's any address, it should be in the documents."

Dylan inspected the papers until he found a contact address on a separate note.

"Ah, yes! I found it here. Thanks!"

They thanked the old man and followed Pradnesh outside. Just in front of the door, he blocked the way and held up his hand.

"I helped you as I promised you. Now please keep your part of the deal."

Dylan looked in his backpack and handed him another gold bar. They thanked Pradnesh and walked out onto the buzzing street. Matteo got startled and searched for the taxi which stood parked further down the street.

"We should go immediately, Dylan. It's not safe here."

Dylan noticed there were several men staring at them and did not feel at ease, either. They rushed to the taxi and got in. They locked the doors immediately. Inside, they discussed what to do next. The driver explained that the address of his birth parents was less than half an hour away from there. Dylan was all excited about finding his birth parents, and they decided to go and check out the address in the document. As the taxi drove away, they did not notice the four shabby-looking men following them on two scooters.

27.

Matteo and Dylan bought some food on the way and had their lunch in the taxi. The sky turned darker. It looked like it was going to rain. At some point, the taxi arrived in a neighborhood with wide boulevards and big houses with gates and walls around them. Most of them had armed guards in front. The driver explained that many rich businessmen and powerful people from the government lived in this neighborhood. They continued a few kilometers further until he stopped on the boulevard at a large yellow gate. He told them they had arrived at the address on the document.

Dylan asked the driver to wait, and they stepped out of the car. He was all excited and even hoped he would meet his parents. The two scooters passed them over on the wide boulevard. There was quite some traffic, and Matteo and Dylan barely noticed them. The four men glanced at them when they passed. This also did not grab their attention, since everybody in New Delhi stared at them as if they were aliens. They crossed and walked over the sidewalk toward the gate. Behind it there was a small guardhouse, and when they rang the front bell, a man came out wearing a respo.

"Hello, sir. I'm looking for Mr. Vikram Singh. Is he in today?"

"No sir! There is no Mr. Singh living here."

"Mr. Singh is my father, and I really need to find him. This is the most recent address I have from him. Look here in this document."

The man looked puzzled. He took the document and checked it out.

"This document is from 2029. My father was working here at the time. He still works here on the premises for Mr. Damani. Just a moment, please."

The guard walked back to the guardhouse and made a phone call. They waited for about five minutes until an older man approached the gate, also wearing a respo. The guard spoke to him in Hindi and showed him the paper. After a while, he came closer and gazed at Dylan.

"Could you take off your respo for a moment, please?"

Dylan took off his respo, but the polluted air irritated his lungs immediately and he started coughing.

"It's okay, you can put it back on. You have your mother's eyes and your father's face. Amazing, what a resemblance! I used to work for your father as a guard over here. Unfortunately, he left and sold the house about twenty-five years ago to Mr. Damani."

"Do you have any idea where he moved to? I really need to find him."

"Well, that's a long time ago. I thought they moved to New York. Or was it to Washington?"

"Do you know where I could find the address they moved to?"

"I'm sorry. I don't," the man apologized, but still looked like he was reflecting on something and after a moment he continued, "Could you give me your phone number? It's a slight chance, but I could have a look at home tonight to check if I kept the address somewhere."

Dylan gave him his phone number, after which the man said, "I'll let you know if I find something."

"Thank you, sir! I appreciate that very much. Thank you for your time."

They turned away from the gate and walked toward the taxi near the sidewalk. Matteo tried to remain positive.

"With a bit of luck, the man calls you tonight with the address. Let's see."

"I hope so, but it sounds like it's going to be more difficult to find my birth parents than I expected," Dylan said and he opened the door of the taxi while Matteo walked to the other side of the car.

Out of nowhere, suddenly a scooter passed Dylan very close, and he felt his backpack ripped out of his hand.

"Shit! They took my backpack, with all the documents and my money!"

Matteo watched them pass and yelled.

"Get in the taxi! Driver, follow that scooter as fast as you can! They stole our bag!"

The taxi pulled up with squealing tires and followed them.

"Faster! Faster!" Matteo yelled at the driver, while he was getting something out of his backpack which looked like some high-tech gun.

Matteo held it out of the window and aimed at the men in front of him. A few seconds later, he fired the gun and Dylan noticed the man on the back got hit by something. For a moment, nothing happened, but then suddenly he fell off the scooter. The taxi had to brake hard to avoid running over him. Matteo and Dylan rushed out of the car, and Dylan took back his backpack from the stunned man.

Out of the blue, another scooter with two men on it showed up, and the one from which the stunned man had fallen also approached. They stopped on both sides of Dylan and Matteo and got off their scooters. The three men formed a circle around them and they all pulled sharp looking switchblades. One of them said,

"Give me the backpack or I'll kill you!"

Matteo did not wait a second. Dylan noticed he was holding a taser in his hand. He aimed at the man in front of him and fired the taser. He dropped the knife as his muscles contracted in agony and he fell to the ground. One of the men behind him immediately approached and tried to stab him. But Matteo turned around just in time to see the knife coming, and he diverted the knife with a swift arm movement. He punched him hard in his face and gave him a kick on the side of his knee, after which he fell down. Meanwhile, the other guy attacked Dylan, who in a reflex threw his backpack hard in the man's face.

The man tried to run away with it, but Matteo fired the taser again and he fell in shock on the floor. Matteo got the backpack and yelled.

"Dylan, get in the car! Let's go!"

They both jumped in the car, and the taxi driver immediately sped away.

"Wow… that was close!"

28.

Elliot was so pissed at his father. He just did not understand him. It had been almost a week since their fight after his trip to the outside reactor. Since then, he had avoided the topic, but today was a special day and he had to bring it up. But why did he yell at him like that? Couldn't he see he just missed his mother and wanted to understand everything? To react the way he did. Ridiculous, he thought. Elliot's frustration boiled up so much that it frightened him. At least, in all his desperation, he had run away and left his father alone. The thought of what he might have done in his anger, if he would have stayed with him in that room, scared him.

Now he was walking between the long rows of tomato plants. He slowly calmed down and tried to grasp the things that had happened in their apartment. The air was fresh, as usual, and the sun shone above his head. As a young child, he realized early on that the presence of plants had a calming effect on him. He would come out here whenever he was angry or stressed and sometimes just to chill out. In between the tomato plants that were hanging from high all the way down in neat straight rows, he felt serene.

The particular smell of them filled the surrounding air. He checked out the tomatoes and picked several ripe ones, which he put in his basket. He remembered coming here often with his mother when he was young. She taught him how to pick the right ones with the best taste. They had spent hours in here, between all the vegetables, herbs, and fruits. Today she would have turned fifty-four. Every year, Elliot would make a small shrine in a corner in the living room and fill it with her pictures. He would put some lavender bags, which his mother used to put in his bedroom on a small table. He adored the smell.

After her death, Elliot and his father had started a tradition on her birthday to honor her and bring up nice memories of his mother. However, for several years now, his father's behavior had changed. He was often depressed, and he had stopped taking part in the commemoration on her birthday. He tolerated his shrine, but quickly got agitated and refused to respond to his questions.

Initially, Elliot thought it had something to do with the surgical interventions his father had gone through. He even had asked his doctor about it, but the doctor actually told him that most patients with a new-grown heart became more optimistic and happier in their lives instead of depressed. Elliot did not understand him and since last week, the question of why his mother had killed herself was troubling him so much that he decided he had to know today. He had to comprehend.

Elliot had come home early from work and decorated the small table in the corner with pictures of his mother. Later in the evening, his father arrived home from work and, after talking about some of their memories of his mother, Elliot asked his father to explain to him why he thought she had done it. Why had she ended her life? Amos exploded this time and raised his voice at him.

"Stop asking me that…you are tearing me apart!"

He continued, though, and tried to explain to his father that the void of answers and lack of understanding was haunting him and made him restless. He had the feeling that his father knew more about it, and he just wanted to understand. Amos got even more upset and yelled again at him with watery eyes. He walked to the corner with the pictures and swept them from the table. Elliot screamed.

"Stop! Don't do that!"

At the same time, he tried to pick up the pictures from the floor and wanted to put them back on the table. His father pushed him away, and Elliot got so angry. He felt like hitting his father with his fists. The thought scared him. In a reflex, he ran out of the room and left their apartment. He ran as fast as he could through the maze of apartments to the staircases. He rushed up the stairs and ran toward the nursery garden. Tears were running down his face.

After picking some tomatoes, he continued walking and looked for some other vegetables, and inside the lettuce house, he ran into Elsa. She just took out a nice crop of lettuce when she spotted him.

"Are you all right, Elliot?"

He had calmed down. Most people would have noticed nothing special, but Elsa immediately sensed something was wrong. He explained to her what had happened, and he felt much better after talking about it. Elsa understood him and took her time to listen.

"I guess it's a difficult topic for your father. I mean, he must have loved your mother a lot and to lose the love of your life is hard."

"I guess you're right. I insisted too much probably."

Elliot tried to look at it from his father's point of view and understood it must not be easy for him. Still, he would prefer him to talk openly, so he could understand it all better. He was happy that Elsa was there for him when he needed her most. They sat next to each other for a while in silence.

Later, they walked back together to the staircases leading to the apartments. They changed topic and talked about Elsa's study. In front of Elsa's apartment, he kissed her on the lips and said goodbye.

He continued to his apartment and in front of the door he hesitated to go in, as he felt the stress and anger coming back to him.

29.

The whole evening, Dylan waited for a call from his father's old guard. After the robbery attempt, they had returned to the hotel. Matteo was the hero of the day, and they celebrated their victory in the hotel bar. Matteo had tried to cheer him up, saying that he was sure the old man would call him. But the later it got, the more he lost hope. Back in his room, he searched online to find any information about his birth parents, but the Singh name was quite common and he did not find much. Around midnight he went to bed, slightly disillusioned.

The morning after, he discussed with Matteo what they would do for that day and they decided to visit the Red Fort and Humayun's tomb. After breakfast they returned to their rooms to prepare their backpacks and get ready. Dylan had just finished brushing his teeth when his phone rang. He rushed out of the bathroom to pick it up.

"Hello?"

"Mr. Myers? We spoke yesterday about Mr. Singh and I had looked for his address, but it was too late to call you."

Dylan's heart skipped a beat.

"Did you find their address?"

"Yes, I did. They asked me at the time to ship some stuff to New York and I had written the address down. Do you have a pen?"

Quickly, he grabbed a pen and paper from the desk in his room.

"Yes, I do. Tell me!"

"The address is 471 Washington Street #PH in New York. I believe the PH stands for the penthouse. I also found an old phone number."

Dylan noted down the address and the phone number and thanked the man. After hanging up, he walked over to Matteo's room and told him the good news.

"Splendid! So, what would you like to do now?"

"I think we earned our touristic outing, so I suggest we start with the tomb first."

They spent the rest of the day sightseeing in New Delhi. He thought several times about his birth parents and had difficulty believing he might have found them. The visit distracted him a bit. The tomb had been constructed in 1572 and it was the tomb of the Mughal emperor Humayun. They built the structure of rubble masonry and red sandstone forty-nine meters high. It was the first Indian building to use the Persian double dome on a high neck drum. It left a deep impression on him, and he felt closer to his roots than ever before. After visiting the Red Fort in the afternoon, he felt proud to be of Indian descent. They had gotten a glance into the rich history of India.

It was very warm and humid again, and at the end of the day, they were happy to be back in the hotel. The entire day, Dylan had felt upbeat because his trip to New Delhi had not been in vain. Matteo had checked with the local authorities and with the Swiss embassy for their trip to the Taj Mahal, but unfortunately, there was negative travel advice on the region around Agra. Apparently, the government had lost control of the region south of New Delhi, and gangs and militia groups had taken over. They abandoned the plan and decided to return home earlier.

In the evening, he called Elizabeth to tell her the good news. He had found the name of his birth parents and even had the address they had moved to after they left New Delhi. She was delighted to hear that they managed to get on a flight earlier and would fly back the next day.

That evening, he had difficulty falling asleep. His search in New Delhi had finished, and it was time to return home. He was happy with the result, but he could not help thinking of the next steps. He realized very well that the address might not lead to much more, since the New York city of 2029 was no more. Still, he was not going to give up easily.

30.

Back in Ikast, Dylan had little time to relax. He got sucked back into his work. The construction of the large solar chimney power plant, which was going to capture nitrous oxide from the air, was well under way and Sorensen had put him on the project team responsible for the construction of the climate plant. He worked long hours but made it a habit now to call Elizabeth so she would not wait in vain for him in the evening.

His relation with Elizabeth had gotten better, and he realized more and more what a special woman she was. She understood how important it was for him to find his birth parents, and she tried to help as much as possible. He had shown her all the information gathered on his parents so far, and she had put it all on the wall above the desk in the study room of their apartment. Since his return from New Delhi, he searched in all online sources together with Elizabeth.

Unfortunately, most of the information they found was about other people with the same name. Every time they found someone with the same name, they tried to gather more information to check if they could be his birth parents. Most of the time they found something that ruled out the people to be his birth parents. The more they continued their search, the more they concluded that their best lead was the address in New York.

The problem was that more than half of New York City had been evacuated and abandoned about ten years ago after several deadly floods and hurricanes. They had tried to protect Manhattan with the construction of a seawall, but during a heavy hurricane the wall had been breached and the seawater had flooded the city, killing many citizens.

Eventually the federal government had decided it had become too expensive to keep on protecting the city, and the lower part of it was declared a national park like most of the coastal area of the United States. All lower regions in and around New York were abandoned. Inhabitants either left the region or moved inland to higher elevated areas in New Jersey. The north and a large part of the south of Manhattan, from Lower Manhattan up to Midtown Manhattan, were all submerged now. If his parents were still alive, they would have left their New York penthouse a long time ago as the surrounding streets were all underwater.

One evening, Dylan entered their apartment and Elizabeth called him from the study room, all excited. She was sitting behind the computer screen when he came in.

"I spoke to Matteo today, and he had a brilliant suggestion about some satellite mapping service. Look here," she said enthusiastically.

He stared at the screen as she typed the address from the penthouse of his birth parents in New York. It showed the map of New York and then she pushed some button and suddenly the entire image switched to satellite mode and he could actually distinguish all the buildings. She zoomed further in on the city, and they noticed many buildings were in ruins. She continued until they could see the exact address and the surrounding streets in detail, and the building that housed the penthouse looked in one piece.

"That's good news, no?" she said proudly.

"Yeah, amazing the detail it shows. It seems the penthouse is all intact."

"Matteo also found a database in which you can search for an address, and then it shows the owners of the property. I ran a search on the penthouse and the current owners are still Vikram and Tanvi Singh, your birth parents. They never sold the penthouse."

"Wow, that's good news. So maybe we can find some clues in the penthouse about where they moved to?"

"Possibly, although Matteo also told me he heard that most buildings in New York have been ransacked and stripped of any valuables. So, the chance we'll find anything is small."

"Yes, I heard something similar from my boss this week, but we are looking for traces of where my birth parents moved to and that could be in documents left behind, which are worthless to looters. Did I understand you correctly? Does that mean that you're thinking of coming along with me to New York?"

"Well, I can't let you and Matteo have all the fun without me every time, right? During your stay in New Delhi, I really missed you and after hearing all your and Matteo's stories, I felt left out. This time I want to come along."

He smiled at her and gave her a kiss.

"We'll have to check when we can take a week off. I need to wait for just the right moment to ask my boss, since I just came back, and it's quite busy now with the construction of the plant."

"You're not in a rush, are you? I prefer to take our time to prepare really well. I'm sure it will be more complicated than your trip to New Delhi."

"Yeah. That's what Matteo said too. I'm also not sure how safe it is in what remains of New York."

"More reason to take our time."

31.

The fresh air did him good, and Amos felt his stress and agony fade away gradually. It hurt him to see his son so upset and angry, but he did not stop asking questions. Every time Elliot asked him about his mother's suicide, it felt like an old wound was ripped open. All the painful memories and feelings of guilt had come back to him. He had lost control in the apartment when he swept the pictures from the table, and he knew he had hurt Elliot's feelings. He had seen the hate in his son's eyes and it had broken his heart.

He walked through the gardens toward the edge of the dome until he arrived at the field with the sunflowers. He took a seat on the bench next to the path and relaxed while his thoughts wandered. The humming sound of all the micro-drones flying from sunflower to sunflower calmed him down. Amazing how this technology took over the pollination function of the bees. His thoughts took him back to the year he met his wife in those dire circumstances. It was as if some higher power had destined him to go through some ironic roller-coaster that year.

It was in the year 2020; the year he had turned forty-one. He was living in one of the better neighborhoods of New Delhi. His career had been very successful and his companies were flourishing, especially one of them. About ten years earlier he had founded a company designing drones, which was off to a rough start at first. But after changing the company's focus onto military and security drones, his business really took off.

The year he met his wife he was already a multimillionaire. That year he made some decisions that made him a billionaire quickly after. Part was luck, part a calculated bet. The years before he had built up a diversified stock portfolio, and he had been betting on the technology, online retail and health sectors. He also owned a company making disinfectant products and hand sanitizer for the medical sector. The years after they flourished and his wealth grew further. But the big jump came when he made that calculated bet at the beginning of 2020.

End of January, he had heard more and more about this new coronavirus outbreak in China. The years before, there had been relatively small epidemics of other coronaviruses like SARS and MERS. The SARS-CoV, or severe acute respiratory syndrome-related coronavirus, was the first one in the year 2002. This outbreak was relatively small and spread mostly in Asia, with the most fatalities in China. In 2012 the MERS-CoV, or Middle East respiratory syndrome-related coronavirus, epidemic followed. This was also a relatively small outbreak, and most casualties were in Saudi Arabia.

This new virus SARS-CoV-2, also called COVID-19, quickly appeared to be different from the other two, especially since the number of infections in Wuhan, the largest city in the Hubei province in China, skyrocketed. This epidemic was much larger and faster than previous ones. Most of the people shrugged their shoulders and did not realize what the implications were. Many people talked about the Wuhan virus, as if they wanted to imply it was something specific to that city.

Amos had experienced the previous outbreaks of the coronavirus from up close since he traveled all over the world for his work. In the middle of January the first infection popped up in Thailand, quickly followed by cases reported in other countries like South

Korea, Japan, but also in the UK and the US. He quickly grasped the consequences of what was happening and in early February he started accumulating short positions on the major stock indices of the world. Initially, he sold futures, but by the end of February he had accumulated large positions of short options as well and the market dropped quickly after.

A month later, after the World Health Organization announced the COVID-19 outbreak as a global pandemic, he closed his positions with a huge profit. Together with the large gain on his other investments, his wealth made a huge jump up and he became one of the many billionaires the world already counted. He continued investing, but also tried to enjoy his wealth along the way. He felt invincible, and at the time, it was difficult to imagine his luck was about to change.

Months later, the global pandemic was well under way and had turned into the biggest one since the Spanish flu in 1918. Most countries had suspended air travel and closed borders. At the end of the official period of confinement, Amos started seeing more people again and even organized several parties. He enjoyed his new lifestyle and the pandemic seemed to leave him mostly unaffected until suddenly the party was over.

The virus caught up with him, and he started feeling sick. The doctor examined him and he tested positive for COVID-19. For a while, he hoped he would be part of the group of people who only had mild symptoms, but soon after, he became really sick. The hospitals were overloaded with patients, but his assistant managed to get him a private room in one of the better hospitals in town.

Quickly after they put him on oxygen as he had problems breathing and the oxygen level in his blood was already dangerously low. He lacked energy and could barely move. Grounded in his bed, he realized that he was no different from any poor soul on the planet. The virus did not discriminate between rich and poor. Never had he been so sick, and he balanced on the edge of life and death for weeks.

Life seemed to throw weird curve balls at him, as it was under these dire circumstances that he met his wife for the first time. She was one of the nurses taking care of him. She wore protective clothing and a mask, but underneath, he noticed her beautiful, large brown eyes. Every time he looked at her, he noticed her warmth and felt safe. She took care of him when he was feeble and bedridden, and his situation looked grim.

After a week, he seemed to have hit the bottom and slowly started to feel slightly better. His breathing improved gradually every day, and his fever went down. He became more aware of his surroundings and slowly recovered every day. He even talked to her from time to time. She was kind, and he liked her from the beginning. His moments with her were short, as she was very busy with the many patients in the hospital. He started looking forward to those moments while he started feeling better.

Eventually, he healed and was discharged, but by then he had already fallen for her. Soon after, he returned to the hospital to bring her a large bouquet to thank her. At home, he could not get her out of his head and he asked his assistant to get him her phone number. After trying to get a date for months, she finally accepted to go for dinner with him. Initially, she had a preconceived idea about rich people like him, and she kept him at a safe distance. She was also very busy with her work and was often too tired to go out. He quickly fell in love with her and after months of dating, she finally fell for him too.

She was an amazing woman, generous and kind, and Amos realized he had met the woman of his life. He was twenty years older than her, but it did not seem to bother her. He proposed two years later, and they got married. She moved in with him and became his rock in the wild sea. In the past, he was only busy making money and contemplated little in life. His wife changed all that and made him aware and more sensitive to the looming problems challenging the world, like poverty, injustice, inequality and climate change.

She made him aware of the price the world was paying for humanity's unbridled hunt for growth and more wealth. Slowly he started seeing the light, but at that moment he could not fully understand what was about to happen. The signs were all there, but he did not grasp the consequences yet. In the year they met, the pandemic preoccupied the world. The urgency of addressing the climate change problem suddenly did not seem important anymore. The lockdown had resulted in a small decrease in air pollution and emission of carbon dioxide, and people continued with their lives with an unfounded optimism that the greenhouse emission problem would resolve itself.

Nevertheless, there were plenty of events showing a different picture, but they barely made the headlines. A slow-moving danger is not interesting news. Australian bushfires on a gigantic scale, with smoke forcing people all over the country to stay inside. Record Amazon rainforest fires in Brazil, encouraged by a government stimulating farmers to exploit the forest. America's West Coast burning like never before. Hurricanes, typhoons, floods, droughts and other catastrophic events all over the world popped up in the news headlines for brief moments to be quickly forgotten soon after. There were melting ice sheets in the polar circle and glaciers disappearing globally. Record temperatures in Siberia of thirty-eight degrees Celsius, eighteen degrees warmer than normal. Reports on thawing of the permafrost barely made the press. Even the spectacular craters formed in Siberia's Yamal peninsula by an explosion of underground methane, and methane bubbling up from the ground on an unprecedented scale, did not get much press attention. People did not seem to care.

Global temperatures were gradually rising, but the speed was slow and even though the rise was accelerating, it did not really alarm people. In the sparsely populated polar circles, the temperatures rose much faster though, but this was too far away from most people to notice it or to worry about it. Amos was no different and it took years before the picture became clear to him, but then he made a decision that changed their future in an unprecedented way.

32.

Dylan and Elizabeth rushed out of the hyper-loop station and took a driverless taxi to Frankfurt airport where they would meet Matteo. Several months ago, they had decided to go all together to New York. Elizabeth's parents had tried to talk her out of it because the trip was not without risks. Elizabeth had countered that apparently it was all right for Matteo to go, but not for her. Her parents had told her it was logical because she was a woman and Matteo a man. That was the last straw for Elizabeth, since she also had done her military service in Switzerland, just like Dylan and Matteo. She had made it clear that it was her decision, and she was going.

Both their bosses at Enviro were not pleased with their plans as they deemed them too dangerous. They had to do quite some convincing, but, in the end, they had accepted to let them go for a week. Matteo had contacted some of his friends in the US army to get the latest security details about their visit. They had thoroughly prepared for their trip and used all the input from experts they could get. The more meetings they had together, the more excited they got, and now it was finally time to go. The time spent waiting for the approval from Enviro to get the days off turned out to be a good thing, since now, at the end of fall, the weather conditions for their trip were getting better. The hurricane season was finished and the heat waves were over. The weather looked good for the coming week.

As soon as they spotted Matteo at the airport Elizabeth ran to her brother to give him a big hug. It felt good to be the three of them, just like the good old days, when they used to go on hiking trips together. They boarded the supersonic stratosphere plane. Dylan was nervous as he still did not like flying, but he was trying to hide it from Elizabeth. Since it was his second time on this type of plane, he knew what to expect. For Elizabeth it was the first time though, and he noticed the excitement on her face when they were pushed backwards in their chairs as the plane took off. The sheer power and acceleration impressed and surprised.

They landed about two hours later at Republic Airport on Long Island, the closest airport to Manhattan. More than ten years ago, the two major airports of New York, John F. Kennedy and Newark Liberty, as well as the other regional airports on lower ground like LaGuardia, had closed. After the breach of several seawalls during a hurricane, they were all closed and abandoned. Sea levels had continued to rise and all these airports were submerged now, like a large part of Long Island. Republic Airport was on higher ground and remained open and was expanded over time.

After collecting their luggage, they headed for the air taxi platform, which was in a different part of the airport. It was an oval-shaped platform with several levels. There were dozens of air taxis parked on each level and some were taking off or landing.

"We are leaving from gate thirty-four," Elizabeth said as they walked through the long corridor on the third floor of the platform.

A robot cart followed them with their luggage on top of it, one of the advantages of a modern airport. At gate thirty-four, they scanned their passports, and the airlock opened. They stepped inside and the luggage cart followed them inside.

"Here we go!" Matteo said with a smile as he put his respo on his face and he pushed the button to open the door.

They stepped outside on the landing platform and walked to the pilotless air taxi. After loading the luggage, they took a seat inside and Matteo closed the door.

"Welcome to the Long Island Air Shuttle. What's your destination?"

Dylan looked on his smartphone and said, "To the Richwood Hotel in Thomaston, please!"

"Richwood Hotel in Thomaston. Confirmed. Your estimated travel time is ten minutes. Please fasten your seat belts."

Elizabeth had forgotten her belt and fastened it immediately. A moment later, the air taxi lifted off and flew away from the platform. Up in the sky, they noticed the ocean was not so far away. Dylan wondered how long before they had to close this airport as well. He noticed the huge seawall they had constructed to protect against the sea.

As they approached Thomaston only thirty kilometers away from the airport, they all peered, astounded, at the horizon.

"Weird to see Queens in the sea," Matteo said, pointing at the horizon, where they saw buildings surrounded by water. "Apparently, most of Queens has been abandoned since more than seventy percent of the streets are permanently submerged in the sea. Thomaston is located higher and has become densely populated. We will meet my friend for dinner later on. He is stationed at the US Marine base, not too far from our hotel."

"Is he joining us tomorrow on our trip to Manhattan?" Elizabeth asked.

"We'll hear that tonight. Perry told me he was trying to get some days off, but he was supposed to hear it today from his commanding officer."

Dylan suddenly felt his stomach twitch as the air taxi descended fast. It landed on the roof of the Richwood Hotel, in between many other high-rise buildings. He understood now what Matteo meant by densely populated.

After landing, they checked into the hotel. In their room, Dylan kissed Elizabeth and pushed her gently on the bed. He started touching her and she enjoyed it for a moment, but then moved his hand away.

"Not now. We have to be down in half an hour for dinner, remember?"

"You're right. These beds are comfy, though."

She smiled at him and disappeared into the bathroom. Thirty minutes later, the three of them were sitting in the restaurant's bar when Perry arrived. He was a confident looking blond American with a square face and he was taller than Matteo, but also muscled. He looked like a guy not to mess with. Matteo introduced Perry to Dylan and Elizabeth, and after ordering some drinks, Matteo turned to his friend.

"And? Are you joining us tomorrow?" Matteo asked.

"Yes! I got some days off and I'm looking forward to go on a mission with you all."

"Great, to our trip to Manhattan then!" Matteo said, and he raised his glass to toast together.

Over dinner, they discussed the plans for the coming days. They had booked a boat that they would pick up in the morning at the harbor not too far from Thomaston. Perry explained that the police and the navy patrolled in the region constantly. Notwithstanding, he warned that there were some gangs active in the area and they should be cautious. They installed a tracking app on their smartphones so they could trace each other, just in case they lost someone.

The boat had several cabins and they would sleep on the boat. Perry told them they would need to take some diving equipment, just in case. Apparently, some abandoned buildings were easily accessible from the surface because the windows on the sea level were broken. But some buildings had special unbreakable glass or had only a wall at sea level. With their satellite program, they could not see what the situation was with the penthouse's building.

That night back in their room, Dylan and Elizabeth both felt better about the trip. They realized there were some risks, but they thought it was like an exciting adventure. If only they knew what a hornet's nest they were stepping into.

33.

I t was a beautiful and calm day. They all stood in the steering cabin while Perry maneuvered the black modern boat from Little Neck Bay onto the East River. Earlier that morning, they had woken up, had breakfast, and then met Perry in the harbor near Thomaston. Perry and Dylan loaded all their luggage and a week's worth of supplies onto the boat while Matteo and Elizabeth picked up the diving gear at the nearby diving shop. Dylan noticed the large green metal boxes on the lower deck and asked Perry about them. He explained they contained tools and some army gear, but he showed a weird grin on his face. They were all excited about the trip and felt relieved when they finally set course for Manhattan.

The boat had a lower deck with several cabins to sleep in and a small kitchen. On the upper deck, there was a steering cabin with a seating area all hermetically closed from the outside atmosphere. The entire ship was equipped with the newest air filtration systems, and as soon as they locked the upper cabin, they took off their respos. Dylan prepared coffee for everyone while Perry steered the boat. As soon as they entered open water, he increased the speed, and it bounced lightly on the waves. It was quite busy on the East River, and Dylan noticed there were several military and police boats.

As they entered the East River, Dylan, Elizabeth and Matteo looked astounded to their right side at what used to be the Bronx. From the air taxi they had seen already how Queens was mostly submerged, but now from the river everything looked even more surreal. As they passed under Throgs Neck Bridge, they noticed how the bridge disappeared in the water on both sides and the entire neighborhood was underwater. Here and there they saw some roofs and some telecom transmission masts sticking out above the water, but most of the houses were completely submerged. On the horizon, they noticed more roofs sticking out in the neighborhoods that were located slightly higher. Perry explained that most of the Bronx was located lower than Queens and both had been uninhabited zones for more than a decade now. The middle section of the bridge had been removed to allow the larger boats to pass. The rising sea level reduced the clearance below bridges.

"Everybody! Buckle up, please! In the middle of the river, I'm going to speed up."

Perry pushed the gas throttle forward, and the boat sped up. They passed at high speed, in between what was left of Queens and the Bronx, until Perry pointed out some building sticking out of the water.

"That's the old air traffic control tower of LaGuardia Airport and I have to navigate carefully since Rikers Island is submerged down here and some buildings still stick out close to the surface so I've to avoid passing over the island."

Elizabeth looked slightly worried after Perry's comment, but he smiled and navigated through the middle of the East River in between Rikers Island and what was left of Hunts Point. He showed her the navigation system on the boat control screen and it indicated all the shallow parts.

"What would we do without technology?" Perry said with a smile to her.

Dylan looked at Elizabeth from time to time, and he was happy to share this experience with her. It meant a lot to him, and he was content that she understood that. She smiled back at him, and they looked at the horizon again. They approached Hell Gate Bridge, and this also looked like a bridge to nowhere as the sides were submerged. The masonry towers and the steel arch were perfectly intact though. They had removed only the part with the railroad on it to allow a passage for larger boats. In front of them they saw the skyscrapers of the Upper East Side in Manhattan on the horizon, reflecting in the bright sunlight.

Perry explained while pointing to the northwest that the streets in East Harlem were submerged in the sea, but that from Ninety-Sixth Street until Thirty-Ninth Street, they had constructed an extra high seawall on the old FDR Drive. It protected the remaining part of Manhattan from the sea. This wall curved westwards at Thirty-Ninth Street and then continued further south, protecting only a sliver of land on the southern part of Manhattan stretching from Park Avenue until Sixth Avenue. They had constructed the wall on the westside of Manhattan on Broadway. Inside the walled area there were still people living, and the only way in or out was by boat or air taxi.

They continued at high speed alongside the massive wall around Midtown Manhattan. The iconic buildings like the Chrysler Building and the Empire State Building were still well maintained and located within the walled area. A bit further the wall turned in town and from that point on the streets between the tall buildings close to the East River were all submerged.

"So, is the Empire State building inside this walled zone?" Matteo asked.

"Yes, it's part of this sliver I mentioned in the middle of Manhattan, which is on slightly higher ground," Perry explained.

"Wow, surreal!" Elizabeth said with her mouth agape as she stared at the flooded streets of Lower Manhattan.

"Post-apocalyptic! I've seen nothing like this," Dylan added.

A while later, they approached the Manhattan Bridge and on their right-hand side, they saw that all the streets in between the buildings were underwater in what used to be the Lower East Side. As they passed under the Brooklyn Bridge, Perry continued explaining how most of Brooklyn was below sea level, but they still inhabited the higher grounds in Brooklyn. However, the area was not protected by a seawall and the streets would often flood temporarily during hurricanes. On the other side, there was another huge wall round the south part of Manhattan. Perry explained that from the World Trade Center until The Battery, another wall completely encircled this south tip of Manhattan. The financial center on Wall Street was still operational, and the police had their headquarters in this part, from where they tried to rein in the power of local gangs. There was a harbor next to the wall, and there were many police patrol boats in it.

"Amazing to see the difference between the buildings within the walled area and outside of it. Outside they're all neglected with broken windows and ruined walls, while inside the wall they're all perfectly maintained," Matteo said while they all stared toward the south tip of Manhattan.

"Oh, look! On the left! The Statue of Liberty, or at least what remains of it. Its pedestal is still sticking above the water while the rest of the island is submerged. How strange," Elizabeth said while she pointed at the half-ruined statue.

Perry steered the boat onto the Hudson River and they headed northbound. They all stared to the left side now toward Jersey City, which was submerged as well, and all buildings looked neglected and half-ruined.

Dylan could not help thinking about the amount of capital that had been destroyed here. But also, in all the other flooded cities around the world, like Bangkok, Singapore, Tokyo, Jakarta and Ho Chi Minh City. He never really had understood why nobody had acted earlier to avoid all this capital destruction. In 1988, the Intergovernmental Panel on Climate Change had been established, and it was already obvious then to many scientists that action was required immediately. If people had taken decisive action in that period, they could have avoided all this capital destruction. Unfortunately, humanity was extremely shortsighted.

34.

A moment later, Elliot had gathered enough courage to open the door and step inside. The apartment was all dark. Maybe his father had gone to bed already. He walked slowly to the kitchen to drink some water, and he noticed the door to his father's bedroom was ajar. He listened at the door, but heard nothing. If he was sleeping, he would have heard him breathe or snore, which he often did. He gently pushed the door to glance around the corner. To his surprise, his father was not there.

This had not happened before, and he wondered if he had pushed him too much. He felt guilty and selfish. He just wanted to understand why his mother had committed suicide. Now he realized that for his father, it must have been very difficult as well. Maybe he did not know why she had done it either, or maybe he felt guilty about her death. Elliot still believed it would be better for both of them to talk about it. It could bring him closer to his father and help them both grieving and possibly to find peace with the past.

Then he heard footsteps in the corridor in front of the apartment, and he rushed to the door. He wanted to give his father a hug and tell him he was sorry. Sorry for insisting too much. He waited in the hall, but the door did not open and the footsteps continued until they faded away.

After brushing his teeth, he checked one more time, but his father had still not come back. He went to bed, but had difficulty falling asleep. He twisted and turned in his bed. Every time he heard a noise;

he thought it was his father. The more he waited, the more he worried.

35.

Slowly, the boat approached the tall buildings in front of them. Perry explained that underneath there was what remained of the flooded Lincoln Tunnel. It connected submerged Lower Manhattan with submerged Newport. On the Hudson River several boats were passing, but close to the tall buildings there were none.

They left the Hudson River and Perry steered gently onto the submerged Canal Street. Dylan felt reassured with Perry on board. He seemed to navigate well and in full control of the boat. Matteo helped him find the right address, using the navigation system and checking the buildings with his binoculars.

"We just passed West Street and the next street on the right should be Washington Street. The building where your father owns the penthouse should be on the corner of Canal Street and Washington Street," Matteo explained while peering through the binoculars.

The buildings next to the Hudson River all looked damaged and neglected, with most windows broken. As they continued along Canal Street, the buildings looked less dilapidated. The boat approached the corner of Washington Street and Canal Street, and Dylan looked at the building on the corner. He was deeply moved when he looked at the place where his birth parents once lived.

"It should be on the corner over there," Elizabeth said, pointing with her finger.

"It looks relatively well preserved. All the windows are still intact. Contrary to the building in front of it," Perry remarked.

They looked at the building on the other side of Canal Street and all the windows were broken, while the ones in the building where his birth parents had the penthouse were dirty, but in one piece. Matteo put on his respo and stepped outside. Perry steered the boat closer until they could almost touch the windows. Matteo stood on the side of the boat and started hitting the window with his fist. It appeared solid. He took a hammer from the toolbox. He smashed into the glass and on the point of impact it shattered, but no pieces fell off.

"It seems to be made of some kind of laminated plastic glass. It does not really break."

He hit the glass a few more times with the hammer, but he failed to make a hole into it. He inspected the glass, and the damaged pieces and concluded.

"It's very thick. That explains why the whole facade is so well preserved. Let's go around the building to see whether there's an easier entry point."

Perry steered the boat away from the windows onto Canal Street. On this side there was no building attached and there were more of the same unbreakable windows, and on one part there was a solid wall. He turned the boat around and onto Washington Street. Here there was another building glued to the one on the corner, but it was a unique structure. A lot of the windows in this building were broken, and they tried to look inside.

"I don't think there's a way through from this building to the other one. Let's try a dive to check whether we can enter through the front door."

He steered the boat back to the corner and attached it to a light pole. They carried the diving gear from the lower deck onto the upper deck and changed into their diving suits. Dylan measured the water quality with the water analyzer they had brought along with them.

"It's quite acid, but with these dry suits, it should be all right since we won't have direct contact with the water."

Dylan and Matteo would dive first to check out the front entrance, while Elizabeth and Perry would wait on the boat. They put the diving suits over their clothes and attached the air tanks on their back. Dylan waved and smiled at Elizabeth just before they flipped themselves backwards over the boat railing into the murky gray water. Elizabeth and Perry looked at them while they disappeared underwater. They followed the trail of bubbles they were leaving behind.

The visibility underwater was poor. Dylan stayed close to Matteo so as not to lose sight of him. There was quite some current and they put on their flashlight to find their way. Underwater they saw how the ground and the first floors were completely submerged, as well as a part of the second floor. They descended toward the front entrance until they were floating in front of the main door, which was marked number 471.

Matteo pushed it, and to his surprise, it was unlocked. They both entered the small hall, where they noticed an intercom and letter boxes from all the apartments. Dylan stared at the letter boxes until he noticed one marked PH-Floor 7. He looked closer, and he saw written on the letterbox: Family Singh. Matteo looked at him and raised his thumb up at him, after which he continued to the next door. It was a sliding door, and he tried to open it, but it didn't move. Dylan tried to help him, but it remained locked.

Dylan searched around while Matteo pulled his knife from his suit and tried to push it through the opening between the two doors. Often automatic doors had some mechanical override system to open the doors in case of a power failure. Suddenly, he spotted the small panel above the doors and tried to pull it open, but it remained tightly fixed with screws. He took his Swiss army knife from his diving suit and pulled out the screwdriver. He started unscrewing the four screws of the panel until he could open it. He smiled at Matteo when he noticed the mechanical override switch inside, and Matteo raised his thumb at him.

After pulling the switch, they tried again to open the door and this time, they were able to open it. Dylan checked the dive time on his watch and continued swimming through the large hall. They looked around in the dark hall using their flashlights and he noticed the elevator and then spotted a door behind the concierge desk. Matteo swam first to the door in the back. Dylan followed him. It was heavy and stuck because of the debris in front of it. They moved the debris away and pulled the door together until suddenly it opened. They both got startled as a large, dark shadow appeared. Dylan's heart skipped a beat as it swept him off his feet under the weight of the dark shadow falling on top of him.

36.

Dylan fell on the floor as he got pushed down under the weight of the dark object. His leg hurt under the weight and he aimed the flashlight at his leg. It was stuck under the dark object, which looked like some tall black filing cabinet. He tried to push the cabinet away, but it was too heavy. Matteo helped him and together they managed to push it off his leg. Dylan felt water coming inside and he immediately checked his dry suit. He spotted a tear on the left leg. He signaled to Matteo that they had to go back to the boat straightaway.

Matteo helped him back on his feet and together they swam back to the front door. Dylan felt the water moving into his suit and he tried to put his hand on the tear to prevent the water from coming inside. They swam through the front entrance. Elizabeth watched them surfacing and immediately noticed something was wrong. She called Perry and together they helped Dylan and Matteo back on board. Dylan quickly started taking off the diving suit while he panted.

"A large cabinet fell on my leg and all the water came into my suit. I should take a shower immediately."

Elizabeth helped him to take off his diving suit and his clothes, and he rushed inside to the shower on the lower deck. The warm water felt good on his skin. The acid and polluted water could cause great irritation and infections, but it looked like he was just in time. He inspected himself and noticed the large bruise on his upper leg and his leg was bleeding. It did not look like a deep cut, though. After his shower, Dylan took some medicine to prevent getting sick from the water. Elizabeth took care of the wound and she wrapped his upper leg in a bandage.

"It is not a deep cut and it should heal quickly."

Dylan smiled at her and kissed her.

"Thanks! I saw the name of my birth parents on the mailbox in the hall."

"That's good news."

Dylan explained what happened to him and he drank some water. His leg hurt him, but he was eager to go back inside the building. He took some painkillers, and then they walked back upstairs. In the steering cabin, they drank some coffee together, while Perry fixed Dylan's diving suit with the repair kit he had brought along. They discussed what to do next and decided this time they would enter the building all together.

After putting on their diving suits and preparing their diving gear, Perry locked the boat and activated the alarm system. Perry took a waterproof bag with him in which he placed their respos. They flipped backwards over the edge of the boat into the water and, after checking everybody was ready, they descended slowly toward the main entrance. Just before descending, Dylan spotted a small boat further down Washington Street, but he did not pay much attention to it.

They swam through the main entrance and through the hall toward the door in the back. Dylan pointed at the large cabinet in the door opening to show Elizabeth what had fallen on his leg earlier on. They continued through the opening and entered the stairwell. Inside, they used the stair railing to guide themselves while they ascended. After passing the door to the first floor, they continued higher. Halfway up the staircase to the second floor, they reached the surface of the sea water. They climbed the last stair out of the water, and now they felt the weight of their diving equipment.

Arriving on the second floor, Perry took off his diving gear and opened the bag with the respos. One of the respos he placed on his face as he took off his diving mask and the others he handed out, while he said,

"We better leave the diving gear down here, as we still have to climb five floors to get to the penthouse."

"Yeah, that equipment is too heavy," Dylan answered after putting on his respo.

"The building looks deserted, so I guess it should be safe to leave it all here," Matteo added.

"Okay, let's go then."

They climbed the stairs up to the seventh floor, and there they paused a moment to catch their breath. Perry looked up at the staircase, which continued further.

"Two more floors above this one. Probably this is one of those amazing penthouses over multiple floors."

"Well, only one way to find out," Dylan said as he tried to open the door on the seventh floor.

It did not open, and Matteo came to help Dylan pull the handle. While they pulled together, Perry took a crowbar out of his bag. He placed it on the side and while the others pulled the handle; he pushed the crowbar in. With a cracking noise, it opened. There was rust on the side of the door, as it had not been opened for a long time.

They stepped into the hall where there was the elevator and another door with a doorbell. Next to the doorbell there was a sign which said Family Singh. Dylan got all excited now, but then he noticed there was something strange about the lock on the door. He walked to it and then he noticed someone had drilled the lock out. While he pushed the door open, he said,

"Apparently, we're not the first visitors."

They peered inside to check whether there was someone inside, but they saw nobody. Nor did they hear any noise. When Dylan looked behind him, he got startled. Perry was carrying a gun in his hand, Matteo a taser and Elizabeth the crowbar.

"Jesus, am I the only one who came unarmed?"

"Yeah, I guess you left the military too long ago," Matteo said with a grin.

Slowly, they stepped inside the penthouse into the large entry hall and they checked all the rooms one by one. They were full of clutter. Broken furniture, papers all over the floors, empty bottles, discarded food packaging. Broken beds, most without mattresses. They stayed together while they checked the rooms. There was a large gym, but they had taken away most of the equipment. There was just a broken treadmill remaining. They entered a room that appeared to be the master bedroom, and it had a stunning view of the Hudson River. Suddenly, Dylan's attention got caught by a broken photo frame in between the mess on the floor. It still had a photo inside. Dylan looked at it and got tears in his eyes. Elizabeth noticed and put her arm around his shoulder.

"Amazing! You resemble him so much. Wow, your mom looks stunning in that wedding dress. A real beauty!"

He turned the picture around and read what was written on the back: *Palace Gardens, New Delhi, 5 August 2022.*

"They married seven years before I was born."

"Well, it looks like we didn't come for nothing, Dylan. Looking at all the papers left behind, we must be able to find out more about your parents."

"Just this picture was worth coming here," and he took the picture out of the frame and tucked it away under his dry suit.

Elizabeth tapped his shoulder and then continued back into the hall. Matteo and Perry had already gone upstairs, and Elizabeth also took the stairs in the hall toward the eighth floor. Dylan realized he was all alone on the seventh floor, and the ransacked penthouse gave him the creeps. He quickly went up as well.

The views were even more impressive on the eighth floor, although that floor had also been plundered. It looked like a large living room with a connected dining room and kitchen. They had left behind a long dining table, as it was probably too bulky to steal. The kitchen had been stripped of all equipment, though. Further on he found what looked like an office, and there the floor was covered with papers. They were going to have a hell of a job going through it all, but Dylan felt lucky all these papers were left behind.

Perry had already continued further up to the ninth floor and suddenly he yelled.

"Wow! Come and look! The views up here are amazing."

They all continued to the top floor, and they arrived in a spacious room surrounded by terraces. The sunny sky offered a stunning view of Manhattan and the Hudson River. Looking toward Battery Park, the view was surreal; many severed tall buildings in front of the small walled area with well-maintained modern buildings behind it. Surreal. They walked on the terraces outside and took their time to enjoy the magnificent view.

Dylan imagined how his birth parents must have enjoyed these views. He wondered where they moved to after living here. Would they still be alive? He hoped the paper mess downstairs would give him some clues. At least he knew now what his birth parents looked like. On the terrace, he took the wedding picture from his dry suit and looked at it again. His mother looked younger than his father. Elizabeth was right; she was beautiful and her eyes resembled his. No, this photo left no doubt. These were his birth parents.

Elizabeth came to stand next to him and, in silence, they enjoyed the view. The city was calm, and there was barely any noise. What a difference compared to New Delhi, Dylan thought. The water through the streets and the flooded Jersey City across the Hudson River provided a post-apocalyptic scenery. New York had paid the price for ignoring climate change. He wondered what would have happened if those people had known thirty years ago that this would be their future. Would they have acted any differently, or would they still have ignored this serious problem? A loud alarm coming from the street and a beeping noise from Perry's wristband abruptly interrupted his thoughts.

37.

I n the twilight, Amos got up from the bench and stretched his legs. He strolled through the gardens until he arrived at the orchard. After wandering for a while in between the different fruit trees, he stopped at a large apple tree and stretched his hand out. He picked an apple and cleaned it with some spit. Then he took a bite and its taste was rich and slightly acid. The abundance of fresh fruit in the community was one of the things confirming he had made the right choice to give up his life outside.

This triggered a flashback, and he remembered how he got introduced to this mysterious group. It all had started when his wife encouraged him to come with her to an exclusive conference about climate change in Paris. Only the extremely rich people on the planet had been invited, and he met many billionaires over there. This must have been in the year 2022, as he had gotten married just before.

It was a vibrant conference, and the drinks and dinner around the presentations were the perfect atmosphere for some great networking. He met Elias there for the first time. Elias was a brilliant nuclear fusion scientist, and it had surprised Amos to meet him there, in between all those super-rich guests. Elias explained that the organizer, a billionaire called Abe, had invited him. Abe was currently the head of the Council in the community.

The conference kicked off with a chart showing the parts per million of carbon dioxide over time. One chart went back about three hundred years and it showed a relatively low carbon dioxide concentration for two hundred years. But then at the start of the industrial revolution, it started rising steadily until the year 1950, when this linear rising trend changed into an exponentially rising trend line. It was clear that the greenhouse problem was completely out of control.

Climate sceptics from all over the world had contested the numbers, but during the conference they refuted all their arguments. One argument was that we had more peaks in carbon dioxide concentrations in the past. For example, about three hundred thousand years ago there had indeed been a spike in carbon dioxide, but it was about three hundred part per millions compared to the four hundred and thirty part per millions measured the year before the conference. The scientist shocked the audience even more when he presented evidence that all the previous peaks had coincided with global extinction events.

To exacerbate the situation, he explained how carbon dioxide added to the atmosphere stayed there for over a hundred years. So not only was the greenhouse problem getting worse fast, it was going to stay with us for a very long time. They explained how the carbon dioxide warmed up the planet through the greenhouse effect. The gases caused the radiation and heat from the sun to remain trapped in the atmosphere instead of escaping back into space. This resulted in heating the planet more and more.

Later, a different scientist presented how the same exponential growth was happening with the other greenhouse gases, like methane and nitrous oxide. The presenter explained how these other greenhouse gases exacerbated the problem even more, as they were more destructive to the global climate than carbon dioxide.

Another scientist presented a piece about the many feedback loops that existed, which made the climate warming problem more complex and bigger than it already was. He talked about the albedo effect and about the thawing of the permafrost, which led to extra emission of greenhouse gases, especially methane. They talked about the feedback loop of water vapor. Warmer temperatures meant that more water evaporated, but also that the atmosphere could contain more water, causing the atmosphere to heat up further. Initially, the seas absorbed more carbon dioxide and slowed down the heating of the planet. The seas were getting saturated with carbon dioxide, and the seas were absorbing less of this additional carbon dioxide. Global warming accelerated more and more. The scientist suggested that humans might have lost control of the climate for quite some time already and that even if they would reduce the global emissions immediately to zero climate change would just continue.

Amos remembered vividly how Abe also presented at the conference. Already then, he was a very charismatic person, which combined with his extreme intelligence, made him an impressive, powerful personality. He ridiculed how governments were arguing over carbon dioxide emission reduction targets, while the data was clear and showed it required drastic action to avoid a catastrophe.

In addition, he attacked scientists who launched ideas that in his view would make the problems even bigger. Some scientists had suggested that injecting large quantities of sulfur aerosols or small particles in the atmosphere would buy the world more time to tackle the climate change problem. The aerosols would create a whitish haze in the sky which would reflect more sunlight back into space and create a global dimming effect. Less of the sun's radiation would reach Earth, and this would have a cooling effect. Similar to what happened during large volcanic eruptions.

The problem with this so-called geoengineering was that it would not last for a long time and after it would stop working global warming would accelerate. It would disrupt the global climate, cause massive droughts, destroy the ozone layer and alter the circulation of the ocean currents and create more stagnant weather. In addition, it would probably take away the urgency for governments to cut back emissions fast.

Abe argued that drastic action was required immediately to prevent the human species from becoming extinct. He invited all participants who were convinced and wanted to be part of the solution to sign up for the follow-up conference. This first conference was an eye opener for Amos. It left him shocked and perplexed, but his wife helped him to go from shock into taking action. Thanks to her, he attended the follow-up conferences, otherwise he would never have become part of the community.

38.

They rushed over the large terrace toward the side overlooking the corner of Washington Street and Canal Street. As they bended over the railing and looked down, the alarm sounded even louder. Dylan got startled when he looked down. There was an old white boat with several men on it. One man was trying to break into the cabin of their boat. It had triggered the alarm. All the lights were flashing, and the sirens produced a deafening sound.

"They're on our boat!" he yelled at Perry.

"Yep, luckily it's equipped with a modern security system," Perry replied while he stared at his wristwatch.

He pushed on it and then they heard a message.

"Intruder alert. Do you want to stun or kill the intruder?"

"Stun, please," Perry answered.

They all peered over the railing toward the boat. A small hatch opened on top. They noticed some sort of gun pointing out. A second later, they saw a flash. The man on their boat fell back on the deck and began convulsing. His body and limbs shook violently for a moment, and then he lay motionless on the deck. The other men were yelling and panicking. They carried the unconscious man on board of their own boat. One man in the steering cabin looked around and then suddenly glanced up. He noticed the four of them watching. After that, he steered away back into Canal Street. A moment later, it turned into Greenwich Street and disappeared out of sight.

"Nice security system, Perry," Matteo said with a grin, while he tapped Perry on his shoulder.

"Yes, only the best for my friends from Switzerland. Let's have lunch on the boat. I don't think those men will come back anytime soon."

They all went back inside and returned to the staircase. They walked down the stairs to the second floor, where their diving equipment was still standing against the wall. After gearing up, they went down to the ground level. They swam through the reception hall and through the entrance door. One by one, they slowly surfaced next to the boat. Matteo climbed on board and helped the others to climb on board. Perry checked the boat, but nothing had been stolen or damaged. He opened the upper cabin, and they stepped inside to have lunch together.

After lunch, Dylan went downstairs to put the picture of his birth parents in his suitcase. Then he checked out his leg, which was still hurting him. He changed the bandage and cleaned the wound. Elizabeth helped him to put back the bandage, and they exchanged some flirting looks with each other. She was an amazing woman.

"I'm really happy you came along on this trip."

"Are you kidding me? Do you think I'd let you guys have all the fun without me?" she joked, and gave him a kiss.

"All right, lovebirds, let's go back to the penthouse to find some clues about Dylan's birth parents," Matteo said.

They put their diving suits back on and went outside. Dylan looked around to check if he could see anything suspicious, but it was quiet all around. Perry locked the boat and activated the alarm. Slowly, they descended underwater and found their way back to the entrance. They surfaced in the staircase on the second floor and put their diving gear on the floor. After climbing the five floors up, they entered the penthouse. Matteo stopped them in the hall.

"Let's do this search in a structured manner. I propose we spread out through the different rooms and gather everything that might contain a clue about Dylan's birth parents' whereabouts, like papers, memory sticks and photos. We pile up everything we find on the large table in the dining room, and then Dylan can already start going through it. After gathering everything, we'll help with the reading. Agreed?"

"Sounds like a good plan. I'll first grab some papers in the bedroom next door and then start reading upstairs," Dylan replied.

They spread out over the different rooms and gathered everything useful. Dylan started in the master bedroom, where he had found the wedding picture. He picked up the documents from the floor until he had a thick pile in his hands. He took the pile upstairs to the dining room and placed it on the table. In the living room, he found a discarded chair on the floor and he put it next to the dining table. He sat down and started sifting through the pile. Meanwhile, the others gathered more papers and pictures in the rooms downstairs.

Most of the papers were useless and old. He found many business documents, like investment proposals and company presentations. There were financial statements from all kinds of companies and he realized his father had been some kind of investor and owned many companies. Dylan mainly focused on dates and addresses in the paperwork. He also found some contracts related to the penthouse, like for cleaning, maintenance and security. He found out that his mother had done charity work and had been a yoga teacher in New York. There were bills and invoices, but he found nothing more recent than the year 2029, the year in which he was born and given up for adoption.

While he studied all the documents, the piles started increasing on the dining table and the others continued combing through the penthouse. The afternoon passed quickly, and at some point, Elizabeth handed him a pile of photos.

"We finished downstairs and everything of interest from the seventh floor should be on these piles now. I found these and couldn't resist going through them. You mother was quite a beauty. She looked like a really kind person. We'll continue on this floor and then upstairs on the ninth."

"Thanks! So far, I didn't find many clues about their whereabouts, but there's still so much to go through."

"When I finish here, I'll come and help you scan through the documents while Matteo and Perry continue upstairs."

Dylan went through the stack of photos. Many were from parties and what looked like charity events. His parents were dressed impeccably. She was right, his mother looked like a kind person. In one photo, a large group of children surrounded her. They looked poor, but seemed to be happy as they gathered around his mother. He even found a picture where his mother looked pregnant, but unfortunately no date was on it. Surprisingly, he did not find any photos of his parents with him as a baby on it. Looking at everything, he would almost conclude they did not have children.

Later in the afternoon, the others had finished searching all the rooms and were all sitting around the large dining table. Everybody was sifting through the documents and from time to time they commented on what they found or made some jokes. It was too much to finish that afternoon and, at some point, Perry got up and looked out of the window.

"It's getting late. We'd better go back to the boat before sunset, since this area is not so safe at night."

They all agreed and got up. Dylan packed all the photos and memory sticks in the waterproof bag of Perry and added a small stack of papers that he had kept aside. On the floor, he had put everything they had already checked. The documents he put in the bag did not give any direct lead on the whereabouts of his birth parents, but had some information on it he wanted to check out later on the internet. They were about halfway through all the paper piles and agreed to continue the next day.

Back on the boat, Dylan put everything in his suitcase and joined the others in preparing dinner. Outside, the sun was setting and it would be their first night on the boat. During dinner, Matteo and Perry exchanged their military anecdotes and they laughed a lot.

Later in the evening, Perry activated the alarm system and made sure everything was well locked. Dylan went with Elizabeth to their cabin and soon after, she was lying in his arms in the comfortable bed. They talked for a while and then Elizabeth fell asleep. Dylan was still contemplating the day. He wondered if he was going to find any clues to where his birth parents might be. He got the impression his parents left in a rush from the penthouse, but where did they go? He heard the water splashing against the hull and the wind blowing hard outside. Then he thought about the intruders and wondered if they would come back.

39.

With the noise of water splashing against the hull of the boat, he woke up the next morning. Elizabeth was still sleeping and he looked at her for a while before he got up and dressed. He felt good and his leg was less painful. Before leaving the cabin, he glanced one more time at Elizabeth. He loved her deeply and was happy to be with her.

On the upper deck, Matteo and Perry were talking, and he overheard them talking about a boat.

"What boat?" he asked curiously.

"You didn't hear it? Last night, someone circled around us for a while and aimed a big spotlight in our direction. We even took out our guns. But then they left," Matteo explained.

"Probably just curious people," Dylan said.

"At three in the morning? No, I don't think they had good intentions and I checked it was no police either," Perry responded fiercely.

"Maybe it's best to make our stay over here as short as possible. I think we should be able to finish today," Matteo said, while looking at the piles of paper left in the penthouse.

"I think that would be better, yeah. This area is not so safe. Last year, the government lost complete control of the region outside of the walled areas, and gangs and militia took over. This year they regained control, although there's still a lot of scum out there," Perry explained.

Elizabeth appeared on the upper deck.

"Good morning! What are you all talking about?"

"Well, that it's not safe around here. So, we want to finish all the work today and then return to Thomaston," Matteo answered.

They sat together at the table and had their breakfast together. Afterwards, they prepared all the gear and put on their diving suits. They took everything outside and while he sat on the edge of the boat, Dylan looked up at the building where his birth parents had lived. It was a cloudy day today. The last day he would be here. He hoped to find enough clues to locate his parents. A moment later, they flipped backwards into the water and descended to the main entrance.

They climbed up to the seventh floor and inside, they all sat together at the large dining table. They continued sifting through the remaining documents. Everything that could be of interest they passed on to Dylan, who after reading the papers put the interesting ones on a small stack that he kept aside. The atmosphere was wonderful, and they joked a lot.

The morning passed quickly and around one o'clock they took a break and returned to the boat. Dylan took the stack with the interesting documents with him in the waterproof bag. After lunch, they went back up to the penthouse. The remaining piles should only take them a few hours to go through.

Before continuing to sift through the papers, Dylan walked through the whole penthouse one more time to make sure they had missed nothing. With all the papers taken away from the floors in the penthouse, it looked less messy everywhere. He double-checked everything. He looked under a mattress which was left behind on one of the beds. On the bottom floor, he found nothing. When he walked back upstairs, he heard a distant noise. He stopped to listen for a while, but heard nothing anymore and continued up.

On the other floors, he found nothing else, and he was convinced they had searched the place well. He returned to the dining table.

"And did we miss anything?" Matteo asked when he came back.

"No, I double-checked everything, and I found nothing useful. Amazing how they have broken into the safe on the ninth floor."

"Yeah, it looked like they used some professional explosives to open it up. Whatever was in there of value has been taken a long time ago," Matteo replied.

They continued going through the remaining piles of paper. At some point, Perry divided the remaining stack into four and gave each of them the last papers to go through.

"The end is in sight," Perry said with a smile on his face.

A while later, Elizabeth got up.

"I don't think I can make it back to the boat without going to the bathroom, so I better go now so you don't have to wait for me after."

"The one next to the master bedroom on the seventh was the least dirty," Matteo said.

Elizabeth smiled at him and left the dining room. All the bathrooms were very dirty, but some were dirtier and smellier than others. They continued going through the last papers, and about an hour later, they finished. Dylan packed all the interesting stuff he had selected in the waterproof bag. He looked around and suddenly realized Elizabeth had been away for quite a while now.

"Maybe I should go down to check if Elizabeth is all right. She has been gone for a long time."

Dylan walked downstairs while Perry and Matteo continued talking in the living room. It was quiet on the seventh floor, and as he came down from the staircase, he called her name.

"Elizabeth? Are you all right?"

He checked the bathroom in the hall, but it was empty. There were four on this floor and he continued to the next one, while he called for her again. After that, he got worried, and he rushed to the next one.

"Elizabeth? Where are you?"

He opened the door to the bathroom next to the master bedroom. But she was not inside this one either. He rushed back to the staircase and yelled up.

"Matteo! Could you check if Elizabeth is in the bathroom upstairs? She is not down here."

"What? Okay, I will."

"I'll check the ninth floor!" yelled Perry.

A few minutes later, Matteo came rushing out of the toilet to Dylan, who had just returned to the eighth floor.

"She is not here."

Then Perry came rushing down.

"She is not up here, either. This is not good."

"No. I don't think she would go back to the boat alone. I'm going to call her on her phone."

Dylan took his phone and dialed her number. It rang, but nobody answered and he got her voicemail. They walked downstairs and Matteo checked all the rooms one more time until he noticed the door to the outside staircase was half open.

"Look, that door is open. I'm sure I closed it when we came up here."

Dylan tried to call her again, but again there was no answer and he got really worried. Suddenly, Perry got a great idea.

"Maybe we can find her with that tracking app we installed on the phone."

They all took their phones out and turned on the tracking app. After staring at the screen, Matteo called out, astounded.

"It looks like she's in the building next door!?"

"How did she get there?"

Perry pushed on his screen.

"There's some three-dimensional view on the app. Let's see if that works."

A moment later, he continued,

"It looks like she's on the sixth floor of the other building. How the hell did she get there?"

Matteo walked to the door.

"Let's go down and have a look there."

They all rushed out of the door and down the staircase. On the sixth floor, the door was open and they ran through it. They entered a long L-shaped corridor and there were several doors to different apartments there. Perry stared at the screen of his phone.

"She's at this level, but in the other building. If I'm correct, the other building is located here at the end of the corridor on the right." They rushed to the corner of the corridor and they saw it continued around the corner. Then, at the end of this part of the corridor, they noticed a large hole in the wall.

"Look! That hole is exactly on the side where the building is attached to the other building. She must have gone through here," Perry yelled.

While they ran to the end of the corridor, Dylan muttered, confused,

"Why would Elizabeth go here? That's not like her."

They stepped through the hole in the wall and entered the other building. Still no sign of Elizabeth. The wind blew through the building. Through one of the open doors, they noticed that the windows were broken. The building was more wrecked and dirtier than the other one. Perry looked back at the screen of his phone.

"She should be about ten meters from here."

Looking left and right in all the apartments, they rushed through the corridor until Perry yelled.

"She should be right here on this spot!"

Confused and stressed, Dylan and Matteo looked around, but no sign of her. They both searched a different apartment next to that spot, but quickly after, they returned to the corridor. They both shook their heads at each other, and then they noticed Perry searching on the floor. He was looking in between the rubbish with his hands. Suddenly, he picked up something. With a shocked face, he held up Elizabeth's phone.

40.

With the smell of lavender surrounding him, Amos passed through the fields further down in the garden. The walk outside had calmed him down, and his feelings of sadness and guilt had faded away. He should probably return to the apartment, otherwise Elliot would get worried. The fight had brought back so many memories. He looked up at the top of the dome. It always made him feel tiny next to this enormous structure. He was among the few lucky ones to be part of the community. He was convinced it had been the right decision. Life outside was rough and difficult. Climate change made it more and more difficult to survive, and life expectancy around the globe plummeted. Inside the dome, it had only gone up.

The presentation that had convinced him was one he would never forget. It had been more than thirty years ago already. Abe had always been a charismatic person, but during that presentation, he was at his best. It was clear to the audience that climate change was happening and even speeding up. Action was required, that was obvious, but most people felt powerless. Governments promised a lot, but were too careful not to antagonize the powerful industries and lobbies they had to deal with. Opponents attacked them and denied climate change. They spread contradicting facts to confuse people and supported people who protected their interests and the status quo. Or they pointed fingers at other groups and simplified the problem by blaming them, like it was the fault of the rich, the poor, the left, the right, the Chinese or capitalism. Whenever someone made firm statements, someone accused them of fear-mongering. Goals of reducing emissions were formulated, but Abe explained how they were not extreme enough to avoid catastrophe. In addition, these inadequate goals were not met the following years and change went slower than required.

Politicians were masters of kicking the can down the road and postponing the tough decisions. Governments struggled to understand all the implications of what was happening. But politicians were only human, and most people struggled to grasp what was happening. They preferred not to believe it, as the predictions showed a dire future. Others preferred to look away and ignore the problem. They thought they would be dead by then anyway, so why worry. Let someone else solve the mess. The timelines sketched by scientists were simply too far away for people to feel a sense of urgency.

The exponential growth of the emissions complicated matters further. It was counterintuitive to the point of being baffling. Scientists predicted what would happen with the climate on Earth by the year 2100. Comfortably far away. The problem was that with predicting exponentially growing things, the margin of error was enormous. The worst-case scenarios were better not spoken about, for various reasons like the fear of creating a mass panic and nobody wanted to be labeled a fear-monger or a pessimist.

Abe predicted that climate change would become a global catastrophe much faster than people thought. He stated that by 2050 already large parts of the world would become uninhabitable or extremely difficult and dangerous to live in. It also amazed Amos how another prediction of Abe had come true. He predicted that by the year 2050 the world population would have shrunk to five billion instead of growing to the ten billion, as many governmental institutions had predicted. During the conference, Abe made it clear he believed it was time to act now and prepare for this catastrophe.

He explained it was in the nature of humans to have difficulty dealing with a problem as big as climate change. Some people believed it was up to the governments to act and solve it. Most people felt powerless. What could one person do against an enormous problem like this? Governments set goals to reduce emissions and most people felt comfortable believing authorities had it under control. We were fine before and we will be fine this time. Other optimists believed technology would provide a solution in time, so why worry. People also suffered from a so-called optimism bias, in which people are unreasonably optimistic about their chances of being a victim. A sense that while bad things happened, they would not happen to me but to others.

Everybody was part of the problem, but one person was not enough to change the course. Abe explained that the step from recognizing the problem to taking drastic action was simply too great for most people. Psychologists described this inaction in the face of danger as negative panic. Faced with a catastrophe, people were often slow to recognize the danger and confused about how to respond. So, they did nothing until it was too late. Another part of the problem was that we got our cues from others. When subjects were in a group, they were much less likely to react: each person remained passive, reassured by the passivity of the others. Then when social cues finally came, we all changed our behavior at once, creating problems. The herd instinct.

After convincing the audience that the problem was huge and complex and that governments were unlikely to tackle it in time, it left everybody with a feeling of helplessness. How do we solve it then? Abe continued and ridiculed the billionaires who were spending their money on missions to Mars and creating a colony on the Moon. Searching for other planets to live on, claiming that soon Earth would be too small for humanity. Or that we needed another planet to survive, like a Plan B. He believed they were simply ignoring reality and dreaming too much; wasting their funds while the world was facing a catastrophe.

Humanity's best chances for survival were here on Earth, not in some dry, barren and inhospitable place like Mars or the Moon. Abe made this point succinctly and convincingly, with facts backing it up. Then came his next point, which proved to be the climax of the whole conference. He still remembered how Abe introduced his dazzling plan. The lights went off and an impressive introduction followed, where Abe exposed his brilliant idea. It had never been done before, but it was so well thought through that he convinced many billionaires in the room with his presentation. It was a drastic plan and required sacrifice and commitment. He first sketched the broad idea, but after that he went through all the details, which left the audience impressed and overwhelmed. That was it. A brilliant solution to face the climate change challenge. That day changed his life forever.

41.

Her head hurt as Elizabeth slowly regained consciousness. She could not move, and it was all dark around her. Vaguely, she heard some dimmed voices and a slow thumping noise, like the noise of some diesel engine. Her ankles were tied together and the strap around them hurt her with every move she tried to make. Her arms were tied with straps behind her back at the wrists. She had some sort of tape on her mouth and had difficulty breathing. She tried to move and get up, but it hurt her everywhere and she had no choice but to stay on the floor.

Her memory slowly came back to her, and she tried to think back about what had happened. She remembered sitting at the dining table sifting through all the documents while Dylan was flirting and joking with her. After that, she went downstairs as she urgently had to go to the bathroom. She remembered seeing the front door ajar, and it surprised her, since she was convinced they had closed it after arriving in the penthouse. She passed the bathroom in the hall and the stink made her continue to the master bedroom.

Matteo had been right about this one stinking less, and she rushed inside to do what she came for. While she was on the toilet, she heard some noises in the corridor and what sounded like whispers. Initially, she thought Matteo and Dylan were trying to scare her, but she had not heard the cracking noise of the wooden staircase. Her heart started beating faster. She quickly finished and put the diving suit back on. She held her breath and listened for a moment, but she heard nothing.

Slowly, she opened the door and peered into the master bedroom. It was empty, and she felt relieved. Maybe she had just imagined it, she comforted herself. She rushed through the master bedroom toward the door to the hall. While she passed through it and continued to the staircase to go back up, she suddenly heard a door on her right open. She noticed some movement behind her. A hand moved her respo from her face and covered her mouth while she felt another arm around her neck gripping her. She tried to scream, but with the hand tight on her mouth, she did not produce more than a muffled noise.

She tried to kick the man behind her with her foot, but the moment she started moving, someone grabbed her leg. Within a few seconds, two men lifted her feet off the ground and a fourth man appeared next to her face. He held some piece of tape in his hands and glued it to her mouth. She panicked completely now and tried to kick around and twist her body, but the four men were holding her tight in the air and started moving fast toward the front door. They carried her by her arms and legs and before she knew it; she entered the staircase.

The men rushed down the stairs with her. A floor lower she noticed the door was open, and they carried her through the door. While they carried her through the corridor, she tried to have a better look at the perpetrators. They were wearing a simple face mask. The type she had seen poor people wear to protect against the polluted air. One man was wearing her respo and she could see his face better. The ruthless look in his eyes scared her. This was not good. She lifted her head to check where they were taking her and at the end of the corridor, she noticed a large hole in the wall.

They carried her through it and the corridor on the other side was windier and looked much dirtier. The more she was carried away from the other building, the more she realized she had to do something. Her adrenaline increased further, and she felt she had to try to get loose. One of the men tripped over some rubbish on the floor and as he fell, he let go of her leg. Elizabeth heard him swear. She realized this was her chance. With her loose leg, she kicked the man holding her other leg very hard in his face. She hit him on his nose. He squirmed with pain and let go of her.

Both her legs fell on the floor now, but the men holding her arms did not let go and tightened their grip. They pulled her a bit backwards, while she watched the two men in front of her getting back on their feet. The last thing she remembered was that the man wearing her respo said,

"Jesus, she's like a cat. Here, take that!"

They must have hit her head from behind, as it was painful on the backside. She had a monumental headache. The thumping noise had stopped, and she heard footsteps. A moment later, she was blinded by the light as a door opened in front of her. A hairy, bearded man with a mask covering his mouth and nose moved toward her. She saw how he was holding something in his hands while his hands moved toward her head. All went dark as they placed a cloth bag over her face.

She was petrified when they lifted her off the floor. The straps on her wrists and ankles hurt her while they carried her away. She felt a light breeze. She had the impression that they carried her for quite some time. The steps of several men around her left her panic-stricken. She realized they were carrying her up several stairs. She could barely breath and sensed she could pass out any moment. Several minutes later she heard a door open. The men put her down on what appeared to be a bed. They were holding her tight and then suddenly her wrists were cut free and she could move her hands again.

Unfortunately, it did not last long, as she quickly felt how someone pushed her arm above her head. Both her hands were attached to the side of the bed. Subsequently, her ankles were cut loose as well and someone pushed her flat on her back on the matrass. She felt hands on her ankles, and they attached her to the bed by her feet. Her heart started beating like crazy now as a horrible thought came to her. Terrified, she feared that they put her in this position to rape her. She tried to scream, but with the tape on her mouth, she barely produced any noise.

To her surprise, the hands let go of her, and she heard how they moved away. In the dark, she heard the door close. Footsteps moved further away outside until there was only silence. Thank God they left, at least for now.

42.

After finding her phone, Dylan panicked instantly, and it was like they swept away the ground from under his feet. Where did Elizabeth go? Who took her? Matteo was freaking out and recognized the desperation in Dylan's eyes. For a moment he remained frozen and did not know what to do. His sister was gone. He screamed.

"ELIZABETH!"

The three of them listened carefully until the echo faded away. Complete silence after, except for the wind whistling softly through the decayed building.

Perry saw the desperation in their eyes and as a trained sergeant of the US Marine Corps he reacted swiftly. He looked at Dylan and took a large gun out of his diving suit.

"Here Dylan, take this! We should search the building. Matteo, did you bring your…"

Perry stopped in the middle of his sentence as he noticed Matteo was carrying a handgun.

"Okay, they went most likely downstairs. Let's search the place. First, I'm going to have a look outside. They probably came here by boat."

Perry rushed through one of the apartments toward the window and looked down on Washington Street. Besides their own boat, he saw nothing else in the street. He rushed back to the other side and looked out of the window there. The building behind was completely in ruins and no way they had come from that side.

"No boats outside, so either they left already or they're still in the building and have no boat. Dylan, follow me to check the lower floors, while Matteo checks the higher ones."

Dylan and Perry walked with their guns in their hands toward the staircase while Matteo continued checking all the apartments on the sixth floor. They searched the entire building for the rest of the afternoon, but there was no trace of Elizabeth anywhere.

Later on, disillusioned, they returned to the penthouse to get their belongings and went on the roof terrace. On the roof, they peered through their binoculars to scan the neighborhood, looking for any trace of her. Unfortunately, everything seemed quiet except for some boats passing on the Hudson River. Further away, they saw air taxis flying back and forth to the walled areas of Manhattan. They decided to return to the boat, but first, to search all the apartments below the penthouse, just in case.

The sun was already low, and it was getting darker. They arrived on the second floor where their diving equipment was. As they geared up, Dylan looked in complete shock at the remaining diving equipment. He stood there frozen for a moment until Matteo took Elizabeth's gear.

"Come on Dylan, let's go to the boat, then we'll search around the building."

Dylan followed Matteo and Perry as they descended the staircase into the water. As they dived through the hall back toward the boat, Dylan stared through the dark muddy water and it all felt so surreal to him. This couldn't be happening.

Back on board, Perry deactivated the alarm and disappeared into the steering cabin, while Dylan and Matteo peered at the surrounding buildings. They called out Elizabeth's name several times through Washington Street and through Canal Street. It echoed between the tall buildings and every time they waited and listened carefully for any reaction. Dylan felt hopeless. How were they going to find Elizabeth in this gigantic city? They could have taken her anywhere. She must be so afraid. He felt he had to do something, but felt crushed and dejected.

"Guys, come inside, quick! I might have something," Perry yelled from inside the boat.

They both rushed inside toward the steering cabin. Perry stood inside and looked up at them, pointing at the screen in front of him.

"This boat is equipped with an excellent security system and when the alarm is activated, it scans and records any movements around…"

Perry looked all excited at them and gestured they should come and have a look.

"… and look what I found on the recordings."

They all watched the screen as Perry played back the recording. On the screen, they saw how a boat circled around their boat about an hour after they had finished their lunch and had returned to the penthouse. Nobody got on board, but the boat continued on Washington Street and stopped at the building next door. It dropped anchor in front of some broken windows and some men put a gangplank between the boat and the building. Four men got off, while one remained on board.

"That's the same boat we saw yesterday when those men tried to break into our boat," Matteo said.

"Exactly, and probably the same one that circled around our boat last night, but look, I'll fast forward," Perry said.

They glanced at the screen, at the accelerated images, until Perry slowed down the video about an hour later. Dylan got startled and shouted.

"That's Elizabeth! Look, they carried her on board. It looks like she is unconscious."

Perry played back the video image for image, and they looked at the screen. They saw how the men carried Elizabeth on board, and then the boat departed through Washington Street. At some point, they turned left and disappeared out of sight. Matteo told Perry to pause the image, and after peering at the screen for a moment, he looked at the map.

"They turned left onto Laight Street."

"All right, let's have a look over there. They are probably long gone, but let's check it out."

Perry started the engine and then turned the boat around. He steered through Washington Street and then turned left. It was getting dark, and they peered into Laight street, but they saw nothing. Perry continued further, and they checked all the side streets. After a while, he looked at Matteo and Dylan.

"No trace of the boat. I think it's better we go to the police headquarters at The Battery and report the kidnapping. They can help us search for her. This way, we increase our chances of finding her."

Dylan did not like the idea of leaving Elizabeth behind, but it made sense to get some help, since they had no idea where they could have taken her. He nodded, and Perry turned the boat and headed back toward the Hudson River.

At the police station, they reported the kidnapping and provided the police with a copy of the video. They took it very seriously and transferred the case to a specialized department. After waiting for quite a while, they met with the police officer, who would handle their case. A heavy, broad-faced man with a large mustache walked up to them.

"Hi, I'm Captain Mike Harris. I'll handle the kidnapping of Elizabeth Muller."

Captain Harris asked them all kinds of questions. He started explaining what the police were going to do. They were immediately going to start a search operation. A picture of Elizabeth was going to be sent to all police stations in New York and New Jersey, and a general alert would be sent out through public news stations. They were going to enter the images of the boat, images of Elizabeth, and the enlarged images of the men onboard into the central electronic observation system. The images of the men were not very clear, since they were wearing masks, but the boat image was very clear. All footage from all cameras in the state of New York and the State of New Jersey would automatically be scanned to check if the boat or these men were spotted somewhere.

In addition, they were going to send out thousands of observation drones to search, especially in the deserted area of Manhattan and New Jersey. Dylan felt reassured with the whole search operation, although Captain Harris also clarified that there was no guarantee they would find her. Night had fallen, and they were not expecting many results immediately, but during daylight, they should be able to search a large area with their system.

Later in the evening, they left the police station and discussed what to do next. Dylan and Matteo preferred to go out and search during the night. They realized it would be difficult to find the boat in the dark, but they felt awful and were worried sick about Elizabeth. Dylan preferred to be busy searching than to stay in the harbor and do nothing. He had to find her as soon as possible. Perry steered the boat away from the harbor and they searched street by street, starting just north of the walled area around The Battery.

Perry navigated slowly through the streets, observing the depth meter as it was not deep enough everywhere. Matteo and Dylan scanned the area using night-vision and infrared scanning binoculars. For hours they continued like this, but after midnight Matteo thought it was better that they take turns. Every two hours one would steer the boat, another would scan the surroundings, and the third would sleep. At some point it was Dylan's turn to sleep, but the empty bed reminded him of Elizabeth and he had difficulty falling asleep. He couldn't stop thinking about her. He was tormented with thoughts of all the horrible things that could happen to her.

The whole night they took turns, but it was relatively quiet and they spotted only a few boats. None of them was the one they were looking for. At sunset they had still not found the boat, and Dylan felt more hopeless with every hour that passed. They continued searching like that, but with no luck. They had arrived at the walled area at Midtown Manhattan and found nothing so far. They continued all the way north, but no boat. Perry suggested searching on the other side of the Hudson River in the old Hoboken area and all the way south. Dylan realized very well that their search was hopeless, like searching for a needle in a haystack.

Later in the afternoon they called Captain Harris to check if the police had come up with something in their search operation. They put him on the speakerphone and they all listened, hoping for any good news.

"We searched all night, but with no results. All camera systems are scanning full time, and at sunrise we sent out thousands of drones over Manhattan and they're searching the area as we speak."

"How much of Manhattan have they scanned so far?"

"Well, at night we did all of Manhattan and almost the complete area around Jersey City. We even scanned large parts of Brooklyn and Queens. Since sunrise we have repeated searching all of Manhattan and we're enlarging the region further. The way it works is that we keep special observation drones constantly high in the sky to give us a continuous aerial view of the region, while other smaller drones scan at street level. We'll continue to search for at least the coming days, but unfortunately, no results so far. For now, that's all we can do. Let's hope we get lucky."

After hanging up, Dylan felt disillusioned. How could they not have spotted the boat if they had scanned the entire region? He looked toward Manhattan while Matteo started blaming himself.

"I should never have allowed her to come along on this trip."

"Matteo, Elizabeth insisted herself, and you know her. When she has her mind set on something, there's no talking her out of it," Dylan tried to comfort him.

"Yeah, I guess you're right, but it's so frustrating knowing she is out there somewhere and that she might be in great danger. The more time passes, the less chance we have to find her alive. It feels so hopeless to navigate through the flooded streets with our boat, hoping to find her by a miracle."

"I don't see what else we could do, and still it's better to search for that boat than to wait," Perry commented.

"We have to stay positive and until we have a better idea, we should continue searching the streets," Dylan said.

"All right, let's continue further south," Matteo said and peered back through his binoculars.

Dylan also continued looking down the streets, although he felt extremely tired. He told Perry and Matteo that he was trying to get some sleep downstairs. He asked them to wake him up when they wanted to change shifts. He laid down on the comfortable bed and was so exhausted that he immediately dozed off.

He slept in a deep sleep for several hours, but then he abruptly woke up. It must have been some movement of the boat that triggered him. His first thought was about Elizabeth. He looked at the empty spot next to him. He had to find her. He had to find a way. He got up and lost his balance as the boat turned and he was still drowsy. He fell back on the bed and then it struck him. How could he not have thought about it earlier?

Dylan rushed to the upper deck, and Matteo and Perry looked startled at him as he stumbled in and yelled.

"I think I might have a way to find her!"

43.

Walking through the gardens and agricultural fields had calmed him down, and time had passed in a blink. Amos couldn't believe how long he had stayed outside. He strolled back to the staircase to return downstairs to his apartment. He thought back to the fight with his son earlier that evening and felt bad about it. Not being able to control his emotions made him feel awful. He knew Elliot had no bad intentions, but he just couldn't deal with his questions. It was too difficult for him.

Slowly, he opened the door of the apartment. It was dark inside, and he did not hear any sound. He wondered if Elliot had returned. He had been so upset when he rushed out after their fight, and he had not seen him outside during his walk.

He tiptoed through the hall until he arrived in front of Elliot's bedroom. He listened at the door, but heard nothing. Carefully, he opened it and peeked inside. It was all dark, and he could not see much. He slid his head through the opening to listen if he could hear anything. Suddenly, he saw some movement in the bed, and a second later, he heard Elliot's sleepy voice.

"Dad? Are you back? What time is it?"

"Yes, it's me. It's after midnight. Sorry, I didn't mean to wake you up."

"It's okay."

"I just want to let you know I'm sorry about my reaction earlier tonight. I overreacted and I'm really sorry about that. I hope you can forgive me."

"It's all right. I also overreacted and I should not have insisted so much."

"Well, anyway, I'll do my best to react better from now on. I love you, Elliot, sleep tight."

"Sleep tight."

Amos closed the door and walked to the bathroom. After brushing his teeth, he went to bed. He felt better now after apologizing to his son. Although deep down, he knew it would just be a matter of time before Elliot would start asking questions again. Since Elias had told his son about the suicide, he felt he had lost his son's confidence. It only made it more difficult for him. He loved his son and felt bad about hiding the truth from him. Despite that, he believed he had no choice. He could never tell him everything.

The next week, their lives went back to normal, and Elliot avoided the topic. They were both busy with their work and time passed. It took several months before Elliot had gathered enough courage to ask his father again about his mother. He had chosen his moment carefully. They had just finished an exquisite dinner when he dared to ask again.

"Do you remember when, a few months ago, we had this fight on mother's commemoration?"

Amos looked anxiously at his son, as he feared something was coming up that he preferred to avoid.

"Yes, I remember."

"You told me you would make an effort to react better the next time I ask questions about my mother."

"Yes, I did," he answered calmly, but he felt like he was walking into some trouble.

"Well, I still have some questions about her. I was hoping you could finally answer me, since I really would like to understand better."

Amos did not like where this was going. Suddenly, his phone started ringing, and he immediately answered it.

"Hello?"

Elliot looked at him while his father listened to the phone.

"What? How did they do that? Are they still alive? All right, I'll come right away."

"Sorry, Elliot. I have to go to the border post. Some intruders have breached our protective walls."

His father rushed out of the door before Elliot could say a word.

44.

I n the darkness, Elizabeth tried to look around the room. Her eyes adapted slowly to the darkness. At some point, the small light coming from under the door was enough for her to see better. She was in a small room with dirty walls with traces left of the wallpaper that had been on the walls. It stunk, and the air felt dusty in her lungs. She had difficulty breathing without her respo, and the tape on her mouth made it worse. Besides her breathing, she did not hear any noise.

She tried to move, but they had attached her tightly to her ankles and wrists. The bed creaked when she changed position. Suddenly, she heard footsteps. They seemed to get closer. She held her breath and listened. The footsteps stopped in front of her door and she noticed that the light under the door got interrupted by two dark shadows. Now she heard the lock, and a moment later the door opened.

The light from the corridor blinded her, and she moved her head away from the bright light. Her eyes started adjusting, and she noticed a dark shadow in the door opening. It was a tall, heavy man. He entered the room and quietly closed the door behind him. He turned on his flashlight and aimed it at her face. Blinded by the light, Elizabeth tried to look next to the beam of light, but she could barely see anything. The man approached.

"So, finally we've some time alone."

The man sat down on the edge of the bed next to her and looked at her face. The bed creaked. She noticed he was breathing through a respo, and she wondered if it was her respo he was wearing. He stroked with his hand through her brown hair and then he caressed her face. His hand was rough and smelled dirty.

"You're pretty."

She moved her face away from his hand in disgust. She felt her heart beating fast in her chest. Now the man looked at her body and her legs. He moved his hand over her legs, over the dry diving suit. Then he slowly moved his hand up over her body and he softly squeezed her breast.

"And you have a nice body. Perfect. Maybe we should have some fun together before."

She tried to scream and yell no, but with the tape on her mouth, her words were not understandable. The man continued to squeeze her breast. He moved his hand down and touched her upper leg. His hand moved under her ass now. She panicked and tried to scream, but she barely produced any noise. She moved her hips away from him, but attached to the bed, she could not move much and when she moved, the straps around her ankles hurt her.

"Still a wild one, not giving up? It's easier if you cooperate, so I don't need to hurt you."

The man moved closer and took off his respo. He moved his face against hers. His breath smelled awful, and she felt disgusted.

"Such a soft skin."

His rough face scrubbed along her cheek. Suddenly, he licked her cheek. She jerked her face to the side and banged with her cheekbones against his face. The man quickly moved away from her face.

"Ah, so you want to play rough, huh?"

With one hand, he pushed her shoulder down while with his other hand, he grabbed her between her legs. She tried to move away, but he was holding her tight. She screamed, but the tape on her mouth muted the noise.

Suddenly, the door opened and the bearded man from before stood in the door opening.

"Andy, we have a video connection with Abdul, and he's asking for you."

The man let go of her and got up. He turned his head to her and looked her in the eyes.

"We'll finish this another time."

Then they both left the room and locked the door. The footsteps faded away. She caught her breath and slowly calmed down. She realized she was in great danger. She had to find a way to get out of here.

45.

Matteo and Perry looked perplexed at Dylan, but he ignored them. He grabbed his phone and dialed a number. Perry slowed down the boat to reduce the noise on the upper deck. Dylan waited for a moment and then spoke on the phone.

"Could you please put me through to Miss Patterson, the head of the Energy division?"

He paused and then continued.

"I know it's late, but it's urgent. It's a matter of life and death. I need to speak to her right away."

He looked outside while he waited on the phone until he got connected.

"Good evening, Miss Patterson. This is Dylan Myers speaking. I'm the boyfriend of Elizabeth Muller. I'm sorry to disturb you so late, but I really need your help."

He listened for a moment before he continued.

"Yes, we're still in New York, but something horrible has happened; Elizabeth has been kidnapped… Yes, it is, and I'm getting desperate. We have been looking all day yesterday and today. The New York police have started an extensive search operation yesterday, but they've not found her so far. We really need your help."

He paused again, while Perry and Matteo were trying to follow the conversation.

"This chip all Enviro employees had implanted in their arm. I heard a rumor that you can use it to locate people. I really need to locate Elizabeth before it's too late. Could you help us find her using this chip?"

He switched the phone to his other ear as it was getting sweaty because of his nervousness.

"… okay, I understand that is the official company answer, but it's really a matter of life and death and if this chip could locate her, it might save her life. The faster we can locate her, the more chance we have to find her back alive… when could you get back to me?… all right! I will talk to you later. Thanks!"

He hung up and explained to Matteo and Perry about the chip that all employees have implanted in their arms. He told them that Elizabeth's boss, Amy Patterson, did not really confirm that they can use the chip to locate people, but he had the impression they instructed her to deny this. That she was going to check internally gave him some hope that the rumor might be true. She was going to try to get back to us this evening.

After explaining everything, Dylan called his own boss, Sorenson, to tell him what had happened and to check if he could help speed up things. He apologized for disturbing him so late, but when he explained the whole situation to him, it surprised him how swiftly his boss reacted. He did not confirm the chip could track people, but he would check with Patterson and also with the head of security, Steve Hawkins. He promised to call back within an hour.

While they waited, they continued further, searching through the flooded streets of New York. They had finished their search in Hoboken and the area south of it and had now started searching the streets in what used to be East Village on the East side of Lower Manhattan. They checked all streets and side streets, but they felt it was hopeless. Still, they continued searching. They had to find her before something bad happened.

Later they spoke again with Captain Harris. But unfortunately, still no trace of the boat. They barely spoke and just stared out of the windows at the tall buildings. Suddenly, the silence was broken by the ringing of Dylan's phone.

46.

Her room was humid and damp as Elizabeth woke up the next day with her hands and feet still attached to the bed. The night before, she was so terrified. She had thought she would not sleep that night. Every time she had heard a noise, she was afraid this man would come back. Nonetheless, she was exhausted and had fallen into a deep sleep after a while.

Now she had a hard time grasping what had happened. The straps around her hands and feet were hurting her. She lifted her head and tried to look around in the room, but it was empty. She had difficulty breathing with the tape on her mouth. In one of the corners, she saw something move in the dark, but she could not see what it was. Something small. Her mouth was dry, and she was thirsty. She thought of Dylan and Matteo. Would they still be looking for her? They must be so worried. She remembered how Matteo and her parents had tried to convince her not to go on the trip. If only she had listened to them.

Her thoughts were interrupted as she heard footsteps approaching. Her heart started beating faster, and the adrenaline rushed through her body. She heard the lock making a noise and then the door opened. She got blinded by the light. She closed her eyes and heard the heavy voice of a man.

"Be careful. She was like a wildcat yesterday."

She cracked her eyes and looked at a shabby-looking man with a mouth mask approaching her. Behind the man she saw someone standing close to the door wearing a respo. She recognized him immediately. Her heart skipped a bit, and she felt adrenaline race through her body. It was this Andy who had assaulted her the night before. He looked better taken care of than the other man.

"If you scream or make any loud noise, we'll hurt you. Will you be quiet?" Andy said, and she noticed the gun in his hand.

The sight of it scared her, and she nodded with her head. With one swift move of his hand, the other man ripped the tape off her mouth. It was painful, but breathing became easier. Although the air was uncomfortable and dusty.

"You'd better be calm today," Andy threatened with the gun.

"I will."

"Cut her loose!"

The man, who had removed the tape from her mouth before, now cut the straps on her hands and then on her feet. She was all stiff and rubbed her wrists. She moved her shoulders to loosen them. She looked at the men anxiously.

"Is it all right if I sit?"

"Yes, go ahead. We brought you some food and water."

He put a tray of food and a bottle of water on the floor in front of her. Then he took the chain that was attached to the bedframe and attached it to her right wrist. Andy kept his gun aimed at her all the time. The man who had put the food on the floor walked out of the room. A moment later, he came back with two buckets. One was filled with water; the other was empty. He placed the buckets next to her bed.

"You can use the water to clean yourself. The other bucket you can use if you need to take a piss or a dump."

She was still petrified and asked, "What are you going to do with me?"

The two men both left the room, while one mumbled.

"Later." and she heard the door locking behind them.

Thank God they left the light on. Her mouth was all dry and the first thing she did, as soon as the men left, was to drink some water from the bottle. She looked at the gray stuff on the plate, which did not look very appealing. Even so, she was hungry. She tried a small bite. It was actually some kind of porridge with little taste. She was so hungry that she finished the whole plate and even licked the plate to finish the last part.

After eating, she washed her face in the bucket of water. She looked around in the room and looked back at the corner where she had seen something move earlier on. There was a small crack in the wall. She saw some dark bugs moving in and out. She peered at the corner and got disgusted when she realized what they were; large brown cockroaches. She pulled her feet back on the bed and sat against the bedframe.

Hours passed, and she either rested on the bed or tried to do some exercise next to the bed. With the chain around her wrist, she could not move much, but she was able to do some exercises, like push-ups, knee-bends and sit-ups. It distracted her from her worries. After the workout, her breathing became more difficult. Without her respo she was out of breath much faster and she feared for her lungs in this polluted air. She had no clue what they were planning to do with her, but she feared the worst.

At some point she heard footsteps again, but this time they did not come up to her door. She listened carefully and heard another door unlock. She heard some noise that sounded like a woman sobbing. A man spoke, but it was difficult to understand anything he was saying. He seemed to get upset with the woman. Then she heard her yell.

"I'm not going to wear that!"

"Yes, you will or…"

"No way! What are you planning to do to me?"

"Put it on!"

"Arghh…"

She heard nothing for a moment and wondered what had happened to her until she heard the man's voice.

"And now do as I told you. When I come back, you better be dressed."

She heard the door lock again, and she heard footsteps until the sound faded away. For a long time, it was quiet outside, and she heard no sounds. Then, after a while, she heard footsteps approaching, and she listened attentively. A door close to her room opened. She heard a man speak.

"That's a good girl. Now cooperate with her or she'll call me and then I'll have to hurt you again. Understood?"

She could not hear the woman answer, but she heard how the door closed again. Now the footsteps approached. Her heart started pounding in her chest when she heard the door to her room unlock. Two men entered. A man with a large scar next to his eye carried a pile of clothes with him. He handed her the pile. Elizabeth looked puzzled at the clothes. She inspected them and held some satin bathrobe in front of her. For the rest, there was only some sexy black lingerie.

"What is this?"

"Your clothes! Put them on!"

She looked at them in disgust and felt horrified. What are they planning to do with her? She thought about the woman she had heard before.

"And what if I refuse?"

"Then I'll shock you with this taser until you listen."

The man held a black device in his hand with two metal pins sticking out. She hesitated for a moment, but thought of the horrible scream before and she slowly started taking off her diving suit. The man looked content and walked out of the room.

"We'll be back and you'd better be dressed."

They closed the door. She stared at the lingerie. She felt appalled and feared something bad was going to happen to her. Notwithstanding, she saw no other choice than to put on the clothes they gave her. After putting on the lingerie, she put on the satin bath robe to cover herself. She felt extremely uncomfortable and anxious about what was going to happen next.

It took quite a while before she heard footsteps again. This time they did not stop in front of her room, but she heard a door open further away. She heard the man's voice again.

"Beautiful. Much better. We'll be back and don't dare to touch your face or I'll hurt you. And you, come with us!"

She heard a door closing and footsteps getting closer until they stopped at her door. The lock clicked, and the door opened. The man with the taser stepped inside and checked her out. A tiny Asian woman followed him.

"This woman is going to clean you up and put some make-up on your face. Fully cooperate with her or I'll take care of you."

The man left the room and locked the door behind him. The woman approached her with her beauty case. Once she must have been a beautiful woman, but one side of her face looked burned and mutilated. She opened the beauty case. Then she started applying some make-up on her face. Elizabeth asked her in a low voice.

"What are they going to do with me?"

The woman whispered with an anxious look on her face.

"They're going to sell you."

47.

S aved by the bell was all Amos could think when he rushed out of the door. He really did not feel like talking about the past again with his son. If only he would stop asking. The thoughts about the past were tormenting him enough. Every time Elliot brought up the topic, those dark thoughts came back to him, suffocating him from the inside.

He rushed downstairs toward the control center. As soon as he arrived, one of his staff members explained what had happened.

"We received a notification that one of our defense drones had intercepted intruders about an hour ago on our compound within the inner wall."

"Within the inner wall!?"

"That's why I called you. I figured you probably wanted to see how they did it. Since this is the first time, we've had someone breaching the inner zone."

"You did well. How many were they?"

"Difficult to tell, since the drones fired at the intruders and obliterated them. They're checking the remainders at the moment."

"How did they get so close?"

"They seemed to have dug a tunnel under both walls."

"What!? But that's a distance of over seven kilometers!"

"Correct. We're still examining it and trying to understand how they did it. Let me show you the footage from the drones that detected the intrusion."

Amos looked at the screen while the staff member launched the video footage. It had happened at night, but thanks to the infrared cameras on the drones, he could clearly see someone climbing out of a hole in the ground. The image was not detailed enough to see whether there were two persons or only one, but he had the impression that right behind the first person there was another one. Suddenly, a bright flash appeared on the red silhouette of the person on the screen. A second later, the whole silhouette had disappeared, and he only saw several small red dots scattered around the area where the person had surfaced.

"Any better image with the night vision camera?"

"This is the best footage we've got. I assume they were wearing black clothes to make it more difficult to spot them, but we'll know more as soon as they've finished the examination. Would you like to check it out?"

About half an hour later, they left the dome through the tunnel and the transporter continued driving for several kilometers south along the inner wall. At some point, they approached the wall, and Amos noticed another transporter parked close to the bottom of it. Several men in suits were standing further in a bright spotlight.

When they arrived at the site, he stepped outside, breathing through his mask. Besides the noise his protective suit made as he walked, it was all quiet around him. At some point, he looked up at the massive wall towering above him in the dark. He still remembered the construction of it almost thirty years ago. After signing up for Abe's brilliant idea, he became more and more involved with the dome's construction. The Council noticed his input and involvement to improve the security early on. Over the years, he upgraded the defensive system tremendously. Still, this breach had shown there was more work to be done.

When he arrived at the site, the men greeted him immediately. There in the ground he saw a hole and around it everything was burned black by the drone attack. At least the drone system seemed to have worked perfectly. Nevertheless, he was troubled by the intrusion. For years, people had dug tunnels under the outer wall to get to the dome, but never had someone dug one so long that it went under the inner wall. They must have used some real professional digging technology.

He looked at the black ground, while the men were still searching for traces. Then he asked the officer in charge,

"What have you found so far?"

"Well, sir, we've found DNA from two people. We're still searching, but at this point, it's likely there were only two intruders. The tunnel itself is impressive and seems to have been built with a very professional machine. Let me show you."

The officer stepped down the ladder into the hole. Amos followed him. Inside, he lit his flashlight and Amos observed the light disappearing into a dark tunnel stretching endlessly. It was not so high inside, and he had to bend deep to walk through it. Close to the exit, he noticed a rail on the floor with some fancy-looking trolley with an electrical engine on it.

"I believe that with this trolley, they were able to move fast through the long tunnel. It's deep enough for them not to show up on our infrared scanners. From the smoothness of the sides, you can tell they've used a professional tunnel boring machine."

"Did we send a team to investigate the other side?"

As they climbed out of the tunnel, the officer answered him.

"Yes, we did. We sent two persons through the tunnel and our people on the outside have found the entry point. It's located in some old barn on the edge of the village Narmik, right next to the outer wall. In the barn they found the boring machine and they're inspecting it at the moment. They believe more people were involved, but they must have gotten away before our men arrived at the barn."

"All right. Finish up the investigation as soon as possible and make sure to destroy the boring machine and the barn with everything in it. Leave no trace."

"What do we do with the tunnel?"

"Fill it up with concrete like we usually do."

"Well, this one is seven kilometers long, not like the usual ones we've filled up in the past."

"I see what you mean. Just fill it up from both sides. The goal is that they can never use the same tunnel again."

"Will do, sir!"

"Tomorrow morning, I will brief the Council about the intrusion. Now I will meet up with my team to discuss how to improve our security system to ensure that an intrusion like this won't happen again."

48.

For the first time since the kidnapping of Elizabeth, Dylan was hopeful. Patterson had called him back about an hour earlier to let him know that the head of security, Hawkins, was going to try to trace Elizabeth. He would call them as soon as they had tracked her down. An hour crawled by, and he nervously strolled back and forth through the upper cabin of the boat. Perry and Matteo were waiting, full of hope, and they jumped up when Dylan's phone rang a moment later. It was Hawkins.

"Hello, Mr. Myers, we have located Elizabeth Muller. I'll transfer the coordinates to you right away. She seems to be in one spot and is not moving. I hope you manage to liberate her unharmed. Good luck and let me know if we can do anything else to help."

"That's terrific news! Thanks for your help, Mr. Hawkins!"

After hanging up, he immediately checked the message on his phone. He looked up at Matteo and Perry.

"They've located her. They've just sent me her coordinates."

"Let's enter them in the navigation system!" Perry said promptly.

He entered them and they glanced at the screen. On the map, a small yellow dot appeared. Matteo pointed at it.

"Look, she's in Jersey City, on the other side of the Hudson River. We searched that area earlier today, but we didn't see the boat anywhere."

Perry nodded and looked at the map. They were in the middle of Brooklyn and The Battery was on the way to Elizabeth's location.

"Let's call Captain Harris. We could meet with him in the police station in The Battery to discuss how to get her out of there."

They all agreed and contacted the police officer to inform him. Captain Harris proposed a rescue operation. He invited them to join the others for a briefing in about an hour. Perry steered the boat in The Battery's direction. The sun was already low, and the sky turned reddish. Matteo was getting all excited about going to rescue his sister.

"Maybe we should go there with our guns and free her now, instead of waiting for the police."

"I don't know Matteo. Somehow it feels better to do this together with the police. We know nothing about the people who kidnapped her. How many people are involved? Are they armed? No, I think we can't take any risks, for Elizabeth's sake."

"The police have a special unit for this. They use the best technologies and methods currently available. Working with them will increase our chances of freeing Elizabeth safe and sound tremendously," Perry added.

"I guess you're right. It's more that I feel so helpless and believe I have to do something," Matteo admitted.

Later they entered the harbor at The Battery and rushed to the police station. Inside, they waited at the reception for fifteen minutes before Captain Harris came walking toward them.

"Good afternoon, gentlemen. I've good news. I just received the green light from the police commissioner to embark on a rescue operation. We're planning to go tonight."

"Can we come along?" Matteo asked immediately.

Captain Harris hesitated for a moment and looked at the three of them with a serious face.

"Well, that is not common, but I guess, given your military background, I could make an exception here. Why don't you join us in our preparatory briefing in about half an hour from now?"

"Excellent! Thanks!" Dylan replied enthusiastically.

Captain Harris brought them to an empty office and had someone bring some coffee. The three of them waited for almost an hour like that until some police officer finally entered to come and get them. He escorted them to a large meeting room filled with a dozen police officers. They took the seats in the back, while Captain Harris started the meeting.

"Welcome everybody. I invited Matteo Muller, Elizabeth's brother, Dylan Myers, Elizabeth's boyfriend, and Perry Jackson, to join us today. They'll come with us on the operation, as they can provide immediate support to Elizabeth Muller afterwards.

According to the GPS coordinates we received today, Elizabeth Muller is located inside the abandoned Goldman Sachs Tower on the corner of Essex and Hudson Street in Jersey City. We have sent an observation drone to the building. So far, we've seen nobody moving in or out."

On the screen behind him, he showed the footage from the drone. It showed a tall skyscraper that was half ruined and most windows on the upper and lower floors were broken. Half of the upper part of the building had collapsed, but the middle floors were relatively intact and even most windows there were still intact. The surrounding streets were all deep underwater. What once was an impressive part of Jersey City, with the best views of Manhattan, was now a desolate and abandoned area.

"We have to be extremely careful in this rescue mission to ensure that we free Elizabeth Muller safe and sound. We have no intel yet about how many people are inside the building, nor if they are armed.

We'll go there in four boats and position ourselves strategically so they can't spot us. From there, we will launch a drone reconnaissance operation."

Captain Harris showed on the map the four positions where the boats would wait until further orders. While he continued explaining the details of the mission, Dylan realized more and more that this could turn bad at any time. Elizabeth was in great danger. Going to rescue her without the police would have been a bad idea. After the meeting, Captain Harris walked up to them.

"I suggest the three of you come along on our boat, so you can follow the operation from up-close."

After a quick dinner, they walked with the group toward the harbor. Dylan looked at the dozen police officers and then he asked Matteo,

"Don't you think they need more police officers for a rescue mission like this?"

Captain Harris overheard what he said and reacted promptly.

"More police officers? This is more than enough for an operation like this. Normally we take even fewer men. With a dozen men, I'm even afraid most won't have much to do."

Dylan didn't really understand, but Captain Harris sounded so sure of himself that he didn't ask more. As he walked along with the heavily armed men in the dark, he felt the adrenaline rushing to his head. This was the moment. He was praying nothing would go wrong.

49.

At high speed, the boat bounced through the darkness over the waves on the Hudson River. Dylan sat in one of the seats on the upper deck, tightly buckled up. The four boats were speeding in formation toward Jersey City. They were on the largest boat, together with Captain Harris. He was impressed with the police fleet, which was extremely modern. When he had gotten on board, he had noticed the eVTOL vehicle on top of the boat. Captain Harris had explained that with that vehicle, they could quickly put police officers on the roof of the building if needed. Inside, it was filled with modern equipment and it reassured him.

As they approached the shore, he distinguished the silhouette of the ruined Goldman Sachs Tower next to the other skyscrapers. The whole tower was dark, and he wondered how Elizabeth was doing. The other boats had disappeared out of sight. Their captain steered close to one of the tall buildings next to the tower and slowed down. He overheard Captain Harris checking with the other boats if they took their positions. After that, he gave an order to one of the police officers sitting behind the large control screen in the upper cabin.

"Send in the reconnaissance bugs!"

He heard a hatch open outside in the front of the boat, followed by a low buzzing noise quickly fading away. Matteo and Perry had gotten up already and were staring at the screen behind the police officer. Dylan tried to look outside, but it was too dark and he could not see anything, so he joined them behind the screen. He looked puzzled at Captain Harris.

"Reconnaissance bugs!?"

Captain Harris turned to him with a grin on his face.

"We have special micro drones for operations like these to check how many people there are in a building and if they are armed or not. Most people think we use thermal scanners to check who's in a building, like they often show in movies. In reality, however, infrared does not penetrate through walls and will just show that the wall is warmer than the surroundings."

He opened one of the cupboards in the upper cabin and returned holding a tiny little thing in his hand. They all stared at his hand. Dylan looked astounded at the thing in his hand and muttered.

"B... b... but that's a cockroach."

"It looks like one, but it's actually a micro drone disguised as a cockroach," Captain Harris responded proudly.

"The buzzing noise you heard before is a larger drone that delivers several micro drones on the first floor above sea level. They crawl like cockroaches through the building and scan the entire building. They are equipped with motion sensors, daylight and night-vision cameras and a microphone. The images are streamed live to our monitor over here and to the other boats."

As they looked at the screen, they listened to the police officer reporting the observations.

"Delivery drone entering the building."

They watched the screen, and they saw how it flew through a large opening in the building. It landed on the floor. On the screen, many dark dots started moving away quickly.

"Reconnaissance bugs deployed!"

Suddenly, all the other screens lit up and the police officers monitored the images streamed from the different bugs. Captain Harris explained to them what was happening.

"The larger drone just dispatched the micro drones and has left the building. It will hoover next to the building and track all the micro drones in the building. This way, we can follow exactly which one is on which floor."

On one of the monitors, they saw the dark silhouette of the tower, and on it there were yellow numbers moving around. Most of them were climbing, although one was going downstairs. Captain Harris pointed at the yellow number five going down.

"Bring the footage of number five on the large screen."

They looked at it, and they saw how the drone was climbing down the wall. Suddenly, the image switched from night vision mode to daylight, as there was some light on this floor. They saw the water below. Next to the staircase, which was half underwater, there were two armed men sitting on the side of a boat. Behind it there was another boat inside the building. Dylan looked astounded at the screen as he recognized the boat. The police officer reported to all the other police boats.

"Two armed suspects at sea level. Two boats floating in the main hall. One of them is the boat used in the kidnapping."

Drone number five stopped walking and observed the armed men. Behind the boats, there were some large wooden sliding doors, hiding everything out of sight from the street in front. The other screens showed images of the other micro drones as they were progressing through the building. They were all climbing upstairs and subsequently spread out to check all the rooms on that floor. Every drone streamed its footage to a distinct part of one of the screens in front of them. The police officer reported the findings of the reconnaissance bugs.

"First floor above sea level scanned completely. No activity observed."

It amazed Dylan to see how efficient and fast the drones moved. They were so small and walked through the opening under a door without problems. On the monitor with the dark silhouette of the building, they observed how the yellow numbers were moving a floor higher, while number five remained at sea level. It took the reconnaissance bugs quite some time to scan the entire floor. After a while, the police officer reported.

"Second floor above sea level scanned completely. No activity. Scan started on the third floor."

While the images from the running bugs kept streaming on the monitors, Captain Harris started explaining.

"They feed all these images into the AIMPS, that is the Artificial Intelligence Mission Preparation System. It automatically creates an interactive map of the entire building and identifies all persons present in the building. It categorizes the persons in different categories, so we know who is armed and dangerous and who is a hostage or a harmless unarmed person…"

Meanwhile, the police officer monitoring the video streams kept reporting.

"Third floor above sea level scanned completely. No activity. Scan started on the fourth."

Captain Harris continued explaining while keeping an eye on the screens.

"All this information we use for the next phase of the rescue operation. Each micro drone that spots a person will remain with that person to record every movement. All this information will be accessible for the entire rescue team and relevant information will be fed to the screens of our helmets."

"Fourth floor above sea level scanned completely. No activity. Scan started on the fifth."

"Impressive! We use drones in the army in Switzerland, but this is quite sophisticated," Matteo said.

Captain Harris smiled proudly, but suddenly he focused his attention back on the screen as the police officer reported.

"One armed suspect in front of the staircase."

One reconnaissance drone stopped moving and kept filming the suspect, who was drinking some water while he sat on a chair next to the staircase. Meanwhile, the other drones explored the rest of the floor. After scanning through the whole place, the bugs continued to the sixth and the officer announced.

"Fifth floor above sea level scanned completely. One armed suspect next to the staircase. For the rest, no activity. Scan started on the sixth."

The bugs raced through the hallway and into the different rooms on the sixth floor until one of them ran into two people.

"One armed suspect is escorting an unarmed woman into a room. Now he leaves her and locks the door. Marking the unarmed woman as a likely hostage," the police officer commented on the video stream.

Dylan glanced at the screen and saw how the Asian woman laid down on the bed in the room. The reconnaissance drone stayed inside, observing her, while another drone followed the armed suspect through the hall. Suddenly, there was activity on another part of the screen and the officer brought the smaller video window up to the big screen. One armed man wearing a baseball cap pushed a blonde woman dressed in a sexy bathrobe onto a large bed on what looked like a stage. Around the stage there were several cameras standing on tripods. It looked like a studio. Several spotlights were aimed at the stage, while the rest of the room was dark.

Another armed man was peering through one of the cameras, while another heavily armed man was standing next to the door. The armed man with the baseball cap was saying something to the woman, who looked terrified. The volume was too low to understand what he was saying. The police officer reported,

"Three armed suspects in the center room on floor six. One unarmed woman. Marking her as a likely hostage."

He increased the volume, and now they heard the woman weep. The armed man yelled at her.

"Stop crying! You're going to ruin your make-up! Do exactly what we tell you to do, or I'll have to hurt you again!"

It shocked Dylan to see the terrified woman on the bed with all the cameras surrounding her.

"Open your bathrobe slowly now and flirt with the camera!" the armed man continued.

The woman looked appalled, but slowly started opening her satin bathrobe. She exposed her long legs and the dark lingerie she was wearing. Dylan was appalled to see how they forced her to undress in front of the camera and, slightly puzzled, he asked,

"What the hell is this? What are they doing to this woman?"

Captain Harris glanced at the screen and, without looking at Dylan, he answered.

"There's quite some abuse of women happening in the region. It could be they're selling video images or worse, they could be selling women on the Darknet."

"The Darknet?"

"Yes, an illegal hidden part of the internet, used mostly by criminals. Weapon deals. Drug deals. But also, human trafficking and selling women. Sometimes, women are auctioned off to the highest bidder."

"And what happens to those women?"

"They often get abused or raped. Sometimes killed."

"That's horrible!"

"Yes, it is. Unfortunately, this is happening all over the world."

Dylan looked at Matteo, who also looked stunned and appalled now. Suddenly, Captain Harris pointed at another screen and commanded the police officers.

"Move that screen up to the primary screen!"

They saw how the armed man, who had escorted the Asian woman, sat down on some chair overlooking the long corridor. One of the drones stopped moving and watched the man, who started drinking from a bottle. On the other screens, they noticed there were more drones running down the same corridor. Matteo suddenly pointed at one of the smaller screens and yelled.

"Enlarge that screen, please!"

The police officer pushed some buttons, and the screen appeared enlarged on the primary one. The drone had just passed under a door opening and walked into a room, where there was another bed. Dylan's heart skipped a beat, and he approached the screen to have a better look. On the bed, he recognized her immediately. She was dressed in a satin bathrobe, just like the other woman. Her face looked different, though. Like she was wearing a lot of make-up. What had happened to her? He noticed she was attached with a chain to the bed. He pointed at the screen while he addressed Captain Harris.

"That's her! That's Elizabeth!"

50.

While the Asian woman cleaned Elizabeth's face, she could not help staring at the woman's mutilated face. She wondered what the woman's role was in her kidnapping. Was she in on it? Was she part of the group of kidnappers? The anxious look on her face told her she was probably not so happy to be involved.

"Are you working here?"

"Lower your voice," the woman whispered and continued cleaning her face. Elizabeth noticed that the woman's eyes were getting all watery and then the woman continued whispering.

"I was like you. They kidnapped me several months ago and locked me up in a room further down this corridor. After forcing me to wear those clothes and those high heels, they took me to some kind of studio on the same floor. They started filming me and wanted me to undress. I refused."

Elizabeth looked at her, and she noticed the tears falling down her face. She felt sorry for her and she put her hand on her shoulder. The woman continued with her story.

"They threatened to shoot me, and I spit in the face of one of those guys. He hit me and dragged me to some room next to the studio. The guy started touching me and he tried to rape me. I got so angry and kicked him several times in his face. The sharp edge of the high heels cut deep through the man's face. When the man realized what a deep cut he had on his face, he went mad. He beat me up very hard and splashed some cup with some kind of acid on my face. It burned so much. I still feel the pain every day."

The woman was crying now, and Elizabeth took her in her arms. A silence fell, as she didn't know what to say to the poor woman. The woman recovered her breath a moment later and continued putting make-up on her face. When she had calmed down, Elizabeth whispered,

"Are there more woman like us around here?"

"Yes, although I'm not sure how many exactly. Next to you there's a young, blond woman in this corridor, but there could be more."

She had finished with the make-up and starting brushing Elizabeth's long brown hair now, when they heard the sound of the lock on the door. One of the armed men entered and looked satisfied at Elizabeth.

"That looks much better. You can stop now and follow me back to your room."

The man looked from the Asian woman back to Elizabeth.

"I'll come and pick you up later. And don't you dare mess up your make-up!"

While the man waited at the door, the woman arranged Elizabeth's hair and when she got closer; she whispered.

"Please, be careful with these monsters."

She left, and the man followed her into the corridor and locked the door. She heard their footsteps fading away. Then she heard some door close further down the hall. The story of the woman had shocked her deeply, and she was horrified. She had to get out of here. Desperation was all she could feel now. She tried to think what she could do, but she felt helpless. If only she could get hold of some kind of weapon. She looked round in the barren room and in the corner; she saw cockroaches crawling.

51.

It was after midnight when Amos left his office in the subterranean complex. He walked through the gardens instead of taking the underground route back to his apartment. After checking out the tunnel from the intruders, he had gone to his office and had worked on a proposal to improve the security. Thanks to this intrusion, he had avoided Elliot's question about his late wife. Nonetheless, he was afraid to run into his son that same evening, so he had worked until midnight.

As he strolled through the gardens, he stared up at the massive dome above him. It still impressed him after all those years. During its construction, he had followed the progress carefully. He had lots of good ideas, especially regarding security and defense, and Abe had valued his input. They put him on a special design team in charge of defense, and that's how his new career in the community started. At that point in time, he became so passionate about the dome it was all he could think about, which had frustrated his wife. This all started after Abe had presented his brilliant plan for an otherwise doomed future. Amos strolled further and thought about that amazing presentation over twenty-five years ago now.

Abe had been so passionate and convincing that day when he presented his solution for the climate change induced catastrophe that was about to hit the planet. The audience was hanging on every word, and professional video footage supported the presentation in the background. Amos had been so impressed that at the end of that day he joined the project and gave up everything he had.

Since Abe did not believe humanity would reduce its emissions fast enough, his solution was the only viable option for survival. With the continuous accumulation of greenhouse gasses in the atmosphere and the unambitious plans of governments to stop the emission of greenhouse gasses, he believed soon we would pass several tipping points. After passing those, even an immediate global elimination of greenhouse emissions to zero would not be enough to stop the climate change. We would need decades of negative emissions to take out the excess amount of greenhouse gases in the Earth's atmosphere.

To prevent the extinction of humans, he believed there was only one viable solution: the creation of a colony on Earth protecting humans from the harsh consequences of climate change. Billionaires and governments were spending billions on space programs aiming to create a colony on barren, harsh planets like Mars or the Moon, while humanity's best chances of survival were still on Earth. His proposal was to create a dome in which a selected group of humans would live and survive until humanity would have solved the climate change problem and restore the natural balance of gases in the atmosphere.

On the large screen behind him, Abe showed the design of this colony, a gigantic dome-shaped structure. They planned to create a completely self-sufficient and self-supporting human colony under this dome. They would supply it with energy by its own nuclear reactor. In the nearby mountains, solar panels would cover large parts of the mountains to have a second energy supply. People would live and work under the ground, while on the surface they would use all space for agriculture to provide the community with an abundance of food. They would take water from the groundwater, and a water purification installation would turn it into drinkable water.

The plan was to create a completely new society and a new political system. The community was going to be ruled by a group of wise men called The Council. There would be no money or private assets in the community. They would provide for everything. Food and water in abundance. The dome was going to be constructed for a population of twenty-five thousand persons.

People were invited exclusively by the Council, and everybody interested in living in the dome had to accept the community's rules and laws. Any habitant would have to renounce all his or her wealth and income to the community. It selected the people in a way that would ensure humanity's long-term survival on Earth.

The habitants of the dome would consist of two types of people. On the one hand, they invited the richest billionaires of the world to join the community and live inside of it. Every billionaire was invited to buy his citizenship inside the dome for a hefty price of one billion per person. The more money a billionaire had, the more spots inside they could buy. On the other hand, they invited the best scientists, doctors and specialists in the world to live inside the dome together with their family. This second group did not have to pay a billion per person for a spot inside. They only had to renounce all their wealth and income to the community and work for them.

All this money was going to be used to construct and maintain the dome. The community would become a shareholder in a fund that would be created. This fund would invest in the dome, but also invest in companies all over the world to have access to state-of-the-art technologies and products to ensure the long-term survival of the community on Earth.

Habitants were not only to renounce all their wealth, but they also could never leave the dome. Abe predicted that the pollution on Earth was going to increase so much that life outside was going to be harsh and difficult. Diseases would proliferate and pollution was going to kill a large part of the planet's population. To keep diseases out and isolate the community from the rest of the planet, no one could go outside. If it was really necessary that someone would temporarily leave the dome to ensure and protect the community's interests, the Council would allow them to go outside in protective suits only.

They designed life inside the dome to become the best place on Earth to live in. With the world's brightest scientists, doctors, and specialists, the aim was to provide all inhabitants with the healthiest and best life circumstances. He gave examples of the best longevity experts which already had committed to join. People inside the dome were going to have the longest life expectancy on the planet. While climate change was going to devastate the world and life expectance was going to drop, inside life expectancy would rise every year further and further.

With the state-of-the-art agricultural and biological methods and agricultural experts inside the dome, the community would be supplied with an abundance of food of the highest quality on Earth. Climate change was going to disrupt the entire food chain on the planet, and food and water were going to be scarce. Crops were more likely to fail or going to be destroyed by disasters, like droughts and flooding, that would increasingly torment the planet. Abe expected climate change to devastate the world. The dome would be the last paradise on Earth.

It was a brilliant idea, and Abe was a genius. After the presentation Amos was convinced and he joined. As a billionaire he had to pay a hefty price and he just had enough money to reserve three places. His wife was expecting at the time, so he reserved a third spot for the unborn child. To give up his wealth and possessions was difficult, but parting with his brothers and sisters and the rest of the family was probably the hardest part. He knew there would be no way back.

In the years after he had taken this decision, he realized the dome would become the world's most desirable place to live in. He had pressed the Council to invest heavily in security and defensive systems. He knew intruders would come and try to enter the dome, or maybe even destroy it. He became so involved and passionate about defense that later on the Council put him in charge. His drone expertise had proven to be a great asset.

After his pleasant stroll through the gardens, he returned to his apartment. He felt relieved Elliot was deep asleep in his room. Intruders had given him a great excuse to leave the apartment just when Elliot was asking those questions that he had so much difficulty with. He knew he would probably have to explain everything to him at some point, but he just couldn't find the courage.

52.

On the screens in front of them, the reconnaissance bugs continued to scan the rest of the building, but above the sixth floor, they did not find anyone else. Meanwhile, the micro drones that had encountered someone continued streaming images, so the police could observe them. When Dylan had seen what the men were forcing the blond woman to do, he started stressing out. Elizabeth was probably going to be next. They had to do something, and fast.

"We should move in now and arrest those criminals before they harm Elizabeth," Dylan said while looking in desperation at Captain Harris.

Captain Harris stared at the monitors and signaled with his hand at Dylan that he should stop talking. He seemed to listen in on the discussion between the men inside the studio with the blond woman. He put on a headset to follow the conversation better. Perry whispered in Dylan's ear that they had to be patient, since a rescue operation was all about timing. Matteo nodded in agreement and the men looked in silence at the monitors for about half an hour until there was some movement on the monitors.

Two men grabbed the blond woman by the arm and took her out of the studio. Captain Harris started talking to all the other police officers through his microphone.

"Everybody, prepare for action! We might get an opportunity for intervention at any moment."

The men showed up on the other monitor where a reconnaissance bug was observing the guard in the corridor, where they had locked away both Elizabeth and the Asian woman. The men pushed the blond woman, who was crying now, through the corridor. Captain Harris was reading something on one screen, after which he suddenly ordered the police officer sitting in front of the control panel.

"Launch the intervention drones!"

The police officer pushed some buttons, and they heard a hatch open in front of the boat. Then there was some high-pitched buzzing, as if a large swarm of wasps flew away. The silence returned when the noise faded away. Captain Harris and the other police officers looked deeply concentrated now. Dylan glanced at the different screens but noticed nothing special. He just saw that the two men in the corridor had opened one of the doors and pushed the blonde woman inside. They locked the door after her and walked further. They talked to the guard seated in the corridor, after which they continued in the direction of the room where Elizabeth was locked up. Matteo whispered to Dylan.

"They're going to Elizabeth."

On the monitor showing the dark silhouette of the building with all the drones marked in yellow, a dozen red numbered dots appeared suddenly at the level of the seventh floor.

Captain Harris yelled through the microphone.

"Start the intervention!"

A police officer pushed several buttons. The red numbered dots moved from the seventh floor down to the sixth floor. Suddenly, they heard a loud explosion. On the different screens, they observed the suspects getting startled by the noise. The lights switched off everywhere in the building. On all the monitors, the images automatically switched to night-vision cameras. Dylan noticed that the two men that were about to open the door to Elizabeth's room were grabbing their flashlights and switched them on. Elizabeth was sitting up straight on the bed, spooked by the explosion. One of the police officers announced,

"Generator taken out!"

The high-pitched noise started increasing, although they could not really identify from which of the screens it was coming from. The guard in the corridor jumped off his seat and grabbed his gun, but just at that moment they heard an explosion and the screen lit up with a flash. A second later the flash disappeared and the guard was lying on the floor, or at least what was left of him. The two men in front of the door grabbed their guns, while the high-pitched buzzing noise got louder again. The man standing closest to the remains of the guard suddenly screamed. They heard another explosion while the screen lit up again. The other man standing in the back fired his gun, while another explosion followed with a light flash.

Dylan looked at the other screens and he noticed that the man who had stayed in the studio was lying on the floor and the upper part of his body had disappeared. A few seconds later there was another loud explosion and, on the screen showing the fifth floor, they saw the guard falling onto the floor and his head was missing. The two guards at sea level had jumped out of their chairs and were looking up. The high-pitched noise increased again and one of them started shooting up in the staircase. Then there was another explosion, followed almost immediately by a second explosion. The screen lit up and a moment later the two men were lying on the floor.

The police officer reported,

"All targets eliminated."

Captain Harris spoke in the microphone.

"Boats two and four, please move in and rescue the three women! Boat three, please remain in position!"

Now he turned his head and looked at Dylan, Matteo and Perry, while he said,

"Our intervention drones have eliminated all suspects. Now our police officers will free Elizabeth and the other women. After they've moved in, we'll also enter the building, so you can take care of Elizabeth as soon as we bring her down."

"What just happened?" Matteo asked, still looking flabbergasted at the screens.

Captain Harris explained how they had first taken out the generator to cut the lights in the building. Subsequently, the drones armed with an explosive charge eliminated all armed suspects. He explained that they tried to use intervention drones as much as possible to minimize police casualties. Dylan was distracted and could not help peering at the monitors. On the one at sea level, he saw how one of the police boats approached the boat inside the building and the officers climbed on board. A moment later, the police officers all entered the building and rushed upstairs.

Suddenly, Dylan felt the boat moving. He glanced outside, but in the dark, he did not see much until they approached the Goldman Sachs tower. There, he noticed a police boat sticking out of a large opening in the building. As they got closer, he noticed how the boat was attached to another one inside the building. They slowly approached the side of the boat. They navigated alongside and then stopped moving. Captain Harris got up and put on his respo.

"All right, why don't you all come on the upper deck and wait with me for the hostages?"

They all put their respos on and left the upper cabin. Outside, Dylan distinguished the silhouette of Manhattan on the other side of the Hudson River. Mostly dark, except for the walled area on the south side at the Battery and the walled area on Midtown Manhattan. All buildings around them were dark. The three police boats were all attached to one another, and the one in front was attached to the two inside the building.

They waited for fifteen minutes there on the deck until Captain Harris finally told them that all three women were liberated and coming down. Apparently, it had taken some more time since the women wanted to change their clothes first. After that, Dylan noticed the Asian woman climbing down the staircase. A police officer helped her get on board, and they walked together over the side of the boats until they both disappeared inside the police boat in front of them.

Dylan looked back at the staircase. He felt shivers up his spine as he noticed Elizabeth coming down wearing her diving suit and walking next to the blond woman. He was so excited and shouted,

"Elizabeth!"

She looked up and waved at him with a faint smile on her face. Dylan rushed over the gangway of the boat toward her, while Elizabeth climbed on the first boat. Halfway, she fell into his arms. They both had tears in their eyes and Dylan felt a wave of relief; she was safe.

53.

The next morning, Dylan woke up next to her in their cabin on the lower deck of the boat. She was still sleeping. He looked at her and realized how lucky they had been. Last night the police had brought them to the station in The Battery. On the way back, Elizabeth talked about all that had happened. She talked about the kidnapping and about the time she had spent locked up in the room. They explained to her how they searched desperately for her and how they located her in the end. After the debriefing in the police station, they thanked Captain Harris and the other officers and said goodbye. That night, they slept on their boat in the guarded harbor. Elizabeth fell asleep immediately and Dylan quickly after her, as he felt exhausted as well. The last few days had been stressful, and he thought about all the events and felt blessed.

After breakfast, they set course for Thomaston on Long Island. Matteo talked for a while with Elizabeth, while Dylan was talking with Perry behind the steering wheel. At some point, Elizabeth descended to the lower deck, and Matteo joined Dylan and Perry. Dylan looked at him.

"Do you think she'll be all right?"

"Yeah, she seems to be fine already," Matteo responded.

"Must not be easy with all she went through," Perry added.

"Well, I know my sister well, and she's very strong. During her time in the military, she had the nickname The Rock, since she could sustain quite some pain and stressful situations."

"She slept well last night, so maybe you're right," Dylan said.

"That's good. I know someone who was kidnapped, and she suffered from anxiety and stress and had a long period of nightmares. Although this person had been abused severely during the kidnapping, so maybe it's different here since Elizabeth was relatively unharmed," Perry said.

"I hope so. It was already bad enough what she went through," Dylan replied.

Out of the blue, Elizabeth joined the conversation.

"Don't worry about me. I'm fine. Those guys didn't do anything to me besides knock me out when they abducted me. You guys arrived right in time though, because I really didn't feel like undressing in front of a camera. That poor other girl. She kept shaking ever after she was freed."

"Yeah, poor thing. Thank god, Dylan came up with this chip in your arm, otherwise you might have ended up like her or worse," Matteo said.

"Yeah, funny how they tried to deny the tracing capability at first, but that chip saved me. I'm surprised they didn't forbid us to tell anyone," Elizabeth grinned.

"Well, they did ask us to come and see them immediately after returning to Ikast. So probably they'll ask us to keep it quiet," Dylan said.

"At least it was quite an adventure this trip, just a pity we didn't find much to locate your parents," Elizabeth said as she placed her hand on Dylan's shoulder.

"Well, I still have to check all the electronic memory sticks, so I'm not giving up hope yet. And even if I find nothing to locate them, at least I've some photos of my birth parents now."

Shortly thereafter, they arrived in the harbor near Thomaston and left the boat. They checked in at the Richwood Hotel. Perry returned to his own apartment but would join them for a farewell dinner in the evening. Dylan, Elizabeth, and Matteo were planning to fly back to Frankfurt the next day. Elizabeth called her parents in the afternoon while Dylan started checking the memory sticks that he had brought from the penthouse.

While she was on the phone, he scanned through the many documents. The more he read, the more excited he became. Elizabeth got off the phone and prepared some tea for both of them. She put a cup of tea for Dylan on his desk and looked over his shoulder at the computer screen.

"Anything interesting?"

Dylan glanced at the screen and nodded.

"I think I might have found a clue of where they went after leaving New York. I focused on the most recent documents. The most recent are from 2029, the year I was born. Look!"

He opened a document on the screen and she leaned forward to read it.

"It's like an invitation or more like an instruction for your parents, signed by The Council, whatever that may be."

"Yeah, it's strange. They were instructed to go to Nuuk in Greenland, where they would be picked up at a hotel to be escorted to the dome."

"The dome? Never heard of it."

"Yeah, I tried to look it up on the internet, but I could find nothing about any dome in Greenland. Look at the meeting date."

Elizabeth glanced at the screen to read and then responded, slightly confused.

"June 26, 2029. What's special about that?"

"Well, that's only two months after I was born, and this is the most recent information on these memory sticks. All the other documents are from before. It seems that right after giving me up for adoption, they had left for New York and quickly after they left for Nuuk."

Elizabeth looked puzzled.

"You wonder what they went to do in Nuuk and what the hell is this dome?"

Dylan pointed at the computer.

"I found some more files with instructions on what they were allowed to bring and also an explicit instruction not to bring anything else. I can tell you it was not much what they could bring with them, almost only objects of sentimental value."

Elizabeth stared at the screen and commented.

"Weird instructions. It doesn't look like some kind of holiday, but more like they were moving somewhere permanently and were not allowed to take much. Like a prison camp or something like that. Strange."

"Maybe I'll find some more clues in the other files. I'll continue my search."

She walked toward the bathroom and filled the bathtub while he continued. The rest of the afternoon he spent going through all the files until Elizabeth told him he had to prepare himself for the dinner downstairs at seven. He quickly freshened up while she brushed her long hair. In the bathroom, he explained what he had found so far.

"It seems to me they went to Nuuk to stay there or somewhere around. Apparently, the months before, they had sold almost all their property and assets. My father owned many companies, and I found several contracts in the files in which either he sold all the shares or he exchanged them for shares in another company called Dominc A/S. I also found a share purchase agreement in which my parents paid a lot of money for shares in this Dominc A/S. It almost seems like they used all their wealth to buy a stake in this entity. I looked up Dominc A/S and all I found is that it has an address registered in Nuuk in Greenland. It seems to be some kind of investment fund."

"Uh… weird… why would they transfer all their wealth into one fund? That sounds pretty risky to me," she responded.

"Yeah, it sounds crazy. Especially since I have the impression that my father was a very successful businessman. It all makes little sense to me. One thing is clear though, everything points to this town in Greenland, called Nuuk."

Dylan looked at her a bit nervously before continuing.

"Probably I should go there to continue the search."

He waited a moment for her reaction, but she just looked at him with a surprised look.

"I checked and there's a flight to Frankfurt with a stopover in Nuuk. Would you like to join me, or maybe it's too much after all you've been through?"

She looked at him for a moment and then smiled at him.

"I've never been to Greenland, so I guess I rather join you to see what it's like. I don't feel like returning home without you."

"Yes! That's what I like about you. I'll try to change the flights immediately," he said enthusiastically.

"We should probably check with Matteo first. Maybe he would like to join."

"Good idea!"

Dylan left and walked to Matteo's room in front of theirs. He stayed away for about ten minutes and then he returned. Elizabeth looked at him.

"No, he would have loved to join, but he has to go back to work. I'm going to reschedule our flights and then I'll join you downstairs for dinner."

She left and went with Matteo to the restaurant while Dylan stayed in the room. About half an hour later, he joined them. Perry had also arrived. Elizabeth looked at Dylan.

"And?"

"I rescheduled our flight and we have a flight now tomorrow afternoon to Nuuk."

"Nuuk?" Perry asked, baffled.

Dylan explained their change in plans and told him what he had found on the memory sticks. When he finished, Perry smiled at them and raised his glass.

"Well, let's toast to your next adventure, then! I hope you'll find your birth parents."

They all raised their glasses and continued dinner. Probably it was the stress from the days before that released, but they laughed and had a great time together. The evening passed in a blink, and that night Dylan lay with Elizabeth in his arms. He was all excited about their trip to Greenland, and he wondered if he finally would find his birth parents.

54.

Elizabeth kept surprising him. After all the horror she went through in New York, she spontaneously came along with him to Greenland. She was a strong woman who loved adventure and was a wholehearted support to him in his search for his birth parents. Before landing at the airport, he had a glimpse of the landscape in Greenland. It was quite green indeed, with gray mountains on the horizon. There was no snow or ice in sight when they landed. Dylan had seen some photos of Greenland covered by a gigantic sheet of ice, but those were from decades ago. Climate warming had melted most of it. While many places in the world had become uninhabitable, Greenland attracted more and more people, forcing the country to tighten its immigration laws.

Nuuk had become one of the world's fastest growing cities. At the beginning of the twenty-first century, Nuuk had an average annual temperature of minus one degree Celsius. All around the world temperatures had increased, but in Greenland and in many other countries close to the polar circles, the rise in temperature had been much more dramatic. He read somewhere that the average annual temperature in Nuuk was currently fifteen degrees Celsius. A dramatic increase, but still a relatively temperate climate compared to many other places in the world.

It was still early in the afternoon when they arrived, but already the twilight was setting in. On the upside, the town had one of the best climates in the world. On the downside, it was close to the polar circle and suffered from a lack of daylight during the winter, and in summer it lacked a proper dark night. As they entered their air taxi, the sky was illuminated in a mystic red glow. The taxi flew them over many colorful houses, most painted red, green or blue in the typical style that Greenland was known for. The center of Nuuk though had grown into an actual city with several modern high-rise buildings. He had booked a room in the most luxurious hotel in town and the taxi landed on the designated spot on the roof of the hotel.

On the rooftop, they enjoyed the beautiful red-colored sky above the ocean. It was still early in the afternoon and it was weird to observe a sunset that early. Dylan hugged Elizabeth while they enjoyed the view for a while. They took their luggage down. Later on, in their luxurious, modern room, he continued his search online for any clues about this mysterious dome. The more he searched, the more frustrated he got, and Elizabeth noticed it was driving him mad.

"Any luck?"

"No, not at all. It's like there is no dome in Nuuk, nor in Greenland. It feels like a dead end."

"Well, the reason we came here was to ask around and search locally, right? So, let's go out and start asking around!"

"Yeah, I guess you're right. Let's go and in the worst case, we get to do some sightseeing in Nuuk," he said with a smile on his face.

They left the room and went down to the lobby. Dylan was almost outside when he noticed she was not behind him anymore. He walked back and saw her talking to the concierge. The man pointed in a direction. Elizabeth thanked him and came walking to him.

"I asked him about the dome, but he didn't know it and suggested we go to the tourist information. It's a bit further down the street."

They left the hotel and walked with their respos on their face to the tourist information office. The air was fresh, and he checked the pollution report on his phone.

"That's what I thought. The air is much cleaner here than in New York. Still not clean enough though, and it's probably better to wear our respos, but I've not seen air this clean for a long time."

"Yes, think back to that horrible air that I had to breathe in New York without my respo. It made me feel sick and dizzy the whole time. I can imagine why people want to migrate to Greenland. The temperatures are more comfortable and the air is cleaner. Ah look, the tourist information office is right over there on the right."

Street lights illuminated the streets and most of the buildings had the light on inside. A moment later, they entered the office and the young woman standing behind the counter smiled at them.

"Welcome to Nuuk. What can I do for you?"

"Hi, we're looking for a place called the Dome. Would you know where we can find it?"

The young woman looked puzzled and shook her head.

"No, never heard of it. Malik, have you heard of a place called the dome?" the young woman asked the older man sitting at a desk a few meters away.

The man looked up and thought for a moment.

"The dome? A while ago I heard something about some dome, but I'm not sure. Someone told me about some large private property near the village of Narmik."

"Narmik?" Dylan repeated, to make sure he understood well.

"Yes, I heard someone claiming there is some kind of dome behind an enormous wall next to the village of Narmik," the older man said as he approached them.

"And where is this village located?" Elizabeth asked the man.

The older man pointed at a map on the counter.

"It's right over here."

The man pointed at a point northeast of Nuuk.

"What is the best way to go there?"

"Well, it's almost two hundred kilometers from here, so probably the fastest way is by one of those air taxis."

"Okay, do you have a list of hotels in Narmik?"

The man grinned.

"A list? Narmik is a tiny village. I believe there's a place called the Narmik Inn, where they have some accommodation and a small restaurant."

Dylan took the address, and they thanked the man. Back in the street, he looked at Elizabeth.

"What do you think?"

"Let's go there! Let's get our luggage from the hotel and make some reservations for the air taxi and the Inn," she said enthusiastically.

He smiled at her, and they walked back to the hotel.

55.

His frustration had grown over the past few weeks and Elliot was really getting fed up with his father's behavior. The night before, he had discussed it again with Elsa, and she had told him to keep on trying. The mystery around his mother's suicide kept tormenting him. The more he tried to talk to his father about it, the more he got the impression he was hiding something from him. Elsa said it was probably best to find a calm moment, like at dinner or breakfast. This morning he was having breakfast with his father and he seemed to be in a good mood, so he figured it was an excellent moment to ask him again.

"Dad, can I ask you something?"

"Of course."

"I would really like to understand better what happened to Mother and why you think she did it?"

His father's face suddenly changed, and he looked anxious. He even started muttering,

"Jesus, I… I… I thought we had finished that discussion. I really don't feel like talking about it. Especially not now. I have to go to work."

"You never want to speak about it, but I really need to understand. When would be a good time to discuss it?" Elliot asked him, frustrated.

"Well, I don't know. I prefer not to talk about it," his father replied, agitated. He got up and continued, "I have to go to the office now. Today is a busy day for me. I'm going to inspect this tunnel signaling measure we took to warn us when any intruders are digging tunnels under the outer walls."

His father rushed out of the door, and Elliot stayed annoyed behind. Later that day at work, he was so upset that he decided to go home earlier to search through his father's belongings.

He told his boss that afternoon that he was not feeling well and left the office. He rushed home and took the interior underground route to his apartment. Normally, he preferred to walk back through the upper gardens, but today he wanted to use all his time to search his father's room. He had the feeling he was hiding something from him, and he had to find out what. Inside the apartment, he hung a bag on the doorknob on the inside. He opened the door, and the bag fell on the floor, making enough noise to warn him if his father returned home. He put the bag back on the doorknob and rushed to his father's bedroom.

It had been a long time since he had been in there. They respected each other's privacy, and he barely ever entered his father's room. It was neat and everything was arranged perfectly. Next to the bed there was a desk, and on three walls all around there were built-in storage cabinets. He figured to take a systematic approach and to go from left to right through all the cabinets and then search the bed and the desk.

The first cabinet he opened had only underwear in it. All the undergarments were perfectly folded, and he took the piles out of the cabinet. He looked behind the piles and in between the clothes. Then he carefully put back the piles in the cabinet and made sure it looked exactly as before. His father had eyes like a hawk and he would notice immediately if something had been moved, so he had to be extremely careful.

His search continued for about an hour until, behind several boxes with socks, he found a closed black box. He lifted it out of the cabinet. It was heavy. He posed it on the desk and opened the lid. To his surprise, there was a black handgun in it. During his trip to the outside, he had noticed that some guards at the climate plants were carrying similar handguns. Elias had explained that they were high-tech handguns that were able to fire laser beams, special bullets or even taser someone. Apparently, his father had one of those guns in his bedroom. He knew nobody inside the dome who owned any weapon. Somehow it did not surprise him that much, since his dad was in charge of defense in the dome.

Elliot took the gun out of the box and held it in his hand. It gave him a strange feeling of power, and he aimed it at the mirror in the corner. After making a shooting gesture in the air, he put it back inside. He closed the box and placed it back in the cabinet. Then he put the baskets with socks in front of it. He continued until he heard some footsteps in the hall in front of the door. His heart skipped a beat, and he immediately closed the cabinet he had just opened. He rushed into the corridor, but then he heard how the footsteps continued further. He checked the time. It was the end of the afternoon and more people were returning home. He should be really careful now.

About two-thirds of the cabinets he had searched and still he had not found what he was looking for. He continued until, at some point, he found a box behind some shoes. It looked like a shoe box, but it felt heavier. He opened it and it was filled with photos. One by one, he started looking at them. Most of the pictures were from his childhood. He remembered how his mother liked to print photos and hang them on the walls. His father had removed most of them from the wall after her death and he thought he had thrown them away, but apparently, he had kept them in this box.

His mother looked so beautiful. No surprise his father had fallen for her. He remembered her as a warm and kind person, always interested in people and in their well-being. After seeing several photos of him with his mother, he got tears in his eyes. He saw in another picture how his mother was holding him as a baby in her arms and his father had his arms around her. What struck him was that his father looked so much happier at the time. Since her death, his dad had changed, and he was often grumpy and distant. Most of the pictures were inside the dome or inside the apartment, but at the bottom of the box, he found a brown envelope with more photos. These he had never seen before. On one of them, his mother was standing next to his father, who was carrying Elliot in a baby carrier in front of his chest, and they were standing in front of the dome.

Suddenly, he heard footsteps again, but this time closer than before. With adrenaline rushing through his body, he immediately put the photos back in the box and placed it back in the cabinet. He felt cold sweat on his hands when he heard the sports bag fall on the ground when the front door opened. No way he would make it back to the living room unnoticed.

"Elliot? I'm home! Where are you?"

Elliot looked at his father's desk and grabbed a pen from his desk.

"I'm here. I was looking for a pen," he replied to his father as he walked out of his bedroom.

His father looked puzzled at him, but then continued.

"I was thinking to cook my Biryani dish for you tonight, would you like that?"

"Sounds good. How did it go on the outside today? I thought you would come home later today?"

"Well, it was just a first test of the system. We designed a system where we drill graphene bars in the soil up to fifteen meters deep. We placed a sensor on each bar that automatically warns us when something touches the bar. Whenever this happens, we have a large robot digging a hole in the breached area, exposing the intruders, and then our drones take care of them. The test worked perfectly, and they'll install those bars in between the outer and the inner wall all around. This will take a few weeks."

"Wow! Sounds sophisticated."

"It is, but our intruders are also getting more and more sophisticated, so we have to stay a step ahead of them."

Elliot continued to his bedroom and put the pen on his desk. Then he helped his father preparing dinner. Slowly he started relaxing as he had the impression his father suspected nothing. He would have to continue his search another day.

56.

Through the twilight, Elizabeth and Dylan flew at high speed inland with the air taxi they had ordered in the hotel. Around Nuuk there had been many houses with lights on, but over here the landscape below them was dark. The estimated flight time was one hour, and Dylan had seen no lights below them for at least half an hour now. He put his arm around Elizabeth while they peered at the horizon through the darkness. It always gave him a strange feeling to fly in a pilotless air taxi, but here in the dark it was even more mysterious. Besides the humming noise above their head from the propellers, there was no other noise.

A while later, he noticed some tiny lights on the horizon, exactly at the same time as Elizabeth, who pointed with her finger.

"Look! Lights!"

"Yes, I guess we must arrive soon. It has almost been one hour since we left."

The air taxi flew relatively low and slowly they distinguished houses in front of them. Then they noticed a huge dark shadow behind the houses extending on the left and right as far as they could see.

Suddenly, they heard through the loudspeaker,

"We will land at the Narmik Inn in five minutes. Prepare for landing!"

Dylan pointed at the dark shadow.

"I guess that must be the wall the man from the tourist information was talking about. It's huge! I wonder what there's behind this wall."

Elizabeth nodded and then grinned.

"Yeah, me too. Let's try to find out!" and then she raised her head toward the ceiling of the air taxi.

"Could you please fly us over that wall behind those houses?"

"Negative. I can't approach the wall as it marks the no-fly zone."

"No-fly zone? What the hell is that?" he looked puzzled at Elizabeth.

The air taxi started descending, and they both looked down at the large red house they were approaching. Light shone off the windows, and they noticed a sign hanging in front of the door. The air taxi landed on the street right in front of it. Now they could read the blue sign on with the yellow letters.

"We've landed at the Narmik Inn. We hope you have enjoyed your flight with us. Press the button on the door when you're ready to step outside."

They both put on their respos and then he pushed the button. The doors opened. The street was empty, and the air was fresh, and further down the street, they noticed the wall towering above the village.

"It looks about ten meters high. Surreal!" Elizabeth said as they both looked at the enormous wall.

"Yeah, what a strange sight. Let's go inside. I'm sure they can tell us more about it."

He opened the front door for her, and they heard voices and music inside. After passing through the double door, they entered the Inn, which had a lively atmosphere and was full of people at the tables and at the bar. Elizabeth turned her head to look at Dylan.

"Thank God we made a reservation."

A bearded, tall man behind the bar noticed them and raised his voice.

"Welcome to the Narmik Inn! My name's Inuk. What can I do for you?"

"Hi, we've made a reservation under the name Muller."

The man checked a screen behind the bar and said something to the woman next to him. He gestured them to follow him and he disappeared through a door in the back. They followed him. In the corridor behind the door, it was much calmer. He continued up a staircase.

"Your room is on the second floor. Here's your keycard. I'll show you the way."

"Thanks, you've quite a lot of people today!"

"Yeah, it's always busy here. We're the only proper restaurant in Narmik, but there's a small snack bar and a supermarket further down the road."

Inuk opened the room for them, and Dylan asked him.

"We came here because we heard about the dome."

"Ha! Why am I not surprised? Most of the guests are here for the dome, but I'll have to disappoint you. Not that you can visit it or something."

"But it exists?"

"Well, I never saw it with my own eyes, but one of my guests showed me some distant images one time, so I guess it exists if those images were real."

"We asked our air taxi to fly over the wall on the north side of Narmik, but it responded that it's not allowed to fly over it since it marks the no-fly zone. Do you know what that's all about?"

Inuk grinned and responded,

"That's what I'm saying. You can't visit the dome. The entire area behind the wall is restricted, private property. You can't fly over the area, not even our government can fly over it."

"Did people try to fly over it?"

"Some people flew drones over the wall and they never returned. One of the hotel guests once tried to fly over the wall himself and we never saw him again."

"What happens on the other side of the wall, then?"

"I don't know what happened to this person, but someone showed me the video footage of a drone that flew over it once. All I saw was a big flash and then the contact was lost. I believe they've some kind of fancy drone security system. I still have the man's luggage in a storage room, but he never returned."

"Wow! Quite a mystery. Any idea who's the owner of this private property?"

"No, I don't know. I'm sorry, but I'll have to go back down now. Breakfast is from eight till ten in the morning and the restaurant is open until eleven o'clock in the evening. If you need anything, just dial zero. I hope you enjoy your stay."

"Thanks."

Elizabeth looked out of the window and she saw the dark shade of the massive wall at the end of the street. Dylan put his arm around her and they both looked outside in the darkness and he said,

"What a strange place this is."

"Yes, mysterious. Maybe we should take the photo of your birth parents with us and ask around if anybody has seen them?"

They went downstairs and ordered a drink in the bar. First, he showed the photo of his parents to Inuk, who was behind the bar.

"Have you seen these people around here? They're called Vikram and Tanvi Singh and were probably transported to the dome about twenty-four years ago."

He looked at it and shook his head. Then he showed the picture to the woman behind the bar, but she also shook her head.

"I'm sorry, never seen them."

Dylan felt he had to try it, even though it felt like a longshot. He looked at Elizabeth and pointed at the only free table in the back.

"Why don't you go sit over there? I'm just going to go around showing the photo to those people and then I'll join you."

She nodded and walked to the table while he continued showing the photo to the guests in the restaurant. They all looked at it, but none of them recognized his parents. Then he joined Elizabeth.

As they sipped their drink, they overheard a young man with red hair at the table next to them.

"Tonight, I'm going to try my new suit. I'm sure it will work! I'll stream everything live, so you can follow and see the images of the dome the moment I see it…"

Dylan immediately reacted.

"You're going to the dome?"

"Yes! Tonight, I'll climb over the wall. You want to come and watch as well? I can send you the link to my video stream."

Dylan gave his details and he send him the link. At the same time, Inuk passed and told the red-haired man,

"You're going through with your plans? You're a fool!" after which he walked away, clearly upset.

57.

The rest of the day, Elizabeth and Dylan spent their time walking through the tiny village. Whenever they ran into someone, they showed them the photo, but nobody had seen his birth parents. They asked at the local police station, but they had no records of his birth parents. After that Dylan asked the police officer about the dome and he answered while he sighed.

"Every year we've a lot of visitors from abroad asking about it. These tourists are good for our local economy, although there're many crazy people who try to climb over the wall. Most of them never return."

"Do the police not search for those missing persons on the other side of the wall?"

"No, we don't have any jurisdiction inside the walled area. Our government has instructed us to prevent people from entering this area, and we are not allowed to enter this area ourselves. It's a forbidden zone. I believe it's some secret military base. Nobody is allowed to enter, and the airspace above it is a no-fly zone. This secrecy feeds speculation, and I guess that's how this myth about this dome got created. Just like what happened in the United States with Area Fifty-one. You will always have weirdos who believe in those things. Like you have many people believing in UFOs."

They left the police station slightly disillusioned and returned to the Inn. Back in their room, Dylan checked the internet and checked out a website giving access to satellite images from all over the world.

He entered Narmik in the search bar and dumbfounded called Elizabeth.

"Come and look! I looked up Narmik on this satellite map software and look over here."

She stared at the screen while he showed her Narmik and then zoomed out. A large circle north of Narmik had been blurred on the map.

"Wow, look at the size of that blurred area! It must be over ten by ten kilometers. It looks like a circle. Maybe that's where the dome myth comes from," she said with a look of amazement.

"Myth? Please, you're not going to believe those stories, are you? I showed you the documents we found in my parent's penthouse. It said clearly in one that they were going to be escorted to the dome, so I don't think it is a myth," he said, agitated.

"I didn't mean it like that. I'm just trying to keep an open mind. Anyway, I'm hungry. Shall we go for dinner?"

"Okay."

The restaurant was almost full. Luckily, Elizabeth had reserved a table. There was a photo of an older man on the wall next to their table. Elizabeth looked at it from up-close for a moment.

"This man resembles the owner of the Inn, doesn't he?"

He took a closer look and shrugged his shoulders.

"Could be… let's check out the menu!"

They sat down and saw an older gray man wearing a dark blue jacket in the corner looking at them. Dylan looked away. At some point, Inuk arrived at their table to take the order. Elizabeth looked at him and asked,

"I noticed this photo on the wall and the man resembles you."

Inuk smiled.

"That's my father. He opened this inn more than sixty years ago."

This triggered something in Dylan and he asked,

"Sixty years ago? He must know more about this dome and this wall, then?"

Inuk hesitated for a moment before responding.

"Well, he was there when they constructed this damned wall. He never saw the dome either, but he used to help people who tried to penetrate the forbidden zone. I even believe that's why he got killed. Although I could never prove it."

"What happened to him?" Elizabeth asked, astonished.

"One day he didn't come back from a walk and I went to look for him. I found him close to the gate. They had shot him in the chest with some kind of laser gun. The police never found the culprit."

"Oh, I'm sorry," she said, when Dylan asked abruptly,

"There's a gate on the wall?"

"Yes, about five kilometers east from here. There's a large double gate in the wall."

"Has anyone ever seen people go in or out?"

"I once saw several large trucks drive inside. It looked like military transport to me. Anyway, enough about this horrible wall. What can I get you?"

While Inuk took their order, Dylan had the impression that the man in the corner in the dark blue jacket was following their conversation. He looked away when he looked at him. Dylan checked his phone. Elizabeth looked slightly annoyed, and he said apologetically,

"Sorry. I just wanted to check at what time this red-haired guy we saw earlier today was going to climb the wall. I checked the link he sent me, but I can't see when he's going to try."

"I guess he cannot really announce it, since otherwise the police might stop him."

"Yeah, probably. I changed the settings and now I'll get a warning when the video stream starts…ah, there's our dinner!"

They enjoyed their dinner and ordered some dessert. After that, they took some tea and saw it was getting late already. They noticed more and more people left. He felt his phone vibrating. The video stream had started. It was all dark on the stream and they could see nothing. He put the volume higher, and they heard someone panting. Now the older guy in the dark blue jacket got up and left.

"I think we should go outside. Maybe we can see more there," Dylan said.

It was colder and very dark outside. The streets were illuminated, and they walked behind some people. At the wall there were no lights, and it was pitch dark. Slowly their eyes adjusted and with the light from the moon and the stars, they could distinguish some vague shapes. They followed some younger people who were walking along the wall westwards until they arrived at a large group of people, all looking upwards. Dylan and Elizabeth also looked up, but they could not see anything.

"You can barely see him, since he has this special suit," a voice in the darkness told them.

It was the older man with the dark-blue jacket from the Inn.

"What's special about his suit?" Dylan asked him curiously.

"He made some suit out of a special black material that absorbs around ninety-five percent of the light. He's hardly visible, even with night-vision. Here you can try my night-vision goggles."

He looked through the goggles and looked at the wall, but he could still not see the man.

"I can't see him, but maybe I'm looking at the wrong spot."

"Here, come closer to the wall and look up."

The man guided him toward the wall, and when he touched the wall, he looked up. Now he saw a dark shadow sticking out from the wall against the star-lit sky, but he could not see any movement.

"Yes, I see a dark shadow on the wall. Here, Elizabeth, have a look!"

He handed the goggles to her, and then he stretched his hand out to the man.

"Thanks, I'm Dylan Myers and this is Elizabeth."

"Nice to meet you both. I'm Jim Richards."

Some people around them were indicating they should be quiet. Jim whispered to them,

"I think he's almost at the top. We have to be silent now."

Everybody looked up, and suddenly they heard a noise like someone was using some kind of spray. They saw some faint fluorescent light on the wall, in the form of a horizontal line. The dark shadow was standing on the wall, and he stepped over the fluorescent line. A moment later, the shadow disappeared. People around them all started staring at their phones. Dylan took his phone out as well and looked at the live stream together with Elizabeth. He increased the volume, but all they could hear was someone panting lightly and some whooshing sound.

After a while, they heard footsteps and some people around him whispered,

"I think he has arrived on the ground on the other side."

The sound of footsteps continued, and they heard his breathing for almost five minutes until they heard a buzzing noise. They saw that the man looked up at the starlit sky and suddenly there was a loud burst and the whole screen lit up. Nothing after, and a message showed up on the screen.

"Connection lost."

It caused some consternation around the other people.

"Poor fellow! It only worked for a moment," Jim said.

"What happened? What worked only for a moment?" Dylan asked him.

"Why don't we go back to the Inn and we talk over some drinks? It's getting chilly here."

"All right. Good idea."

They walked back with Jim while he explained what just had happened.

"The red-haired man who just died was called Rick Young. I spoke with him on several occasions. Rick figured he found a way to cross the plains behind the wall without getting noticed by the drones. Apparently, his suit was not good enough. We know they equipped the drones with normal and special cameras with night vision and infrared."

"Infrared as well?"

"Yes, and I believe that it probably went wrong there. I had asked him last week how his suit worked and he explained about the blackness and how it would not reflect light so the night vision camera would not detect him. The infrared was a much bigger challenge. Rick explained how he had developed a suit with a cooling function. The outside temperature would counterbalance the body temperature and make him undetectable."

"How did he do that? I mean, that must be quite difficult since he exhales constantly. His breath is warmer than the air around him and would probably get detected. Or did he have a solution for that?"

"That's a good question. I asked him and he explained to me that the exhaled air would pass through his cooled suit."

"Did he test the suit thoroughly before? I can image the effectiveness could be different during physical effort."

"I don't really know, but climbing the wall and walking must have increased his body temperature a lot and probably that's how the drones detected him," Jim responded while they entered the Inn and sat down at a table in the back.

"And what was this faint fluorescent light I noticed?"

"There's some kind of laser detection system on top of the wall. If something interrupts the light, it triggers an alarm. Rick used some special fluorescent spray to make the laser beam visible. This way, he could carefully step over it without breaking the light stream."

"Smart! Although not smart enough, since he got detected later on."

"It's sad to see these young people trying and dying," Jim sighed.

"You mean there were more like him?" Elizabeth asked.

"Yes, several people have tried over the years. Almost all died trying, although some simply never came back and nobody knows if they succeeded or not in reaching the dome."

Inuk came to the table to take their order. He listened to their conversation and asked, clearly annoyed.

"Did that red-head go over the wall?"

"Yes, poor soul. He didn't make it far."

"Pfff… well, I guess I'll empty his room then and add his backpack to the pile in the storage room. Soon I'll need more space. Anyway, sorry about that. What can I get you?"

He took their order and walked back to the bar. Dylan asked Jim as soon as Inuk was far enough,

"There're so many people that have tried?"

"Yes, this year alone, more than twenty already, and I probably missed a few."

Elizabeth looked puzzled and asked,

"If I may ask, Jim. How come you know so much about all this?"

Jim grinned and moved in his seat. Inuk came with the drinks and he waited for him to leave before answering.

"Well, that's a long story."

58.

Jim explained he was a reporter. A young man had approached him last year and told him about the dome. At first, he did not believe the story, but the man provided him with some video footage and this triggered his curiosity. He worked at The Times in London at the time. He convinced the managing editor to investigate the story, and soon after, he made his first trip to Narmik in Greenland.

There, he investigated the rumors about the dome and interviewed the villagers and the people who visited the village. People from all over the world regularly visited because they were curious about the myth of the dome. Some of them attempted to reach it. Dylan and Elizabeth listened with fascination to his story. Jim had met people who had sent drones over the wall to get a glimpse of the dome, but also people like Rick, who were courageous and foolish enough to climb over it. Jim explained passionately.

"I was still naïve at the time, and I didn't realize quick enough that I was stirring up a hornet's nest. I had found nothing online and believed I was onto some major scoop. I published an article in my weekly column for The Times. A day later, I arrived at the office expecting compliments from my boss. Instead, I found out that they had taken my article offline. They summoned me to the managing editor at once, and he told me they had to let me go. I asked him why and he could only tell me it was a decision from higher up and that he felt sorry. If he would have known, he would have warned me. I never really understood who was behind all this, but I realized at some point that there was no information at all online about the dome, nor about the people who went missing after trying to get over this wall."

"Yes, that also struck me. I couldn't find a thing online," Dylan said.

"I believe there're some powerful people trying to keep the existence of this dome secret, and they got me fired. Luckily, I found a new job as a reporter for the Arctic News and I moved to Nuuk. Once I suggested to my boss to do some article on the dome and he told me that they could not cover this topic. When I asked him why, he told me to stop asking or he would have to let me go."

"Amazing! But what are you doing over here then?" Elizabeth asked.

"I guess that is the journalist in me. I just can't let it go. I'm here in my spare time. Most of my holidays I spend over here investigating. The topic is simply too fascinating. Anyway, enough about me. What brought you two over here?"

They explained how they had searched for Dylan's birth parents and how they had ended up here. Jim was very interested in the documents they had found, and they invited him to their room to have a look at them on Dylan's laptop. After scanning through the documents, Jim looked at Dylan.

"It seems that they transported your parents to the dome right after they had finished its construction. The outer wall was constructed twenty-eight years ago, and they probably constructed the dome after that. I found more evidence of people who moved to the dome in the same year as your parents. Strangely enough, I found no evidence of people moving in the years after."

"I'm convinced my parents live inside this dome."

"You could be right, since I have found indications that many people moved in the same year and never came back."

"Where did you find all this information, Jim?" Dylan asked, intrigued.

"Well, since I lost my job because of it, I became even more intrigued by the dome. I applied for jobs in Greenland and I came back here to talk to people. I started asking people where they had heard about this dome, and one day someone showed me how to access the Darknet."

"The Darknet? I thought that was for criminals?" Elizabeth said, surprised.

"Yes, the Darknet is like an overlay network within the internet. This encrypted network can only be accessed using a unique customized communication protocol. The Darknet is actively used for illegal activities by criminals, but I also found that some people posted information about the dome there. Contrary to the general internet, the information here is not automatically removed. I can show you on your computer how to access it if you like?"

Dylan nodded and handed his computer to Jim, and he started installing some software on it.

"I use a special software to divert the access points so it's more difficult to be traced, and then I use another software application to access the Darknet. Everything is installed now. I'll show you how it works."

He typed some more on the laptop and then he turned the screen toward Elizabeth and Dylan.

"We're on it now. I use this special browser to search. I'll demonstrate it by looking up a post."

Jim typed the words "tunnel" and "dome" in the search bar, and it showed several results. He clicked one of them.

"This is a post I placed on it under an alias. It's about two men I interviewed last month. They tried to reach the dome by digging a tunnel under the wall. First, I didn't really take it seriously, but later I understood from Inuk that someone in the village had seen them passing with a truck with professional drilling equipment on it. They took me to the shed outside the village one evening and showed me how they had started drilling under the wall. There had been other people in the past who had dug tunnels, but these two men were planning to dig one longer than anyone else ever had done. They were aiming to dig over a length of over seven kilometers, which they estimated would get them under the second wall."

"The second wall? You mean there's another one?" Dylan interrupted Jim.

"Yes, let me show you a drawing I got from them."

Jim scrolled down in the article and showed them a drawing on the screen.

"Apparently about seven kilometers behind the wall you saw today, there's another one."

"How did they know about the second wall? I mean, seven kilometers is quite far," Elizabeth asked.

"I asked them the same question and they had found video footage from previous attempts from other people. Apparently, some guy had flown in a turbojet pack at a height of almost one kilometer. The drones shot him out of the sky as soon as he crossed over the outer wall, but on the live stream video footage from the camera on the jetpack, they had seen the dome and the second wall in front of it. They had analyzed the video footage and calculated that the distance between the two walls is more than seven kilometers. I should be able to find this video again."

Jim searched on the Darknet and after a while he found a video post. He showed it to Elizabeth and Dylan.

"Look here in the back, it goes quick and it's difficult to see."

They stared at the screen and suddenly Dylan pointed.

"Ah, there! I see something looking like a dome and I guess that stripe in front of it's the wall then!?"

"Exactly, I know it's not very clear, and only a glimpse, but this is what they showed me at the time."

"Amazing! What happened to the two men and their tunnel?" Elizabeth said as she glanced at the screen.

"They went missing. I returned to their shed, but they were not there. The hole in the ground to access the tunnel had been filled up with concrete, and there was no trace of the equipment or any of their belongings. It was like someone had cleaned out the place. They did not post much on the Darknet, but there're quite some other people who did."

"Why do these people risk their lives to get to the dome?" Elizabeth asked, puzzled.

"Different reasons. Some are just curious or sensation seekers. Some of them believe the dome is like a paradise on earth where they could live safely, protected against the destructive forces unleashed by climate change. Others are looking for missing relatives. Just like you are."

Dylan had continued reading the articles on his laptop, while Jim answered Elisabeth. He looked up and with a sparkle in his eyes he said, "This is really interesting stuff, Jim!"

"Just make sure to use this diversion software. You can't be careful enough. It's getting late. I'm going to sleep. I guess I'll see you tomorrow?"

"See you tomorrow, Jim, and thanks for your help!"

Jim left the room. Dylan continued searching the Darknet, while Elizabeth brushed her teeth. The more he read about all the attempts and about the dome, the more convinced he became. Although he was worried about her reaction to his plan.

59.

S he snapped at Dylan, clearly upset about his announcement, while she nervously paced up and down through the hotel room.

"You want to do what? Are you crazy? You're going to get killed for sure! Didn't you listen yesterday? None of those people returned, and we've seen on several videos what happened to them. Those drones shot them to pieces."

Dylan had expected she would not be happy with his decision, but he had never seen her so agitated. He understood her worry, and he tried explaining it again.

"Please, Elizabeth. I won't go if I'm not a hundred percent convinced it will work, but I think there might be a way to get to the dome safely. It's just that I have to try. I feel that I've no other choice."

"Of course you do! You always have. This obsessive search for your birth parents is getting completely out of control."

"Please, you know how important this is for me."

"I know, but I don't want to lose you like that and I'm sure your birth parents won't be happy when they find out their son died trying to get to them."

"I'm not going to die. I'm not crazy! I just want to explore if I can find a way to get to the dome alive. I promise you I won't try to go there if I'm not a hundred percent sure that I'll get there alive."

"How can you promise something like that? You can never really be sure. How are you thinking of getting past those two walls alive, anyway?"

"I don't know yet. I see several possibilities, but I'll have to do much more research to check if it's possible. It's not like I would try tomorrow. This could take quite some time preparing, and if I don't find a safe way to get to the dome, I won't go! Okay?"

"That sounds nice, but even if you think it could work, there could still be something new you didn't anticipate. I'm sure those people who have died trying were convinced it would work."

"All right, let's just explore the possibilities and if I can't convince you, then I won't risk it."

"Well, I guess I can't stop you from exploring the possibilities."

She still didn't look convinced, but she seemed to calm down a bit. The day before they had discussed together that they would walk around the wall to check out the gate. After breakfast, he had mentioned his plan to try to get to the dome, and they had been fighting ever since. It was getting lighter outside, and they had to go now if they wanted to profit from the few hours of daylight. They stopped arguing and agreed to go for the walk.

Outside it was gray weather. They walked toward the wall with their respos on. There they continued walking eastwards, like Inuk had indicated. It was light, but it was as if the sun had gotten stuck low on the horizon and it would not go much higher. Soon it would set again. After walking for almost an hour, they suddenly noticed the gate. It was as high as the wall itself and made of some kind of solid metal. There were several glass hemispherical bowls on both sides of the double gate.

"Look, there are probably cameras inside those bowls, but for the rest I don't see any doorbell or guard post anywhere."

"Yeah, strange. Looking at the weeds in front of the gate, it must have been a long time since someone passed through here."

"These cameras are good news."

"Why?" Elizabeth asked, puzzled.

"Well, it suggests there are people behind this wall."

Dylan knocked on the gate, and then he picked up a heavy stone and threw it against it. After the loud bang, Elizabeth glanced at him with a baffled look on her face.

"Are you having fun?"

"Just wanted to check what would happen. It looks very solid. I wonder if someone ever tried to drive through it with a heavy truck or something."

"You should ask Jim. Maybe he knows. Shall we go back? I would prefer to be at the Inn before it gets dark."

They walked back to Narmik along the towering wall. He felt small next to it and while walking; he wondered how to prepare for his attempt. Back in the Inn they joined Jim at his table and ordered some drinks. He seemed happy to see them and they talked about their walk. Jim explained that a couple he met several months ago had mountain biked all around the wall, and apparently there was another gate on the other side.

"Did someone ever try to ram through the gate with a truck or a car?" Dylan asked, eager to know more.

"I have seen a short movie on the Darknet once, where some guy rammed into the gate with a heavy tank truck filled with water. The whole truck's cabin was squashed together. The driver died instantly and they towed the truck away. The gate had not moved an inch and only had some scratches. I believe there's some special reinforced construction behind."

"Mmm, that's another option deleted from the list," Dylan mumbled.

"You're considering trying to get to the dome yourself?" Jim asked, astounded, and then looked at Elizabeth.

"Don't look at me! I think it's crazy to even think about it," Elizabeth said, dismayed.

"Well, I'm not sure I'll do it, but I'm going to explore the possibilities. I believe it's the only way to find my birth parents," Dylan responded calmly.

"Interesting! Let me help you assess the different possibilities. It would be nice if someone would succeed for a change," Jim offered.

They continued talking about all the possible ways for hours, and during the conversation, Dylan got another idea. He waved at Inuk and when he arrived at their table, he asked him,

"Inuk, I remember you told me yesterday that you have a storage room where you keep all the belongings from your missing guests."

"Yes, I keep everything in the back."

"Could I have a look?"

"I don't know Dylan. It's more for relatives or for the owners of the luggage."

"I'm sure we can work something out."

Dylan got his wallet out and smiled at Inuk.

They spent the rest of the afternoon going through all the backpacks and suitcases in the storage room. Dylan figured that all those people who had tried to get to the dome must have prepared their attempts carefully. They looked on smartphones, laptops and went through all documents they could find. They copied all electronic files on a memory stick and scanned the interesting documents. Jim helped them go through all the luggage and also got a copy of everything. They thanked Inuk afterwards and since it was their last evening in Narmik, Jim invited them for dinner.

At dinner, they agreed to stay in touch and exchange ideas. Jim was impressed with Dylan's determination and agreed to help him out as much as he could. Elizabeth was still disconcerted by his plans, but his promise to involve her in the final decision had calmed things down. The next morning, they said goodbye to Jim and Inuk and got in the air taxi that was waiting for them in front of the Inn. When it lifted off, Dylan glanced one more time at the wall in the twilight. He caught a glimpse of the flat plains behind it when they gained altitude. Shortly thereafter, the air taxi sped up in the southwest direction toward Nuuk. Dylan peered at the horizon as the wall disappeared out of sight, wondering if he would ever see the other side of it.

60.

Several days after his interrupted search of his father's bedroom, Elliot saw another opportunity to leave his work earlier in the afternoon and to continue. His father had told him he probably would be home late that day and that he did not have to wait for him for dinner. Elliot asked Elias in the morning if he could leave earlier that day. Unfortunately, Elias insisted he finished a report before leaving, and it took him more time than expected. At five o'clock, he arrived home. He drank some water and then opened the door to his father's bedroom.

This time, he was less nervous as he started going through his father's belongings. The previous time he had searched two-thirds of the cabinets and he recalled he had not looked at all the photos in the brown envelope he had found in the box in one of the cabinets. He grabbed the box and took out the envelope. One by one, he looked at the photos. On one of them, he saw a crowd inside the gardens of the dome. His father and mother were posing in front of it. He was sitting in the baby carrier his father had strapped around him. He recognized Elias with his family next to them. In the back he saw a stage with a large table with what looked like The Council sitting behind it.

There were many other pictures taken inside or in front of the dome. In another picture, he saw himself sitting on his mother's lap and she was holding him tight inside what looked like a large bus. In the background, he noticed the wall he had seen outside. It was taking him quite some time to go through the pile of photos, but it gave him a good feeling as he realized how happy his parents must have been. This puzzled him, since it made it even more difficult to understand why his mother had taken her own life.

At some point, he finished looking at the photos and put them all back where he had found them. He continued going through the remaining cabinets, but found nothing interesting. He started searching through his father's desk. In the top drawer, he saw several keys in between some pens and other writing tools. He inspected the keys but could not figure out what they could be for. He found lots of papers in the bottom drawer with what looked like work-related documents. He went through all the paperwork one-by-one, hoping to find some letter from his mother or something else explaining her suicide. He looked at the clock and realized it was getting late.

The only place he had not searched yet was his father's bed and the nightstand next to it. First, he looked under the bed. Subsequently, he opened the drawer of the nightstand and the moment he looked inside, he heard the front door slam. His heart started pounding in his chest. His father had come back already. In a rush, he closed the drawer and moved back to the desk. The papers from the drawer were still on it. He grabbed them and tried to push them back in.

"What are you doing in my room?"

Elliot did not know what to say and muttered, "Uh…I…I was…"

"Why are you going through my stuff?"

"…uh, I…I…"

Amos looked unamused and stared him deep in the eyes. A silence fell as his father waited for an explanation.

"I… I'm sorry, but since you never answer my questions, I started looking for answers myself. I'm sorry to disappoint you," he answered while he glanced at the floor, too afraid to look him in the eyes.

His father sighed deeply and a long silence fell until he spoke.

"I know you've questions about your mother's death, but you've to understand it's very difficult for me to talk about it."

He noticed a tear appearing in the corner of his father's eye, and he gave him a hug.

"I understand it's difficult for you, but I want to understand better."

"All right, let's sit down in the living and I'll try to answer your questions."

They sat down on the couch. His father looked sad and down.

"So, what would you like to know?"

"What I don't understand is why mom committed suicide? We have this privileged chance to live inside this dome, while the rest of the world has to live in a harsh and polluted world. We were together as a family, so why would she kill herself? I don't get it."

His father sighed again and looked down. Elliot noticed his hands were trembling.

"Your mother… well… it was not so easy for her to come and live in this dome. Initially, she wasn't so sure she wanted to live here. I mean, leaving behind our previous life outside the dome was not so easy…"

His father hesitated and was clearly nervous.

"… I guess I put quite some pressure on her to come here. I know I can be like a steamroller with people sometimes. If I decide something, I go for it. Your mother found it hard to live inside the dome…"

All of a sudden, his father's phone rang and broke the tense atmosphere. He responded immediately.

"Hello?"

"Yes, okay. An intruder? Why do you call me for that?"

"Ah, I see. That's exceptional, yes. You did right to call me. I'll be right over."

Elliot felt his hope sinking. Not again, he thought. Amos hung up and got up.

"I'm really sorry, but I've got to go to the front guard post. Something alarming has happened. I'll be back as soon as possible and then we'll continue our conversation, okay?"

"Okay, I guess," Elliot responded, doubting his father would really continue his explanation later on. It was not the first time he avoided the topic like this.

61.

Back in Ikast, they got back into their usual work rhythm, and for a while Elizabeth thought Dylan had forgotten about his daring and dangerous plan. Life had returned to normal, and she started feeling better. She had digested the dreadful ordeal she had gone through in New York and realized how lucky she had been to come out unharmed. They had not talked about Dylan's plan to reach the dome anymore since their trip to Nuuk, which had been several weeks ago.

He worked long hours at the Environmental Technology Division, and in the evening, often talked enthusiastically about the solar chimney power plant they were working on. One evening, he arrived late at home again. At least he warned her now every time, so she did not have to wait in vain for him for dinner. Dylan heated up the meal she had left for him, and she kept him company in the kitchen. He must have been starving, because he walked back to the stove to refill his plate.

While he was with his back to her, his phone buzzed a few times. She saw the screen lighting up and, to her surprise, noticed a message from Jim popping up. He turned to check his phone, and she stared at him.

"You're in contact with Jim?"

"Uh… yes," he answered.

She looked surprised at him, and on purpose, she let a long silence fall. He got visibly uncomfortable and muttered,

"Well, in Narmik we agreed to stay in touch with him, right?"

"I know, but this is the first time in weeks we've talked about him. How long have you been exchanging messages with him?"

"Since we left Narmik," he responded nervously, and looked away.

"Why didn't you tell me?"

"I don't know. I guess because you were so against my plan to try to get to the dome."

"But you promised to involve me in the decision to go or not?" she looked annoyed at him.

"Yes, I did, and I was planning to, but I thought it would be better to work on the preliminary ideas first before talking about them."

Another silence fell, and he looked at her, uncomfortable with the whole situation.

"I'm sorry, okay? I realize it was wrong."

She looked at his face and couldn't really stay upset.

"Okay, but from now on, you involve me. Agreed?"

"Yes."

"So, tell me, what ideas you've been working on?"

"Initially, I started with a long list and I've been working on them to assess which one has the highest chance of success. Last week, I still had three options left. The first is what I call 'invisible suit'. The second is the idea of digging a tunnel, and the third was to fly with a heavy armored helicopter at high altitude over the walls and descend above the dome."

He paused to take a bite of his food while she sipped her tea.

"The third idea I killed this week after I found out someone had tried that already. I figured it would be difficult for the drones to shoot down a heavily armored helicopter, but I found a video on the Darknet of someone who tried something similar. Apparently, next to the drone security, there's also a very heavy air defense system.

The helicopter got shot out of the sky by a missile. And a few years ago, they shot down a plane that passed at a height of ten kilometers. No, this no-fly zone is a tightly controlled airspace."

"And the two remaining ideas?" she asked eagerly.

"Yesterday, the tunnel idea got killed. Jim called me after he had spoken with a man in Narmik, who had tried to dig a tunnel like the two men had tried before. He had bought similar equipment. He stayed behind, while his brother went into the tunnel after the drilling equipment had gotten stuck a couple of hundred meters behind the wall. His brother phoned him over the wired phone he had taken into the tunnel and told him they had hit some kind of strong metal bars. A moment later, he heard his brother scream, followed by a loud explosion, and that was the last he heard from him. The man freaked out and rushed out of the shed. Just in time, apparently, since shortly afterwards, he observed from a distance how several vehicles stopped at the shed. It looks like the people inside the dome installed bars to impede tunnels to be dug."

"That leaves only your 'invisible suit' idea," she concluded.

"Exactly. I studied all the files we found in the storage room at the Inn. I learned a lot about the drone security system, which uses ordinary cameras, but also night-vision cameras combined with infrared. Night-vision basically uses an image intensifier tube to amplify exiting light. The faintest light becomes detectable this way. Rick, the red-haired guy, tried to tackle this with his special black suit and by going in the darkest of the night. The infrared measures the radiation. Basically, the heat emitted from objects measured relative to their surroundings. He tried to tackle that by cooling his suit with an air fan."

"Why did he still got shot down then?"

"That's exactly what puzzled me from the start. I studied all his design drawings and specifications. I believe the whole design can be improved significantly, but his biggest mistake was the cooling system. He used a constant air-cooling system, and that would have worked fine if the heat he emitted would have been constant. He cooled the heat of his body through his suit and the heat from his breathing, he redirected into his suit where it would get cooled. I guess he must have tested it in stable conditions where his heat did not fluctuate that much. That was his mistake. Climbing the wall and the added stress must have produced much more heat than expected, too much for his cooling system, which didn't adapt to it and that was the end of him."

"Poor guy! Sounds like this suit isn't such a good idea either."

"His suit maybe, but I think mine will be much better without those flaws. I believe I can improve it significantly."

"How are you planning to do that?"

"With a long list of improvements, but two major ones. First, I'm working on a new design for the cooling system to make it adapt automatically to the heat produced and ensuring that the external temperature of the suit stays equal to the temperature of its surroundings. Second, I'll increase the blackness of the suit significantly to get it closer to a hundred percent light absorption."

"But he already had it around ninety-five percent. How can you increase that further?"

"Ha, I can do much better than that! Look!" he got up to get his laptop and sat next to her to show her something.

"One thing is the visor he used to look through. The blackness of the suit is important, but around his eyes he kept a small horizontal opening to look through, which resulted in more light reflected around his eyes. I'll work with a system of mini cameras that will project their images on the inside of the helmet. This reduces the light reflected tremendously. In addition, I'll receive a new material next week for the exterior of the suit. You know that even black material can still reflect some light. The particles of the suit always reflect some light. This new material is based on the Pacific Black dragon, a fearsome-looking creature and one of the ultra-black fish that live in the deepest and darkest parts of the ocean."

"Wow, that's one ugly creature!" she said when he showed a picture of the fish on the screen.

"Yep, and it's one of the blackest creatures in the world. It absorbs ninety-nine-point-five percent of all light, making them appear as little more than silhouettes even in direct light. It absorbs almost every photon of light. Light doesn't bounce back and doesn't go through. The fish uses a melanin-based system that they copied into a new material, making an ultra-black suit thinner and more durable than any other material."

"Impressive! How will this work with your cooling system?"

"Good question! I designed a completely new adaptive system which will be fitted as an interior layer inside this black suit. I'll breathe compressed air from a tank. The exhaled air will go through the cooling system inside and leave the suit at my feet, but only when it has been cooled down to the outside temperature."

She studied his design on the screen. After explaining all the details to her, she relaxed further.

"You've made quite some progress already, but still, I'm very worried about this entire plan."

"Don't worry, from now on I'll involve you in the entire process and I won't go if I'm not completely sure it'll work."

She nodded, slightly reassured, but she still had a bad feeling about the whole thing.

62.

Several weeks later Dylan had finished the suit, and they were going for a last test. This was the fifth version of it since in the previous tests, some flaws had popped up and he was frantically trying to make it perfect. Last time, Elizabeth already had told him he was testing it under too extreme circumstances. Nonetheless, he had insisted on improving it further. Tonight, they were planning to do another one in an open field around Ikast.

After work, Elizabeth arrived home that evening and, to her surprise, the table was all set and dinner was waiting for her.

"What a pleasant surprise! I thought you would work late again tonight?"

"We've made quite some progress with the construction of the climate plant, and we're ahead of schedule. So, I thought, it's about time I cook, since you've been cooking so often lately."

"Nice. You can do that more often. Are we still on for tonight?"

"Yes, the circumstances are good. It's a clear sky tonight, and the moon is thin at the waning crescent phase."

"I thought you would only do the attempt when there would be no moon?"

"Yes, the plan is to aim for the New Moon phase, but I'd like to test with more light to make sure it's safe. If it's safe with little light, it should be even safer in complete darkness."

"Tonight, I also want to test the climbing assistant on a higher wall than last time. I found a wall of six meters high, not too far from here."

"All right, well, let's have dinner first."

They enjoyed the exquisite meal he had prepared and, after cleaning up, they started packing all their equipment. They had bought very sensitive night-vision and infrared cameras to test if they could detect Dylan in his suit. They put everything in the driverless taxi and drove to a field about five kilometers away from Ikast. The taxi stopped right in front of the six-meter-high wall. Tonight, they had planned a long test run. First, he would walk at a normal pace for about two kilometers. After this, he would climb the wall two times to test the climbing device that he had adapted several times already. Next, he would run at a high pace for about five kilometers; followed by another climb. And last another high pace run of one kilometer.

The climbing device was based on the design that Rick had used in Narmik, but Dylan had improved it. He also had covered the whole device with the black fabric. For this test, he would breathe using the compressed air in the double tank on his back. In theory, it had enough air for two to three hours, but he wanted to see how much he would use if he ran and climbed intensely. Together they had installed cameras along the route, and Elizabeth would follow him the entire route with a camera. It was quite dark except for some light from the moon and the stars and some light coming from the nearby village.

Almost three hours later, they had finished the test and returned to the taxi with all their equipment.

"Impressive, Dylan! No detection at all along the whole trajectory. How did you feel?"

"It was comfortable, still a bit chilly, but much better than last time. The cooling works well, and I was finally wearing the right amount of clothes under it, not to get too cold with the cooling unit doing its work."

The taxi drove them back to their compound. Back in the apartment, he immediately went to check something on his computer while she prepared some tea. The moment she came out of the kitchen, he looked up with a strange look on his face.

"Next weekend it's the new Moon phase in Narmik and it's relatively warm at night. Ideal circumstances."

A silence fell and she glanced anxiously at him.

"You want to try already?"

"Well, we agreed that I would only do it when the suit is perfect. I think tonight's test proves it is."

She looked uncomfortable and sighed.

"I don't know. I still feel uncomfortable with the whole thing."

"You saw tonight that it should work."

"I know, but so far, nobody has succeeded."

"That doesn't mean it isn't possible. I mean, I understand you're concerned. I'm worried as well. I think that is normal, but you know how important it's for me to find my birth parents."

"I know, but what if you do succeed in reaching the dome in one piece and they shoot you when you get there?"

"Why would they shoot me? Especially when they hear that I'm the son of Vikram and Tanvi Singh. No, I'm not afraid of that."

"I don't know. It's just that so many things could go wrong."

"Of course. I could die tomorrow in an accident as well. I have to try. I prefer to die trying than to live with the regret of not having tried. That would haunt me for the rest of my life."

She was silent for a moment and then reluctantly said,

"If it's really that important to you, then I guess you should go for it. I agree life is too short to live with regrets. All right, I'll accompany you to Narmik."

He gave her a big hug, and they kissed.

"Let's ask for some days off tomorrow and then I'll book the flight right after."

63.

In the twilight, Dylan distinguished the massive wall on the horizon. The sheer size of it still overwhelmed him. The entire village still had this mystical aura in the middle of nowhere. The air taxi landed next to the Narmik Inn, and it felt weird to be back. He was more nervous than during his last visit, and he noticed Elizabeth was also tense. They unloaded their luggage and carried everything inside. As soon as they opened the door, the buzz and liveliness of the place made them feel at ease.

Inuk welcomed them and gave them the key to their room. Dylan noticed Jim in the back and he waved at him. They first brought all their luggage to their room and Inuk helped them carry it upstairs.

"What do you have in this large box? It's heavy and well packed."

"Oh, just some extra clothes."

"Extra clothes? So much? What are you planning to do?"

Dylan ignored his question in the hope he would stop asking, but it had triggered Inuk's curiosity.

"You're not going to try to get to the dome, are you?"

Elizabeth glanced at Dylan and told him,

"Maybe you should just tell him? He'll find out anyway."

Dylan sighed and responded to Inuk, who waited at the door.

"Please Inuk, I want to keep it quiet. Promise me you won't tell anybody."

"Uh, okay, no problem."

"I've developed a special suit."

"A special suit? No!? So, you're going to try to get to the dome? You're crazy! No one ever comes back."

"I know, but someone has to be the first."

"Yeah, that's true. Well, I've got to go back to the bar now. Please come and say goodbye before your attempt."

"I will! And Inuk?"

"Yes?"

"Please keep it quiet."

After unpacking, they went downstairs to meet Jim for dinner. It was nice to see each other again, and they talked about lots of different things. Dylan tried to relax, but his mind wandered off several times. Doubt came back and forth in his mind. Should he really attempt to get to the dome? What if he had overlooked something? Elizabeth noticed and touched his hand. At some point, Jim asked,

"When are you planning to make your attempt?"

"It depends on the weather, mostly. Tonight, we'll go out to check the circumstances and compare with the forecast for coming nights. Maybe tonight, maybe tomorrow night."

"Makes sense. Do you have a link where I can follow your live stream?"

"A link? There will be no link," Dylan responded bluntly.

Elizabeth noticed the surprised look on Jim's face and added,

"We analyzed why it might have gone wrong with Rick, and most likely it was his extra body heat that gave him away. But there is another possibility. Maybe the drones picked up the radio waves emitted from the camera streaming the images. We're taking no chances, so he's not taking anything that could emit any signals."

"Radio waves? Makes sense. I had not even thought of that, but you could be right. Poor Rick!"

"Believe me, I've tried to shoot holes in Dylan's plan any possible way I could, but he solved all issues."

"You'd better, given the risks. Sorry for asking a blunt question maybe, but how is Elizabeth going to know if a drone got to you or not?"

Dylan looked uncomfortable now, and slightly annoyed. Elizabeth noticed and answered for him.

"After his departure, I'll steer a small drone up in the air with a sensitive microphone aimed over the wall. This way I should be able to pick up any explosion or loud sound."

"Ah, yeah. That could work. Well, I have to give it to you, Dylan, you have guts. I'd never dare to do what you are planning."

"Thanks, Jim! Although it feels like a questionable honor."

After dinner, Dylan and Elizabeth went outside to check the weather. It was pitch dark. Since it was the New Moon phase, there was no light from the sky. It was cloudy and they could not see any stars either. As they walked toward the wall, they left behind the light from the streetlights in Narmik and it was getting so dark they could barely see where to walk. Dylan measured the air temperature with his phone.

"The weather conditions are even better than I had expected. I think I should go tonight."

"Are you sure?"

"Yes."

They walked back to the Inn and agreed with Jim to meet up later in front of the Inn. Upstairs, Dylan opened the box and changed into the clothes he had selected to wear under the suit. Elizabeth prepared the small drone and an infrared camera to take with her. He carefully put the suit on. The helmet he was going to put on outside. After preparing everything, he kissed her passionately, and they hugged for a while. She did not want to let go of him and got tears in her eyes. He hugged her again.

"Don't worry, I'll make it and will get back to you!"

She sighed and dried her eyes. They went downstairs and signaled Inuk to come to the back. He helped them go out through the back door to prevent the guests in the Inn from seeing them and he wished them good luck. Jim was waiting outside already and together they walked toward the wall. Elizabeth and Jim both put on their flashlights to find their way in the dark. The closer he got, the more nervous he felt. In front of the wall, he checked the climbing device one more time, and then he took a deep sigh. Elizabeth looked at him in the dark.

"You can still decide not to go. You know I prefer you don't."

"No, I have to try. Don't worry. I'll put on the helmet now. We can do a last check and then I'll go."

He said goodbye to Jim and kissed Elizabeth one more time. He put the helmet on and they both made sure it was well glued to the rest of the suit with the Velcro system he had designed. He was shivering. He put his hand and feet on the climbing device and looked back at Elizabeth.

"All right, I think it's well closed. My night-vision camera is working. Let's do a last check!"

Elizabeth took the infrared camera out of her pocket and checked at a distance and then up-close to see if she could detect anything.

"Nothing. The suit still seems to work well."

"All right, wish me luck! I love you, Elizabeth."

In the dark, he could not see her tears when she responded.

"Good luck! Please be careful!"

"Good luck, Dylan! I hope to see you again soon," Jim said.

Dylan was happy Jim was there. At least Elizabeth would not be alone. He turned his back to them and put his hand on the wall. The device attached itself to the wall, and he started climbing. His heart was pounding, and he realized his breathing was too fast. He told himself to calm down and tried to use one of the meditation techniques he learned in the past. Slowly, he seemed to regain his composure and felt more focused on his task. He had put his feet against the wall and, thanks to the climbing device, he had a solid grip now.

He climbed carefully. It was higher than the walls he had climbed during his practice runs. The physical exertion was increasing his body temperature, and he felt the engine of the cooling system increasing its speed gradually. He knew nothing in the system could break down or he would be a dead man.

At the top, he noticed the sheer thickness of the wall. It looked like two meters thick. He looked over it and could vaguely see the dark plains ahead of him. This was a crucial moment since he had to be careful with the laser detection system. Contrary to Rick, he had not brought a can with spray, but had built the spray into his suit. With his left finger, he triggered it and sprayed on top of the wall. Immediately, he noticed the beams. There were two laser beams. First, he carefully climbed on top and then he stepped over the laser beams.

Cautiously, he turned around and started descending to the other side. Slowly, he crawled down and moved his hand and feet one by one down. At some point, the wall was towering above him and he started wondering how far he still had to descend. Suddenly, he touched the ground with one foot. He had arrived at the other side. He turned around and took off the climbing device and held it in his hands. In front of him, he faced the dark plains. A bare field stretching as far as he could see. Calmly, he started walking away from the wall. Slowly, he recovered from the physical effort of climbing and he felt his body temperature going down slightly.

It was strange to walk through the field in the darkness. The further he got, the more he relaxed. He increased his pace a bit, but after walking for a while, he lost track of time and wondered how far he had already walked. It must have been more than an hour, maybe two, he thought, but he had no clue and could not check it in any way. He just continued going until, at some point, he vaguely noticed a dark strip on the horizon. After continuing further, he realized it was the second wall. He was getting close. He felt exhilarated but also realized he was not there yet. He walked slightly faster in his excitement.

About two hundred meters away from the wall, he suddenly hit some kind of stone and it flew away and hit another rock. In a blink, he saw a bright spark in front of him. The clacking noise startled him and he immediately stopped. He looked around, but he could not see anything. Just at the moment he was about to continue, he got startled. He heard a buzzing noise in the distance. It was getting closer and his heart raced in his chest. He felt adrenaline rising through his head. A drone was coming toward him.

64.

Petrified, Dylan stood frozen to the ground and looked up. Out of nowhere, he saw the drone appearing above him. It flew toward him and he held his breath. Seconds seemed to pass like minutes, and it was as if time stood still. He didn't move an inch. The drone passed overhead and continued further. Slowly, he started feeling relieved as the drone disappeared out of sight. That was close, he thought, and he decided to avoid the rocky pieces. He continued on what felt like grass.

Quickly after, he reached the second wall and put the climbing device back on his hands and feet. He climbed up and on top he tried to avoid looking down, as he knew he was high above the ground. There he applied the spray, and again he observed two laser beams in parallel. Carefully, he stepped over the beams, avoiding getting close to them. Just before starting his descent, he peered at the horizon and in the distance he distinguished what looked like a faintly illuminated reversed half bowl: the dome! For the first time, he saw it with his own eyes. He got shivers along his spine.

A moment later, he descended slowly on the other side. With a feeling of relief, he touched the ground. If all the stories were true, there were no more walls between him and the dome anymore. From the ground he could barely see it, just a faint light at the horizon. Still quite some distance to cover, he figured.

The closer he got, the clearer he could distinguish the shape of the dome. Its sheer size made a deep impression on him. It was even bigger than he had imagined. He must have been about five hundred meters away from it, when he realized that gradually the light coming from the dome was illuminating the surrounding plains. He looked back at the horizon behind him and then noticed his shadow. There was so much light now that his shadow had become sharper and visible.

Frightened, he realized that in all his test runs they had measured with the cameras sideways. The drones observed from the sky and a clear shadow meant variations in light. He comprehended the risk he was exposed to. He decided to continue crawling to minimize his shadow.

It frustrated him as he progressed much slower than expected on this last stretch of his long walk. Still, gradually he got closer and closer. The light became brighter and brighter the closer he got. At some point he was less than hundred meters away from the dome. He paused for a moment and glanced up. The dome looked enormous from here, and he could even see where the faint light was coming from. Inside, he distinguished the shape of plants, and there were lights aimed on them. It seemed like some kind of giant greenhouse.

Fascinated, he continued crawling. The dome was standing on a concrete structure of about three meters high. At a certain point he got so close that he entered the shadow of this structure. As he was out of the bright light now, he got up and took a good look around him. To his surprise, he did not see any gate or entrance; just this concrete structure all around with the dome on top. He had to choose which direction to take and he realized that his choice could determine his fate; he tried to think first. The gate on the outer wall next to Narmik had been on the east side, so he concluded his best chances were to walk eastwards.

After a while, he felt a vibration on his back. Puzzled, he paused for a moment. A minute later, there was another vibration on his back. In a blink, he realized what it was and started getting all stressed out. He was running out of air. The vibration he felt was the programmed warning signal from the air tank. He had not anticipated this. According to his estimates, he should have had more than enough air to traverse the estimated ten kilometers to the dome. But the crawling must have taken more time than expected, and he had not taken into account the distance walking along the dome.

Worried, he continued walking. He realized that if he would run out of air, he would have to take off his helmet, and then the drones could detect him easily. Since he had passed the second wall, he had seen several drones passing through the sky. With increased pace, he continued along the wall. Still, there was no sight of any entrance and it took him too much time, so he started running.

Sometime later, he spotted the shape of some buildings vaguely in the distance. His air tank vibrated more frequently now, and he knew he would soon run out of air, but the sight of buildings made him hopeful. He continued running until, all of a sudden, he stepped into some kind of hole and he fell with a big smack on the floor. A drone passed through the air not too far from him and he held his breath. As soon as it was out of sight, he got up and continued walking at a high pace.

As he approached the buildings, it surprised him to see that there was no light in any of them. As if there was nobody inside. There was no movement anywhere, just the occasional drone passing through the sky. He continued until he noticed a lower wall perpendicular to the one that he was walking along. This wall was about one meter high, and when he reached it, he peered over it. Behind there was a deepness with a faint light coming out of some kind of tunnel. He realized it was a road coming from under the dome; he had found the entrance.

The road was long, and he preferred not to step out of the shadow, so he decided to descend along this wall. It looked quite deep, maybe fifteen to twenty meters. After putting the climbing device on his hands and feet, he started descending into the tunnel. His air supply vibrated again.

Cautiously, he climbed down along the concrete wall. About halfway through, his air supply vibrated one time, but now longer than before. Dylan felt terrified as he realized what this meant. He had run out of air and he was hanging halfway on the wall. Way too high to jump and, with his hands and feet glued to the wall, it would be difficult to take off his helmet. He held his breath and continued downwards. Stars started appearing in front of his eyes, and he felt he could faint anytime. He detached one hand from the wall and tried to pull off his helmet, but the double Velcro system made it very difficult. He took the hand out of the climbing device and tore the Velcro open. With a firm jerk, he was able to remove his helmet, and he took a deep breath.

All of a sudden, he lost his balance and fell backwards. The climbing device gave in under his weight and he fell down the remaining meters. With a big blow, he smacked on the hard floor. He tried to get up, but his ankle hurt like crazy. In a haze, he looked around and noticed the guard post inside the tunnel only ten meters away from him. It was all lit, and he noticed someone inside looking through the window. Afraid of the drones, he started dragging himself desperately along the floor toward the guard post.

A large spotlight went on inside the tunnel. Just as he had dragged himself close enough toward the door and he was about to bang on it; the door opened. A heavily armed man in a black uniform looked into his desperate eyes and yelled,

"What the hell?"

65.

How could this be possible? This had never happened before, Amos thought, while he rushed through the maze of corridors under the dome. Someone had reached the dome alive for the first time since it closed for the outside world. The Council was not going to be pleased. After taking the elevator downstairs, he rushed into the tunnel where a small transporter was waiting for him to drive him to the front guard post. As soon as he sat down in the transporter, it drove away. They had told him they kept the intruder in one of the special visitor rooms.

Close to the outside guard post, there was a dedicated visitor area. It contained several rooms that were originally constructed to make it possible to meet with people from outside the dome in a room separated by a glass wall, eliminating any risks of contaminating the dome with any disease spread through viruses, bacteria or other germs. On arrival at the guard post, one of his staff members greeted him. They walked together toward the visitor area.

"We found him wounded in front of the guard post, wearing some kind of strange black suit. Apparently, the intruder was unarmed. The guard carried him inside and locked him in one of the visitor's rooms. Since it's the first time someone made it alive to the dome, we immediately called you, sir."

"You did well. Who's this young man?"

"He told us his name is Dylan Myers, and he came to find his parents. He's convinced his parents are inside the dome. It looks like he has broken his ankle. The guard gave him some painkillers."

"Did this Mr. Myers say who his parents are?"

"Yes, he told us, they are Vikram and Tanvi Singh. The guard checked in the system and explained to Mr. Myers that we don't have a Vikram and Tanvi Singh living inside the dome."

Amos's heart skipped a beat. He couldn't believe what he was hearing. Suddenly, he felt weak in his legs and his mind wandered off. In a haze, he thought back to the instructions they had received when they moved in here. Another brilliant idea from Abe. Everybody who came to the dome got a new name on entry. The old name was no longer to be used. They had done this to make a clear cut with the outside life and to prevent people from the outside contacting someone in the community. Everybody started all over in a new life with a new name. Hearing his old name shocked him, and he felt overwhelmed as he realized who this intruder might be.

"Are you all right, sir?"

"Uh… yes, I'm fine."

"We have put the suit he was wearing in room one. I show you that first?"

"Okay."

They both entered the room. Behind the glass separation, there was a black suit lying on a table with a black helmet next to it. A guard stood on the other side of the separation. He explained what he had learned from the interrogation.

"The suit was designed to be invisible for night-vision and infrared cameras and successfully, since our drone security system did not detect him. It's quite a sophisticated suit and automatically adapts to the outside temperature, rendering it undetectable by infrared. I asked him who he was working for, but he claims to act on his own and that he designed the suit himself."

"I guess we'll have to upgrade our security system now?" his staff member asked.

"Yes, and looking at this suit, I believe we should probably install a minefield between the two walls to prevent this from happening again," Amos responded.

"He had nothing on him. No ID, no phone or other belongings, except for this photo," the guard said, and he put the photo on the table against the glass wall.

Amos approached the window to look at the picture, but he quickly recognized it. His wife looked beautiful, exactly the way he remembered her. The feeling of emptiness and guilt he hated so much came back to him in a wave. He felt swept off his feet, and he could not believe this was happening. How was this possible? If only she would have still been alive, she could have guided him to make the right decisions.

"The man in the picture looks a lot like you, sir?" his staff member said after taking a good look.

"Where are you keeping the intruder?" Amos asked.

"He's next door in room number two."

Amos walked next door and entered the room. Inside, he noticed the young man sitting behind the glass partition. He was touching his ankle and looked up when he entered. Amos looked straight into his eyes, and he could not believe what he saw. The intruder looked exactly like Elliot and had his wife's eyes, just like his son.

Dylan looked up after rearranging his sock around his swollen ankle. Thunderstruck, he looked at the man on the other side of the glass. That was him, the man in the photo, his biological father. There was a moment of silence as they both glanced at each other. Amos was speechless and could not believe his eyes. Dylan smiled at him and broke the silence.

"You are not an easy man to find, Mr. Singh. I believe you're my biological father. My name is Dylan Myers and I'm born on the seventh of April in the year 2029 in New-Delhi. I learned that the original name you and my mother gave me was Yagnesh."

Another silence fell as Amos stared at the young man.

"Yagnesh? But that is not possible. Yagnesh died in the great heat wave in 2039."

"No, I didn't. I was already living with my adoptive parents in the United States. How is my mother Tanvi doing?"

Amos's head started turning. What was this young man telling him? This could not be true. He suddenly felt terrible. If they would have known this before, maybe his wife would still have been alive. It was his fault he had not checked properly at the time and assumed their son had died in the heat wave. That is what he had told his wife. What was he supposed to do now? He was the head of defense, and he knew the rules. He had no choice. He had to be exemplary. No, he could not deal with this, not now. Suddenly, he felt very weak and his head started turning. He felt tears in his eyes.

"Your mother is dead. I'm sorry, but I've to go."

Dylan looked shocked and jumped up from his chair. His face showed the pain he felt from his broken ankle as he screamed after his father.

"You can't leave me like this!? I'm your son! I risked my life to come and see you! Please! Please come back!"

His father had already turned his back on him and left the room. With a big bang, the door closed behind him. Amos had tears running down his face. Outside, he saw his staff member coming toward him. He did not want to be seen like this. He turned and started walking away through the corridor in the direction of the transporter.

"Sir? Sir? What do I do with the suit?"

"Decontaminate it and bring it to the laboratory for examination after."

As the distance had gotten bigger, the staff member yelled through the corridor.

"And sir? What do you want us to do with the intruder? Shall we terminate him, sir?"

66.

The drone flew steadily above the wall. Elizabeth made sure not to fly over it to prevent the drones from detecting it. She felt extremely stressed and worried about Dylan. She should never have let him go. She had a bad feeling about the whole attempt. It was a crazy and suicidal venture, but it was too late now. She had put on her earphones to listen to the drone's microphone. She could also look at the video images on the controller, but the screen was dark, like her surroundings.

Suddenly, she heard a high-pitched noise and stared at the controller. She heard a loud explosion right after that and, on the screen, she saw a flash far away. This could not be happening. No! Not Dylan! And she screamed,

"No!!!"

It was all dark, and the room was silent as she looked around drowsily. She turned on a small light and she glanced next to her in the bed. Dylan was not there. Was it a nightmare, or did Dylan really die yesterday? Slowly she remembered walking back with Jim to the Inn after they waited for two hours next to the wall. Now she heard a noise, like someone was trying to open the door to her room. She turned on the main light and saw the door handle move. Someone knocked on the door.

"Elizabeth?"

She rushed out of bed and couldn't believe what she heard. Again, someone knocked on the door.

"Elizabeth?"

Promptly, she opened the door and there he was.

"Thank God! You're alive!" and she embraced him. They kissed and hugged until she bumped against his leg and he screamed out of pain. His ankle was all swollen, and she could see the agony on his face. She helped him limp to the bed so he could lie down. She put a pillow under his head and looked at his ankle.

"What happened? Did you make it to the dome?"

"Yes, I did. I even met my father, but it was rather disappointing."

"How come?"

"Well, I think he recognized me, but I got the impression that he thought I had died in the great heat wave of '39. I asked about my mother and he told me she was dead. Then, out of the blue, he told me he had to go and left. I noticed he had tears in his eyes. He didn't give a reason, though, and I was completely dumbstruck. He walked out of the door and I was so shocked that I yelled after him. He just left like that. Can you believe it?

"About fifteen minutes later, they put a black bag over my head and I think they put me in some kind of truck. They told me I should tell no one about the dome or they would come after me. After a while, they pushed me out. By the time I managed to take off the bag, I was standing outside the closed gate. It took me a long time to limp back to the Inn and I'm dead tired."

"Try to sleep then! I'm so happy you made it back!" she said with tears running down her cheeks, and she kissed him.

Dylan quickly fell into a deep sleep. The next day they left the Inn for the hospital in Nuuk, where they took care of his ankle.

On the plane on their way back home, he thought about everything that had happened. On the one hand, it disappointed him that his father had cut off the contact the way he did. On the other hand, he was happy he had made it to the dome. At least he had met his father, and he felt he had filled the void in his life.

67.

After his father had left abruptly during their conversation, Elliot went to bed. In the middle of the night, he woke up and went to the bathroom. While he was washing his hands, he heard the front door open. He looked at his father entering the hall and noticed he looked very affected. He even had the impression he had tears in his eyes.

"Dad!? Are you all right?"

His father looked away and rushed to his bedroom, while he mumbled,

"I'm fine, but I'm dead tired. Good night."

Elliot had the impression something shocking had happened.

"Are you sure you're okay?"

"Yeah, yeah, I just need to be alone and get some sleep."

His father was acting strangely and more bluntly than usual. Why did he return home with tears in his eyes? He went back to bed. In his bed, he kept thinking about what had happened and he vowed to find out what he was hiding from him and why his mother had made that tragic decision. He had to know.

BY THE SAME AUTHOR

Rejuvenation is a gripping scientific thriller about a journalist's investigation into a promising new drug, that is about to change the human race forever.

ISBN: 9789464007329 (paperback)
ISBN: 9789464007336 (hardback)
ASIN: B082MR9SV5 (eBook)

The Breach is a thrilling story about a young man's immersion in the world of refugees suffering from the catastrophic consequences of climate change. The second book in the Dome series.

ISBN 9789464007367 (paperback)
ISBN 9789464007374 (hardback)
ASIN: B09L64DTN3 (eBook)

Nemesis is a fast-paced thriller about revenge, love and hope in a world where shocking events are taking place. The third and final book in the Dome series.

ISBN 9789464007381 (paperback)
ISBN 9789464007398 (hardback)
ASIN: B0BKLQ5JBJ (eBook)

www.ingramcontent.com/pod-product-compliance
Lightning Source LLC
Chambersburg PA
CBHW021940120726
47992CB00001B/65